Mary Sweeney, nee Scully.

One More Day

Emma Heatherington is from Donaghmore, Co. Tyrone. She is the author of fourteen novels, including the bestsellers *The Legacy of Lucy Harte* and *Secrets in the Snow*, and novels written under the pseudonym Emma Louise Jordan. Emma is also an accomplished scriptwriter, and a ghost-writer for country music legend Philomena Begley on her autobiography, *My Life, My Music, My Memories*, and Liverpool-born country singer, Nathan Carter's, *Born for the Road*. She is a regular contributor in magazines and newspapers and has appeared on numerous TV and radio chat shows in the UK and in Ireland. Emma is a mum/stepmum of five, and her fiancé is artist and singer/songwriter Jim McKee.

f /emmaheatheringtonwriter
◉ @emmaheatheringtonwriter
🐦 @EmmaLouWriter
www.emmaheatheringtonwriter.com

Also by Emma Heatherington

Emma Heatherington

One More Day

HarperCollins*Publishers*

HarperCollins*Publishers* Ltd
1 London Bridge Street,
London SE1 9GF

www.harpercollins.co.uk

HarperCollins*Publishers*
1st Floor, Watermarque Building, Ringsend Road
Dublin 4, Ireland

First published by HarperCollins*Publishers* 2022
1

A catalogue record for this book is available from the British Library

ISBN: 978-0-00-843519-6 (TPB)
ISBN: 978-0-00-843518-9 (PB)

Typeset in Birka by Palimpsest Book Production Ltd, Falkirk, Stirlingshire

Printed and Bound in the UK using 100% Renewable
Electricity at CPI Group (UK) Ltd

MIX
Paper from
responsible sources
FSC™ C007454

This book is produced from independently certified FSC™ paper to ensure
responsible forest management.

For more information visit: www.harpercollins.co.uk/green

For Aurelia – in loving memory

My husband sits right here beside me. I can hear him breathe, I can touch his skin, I can smell his cologne on his skin, yet I still feel so painfully alone.

I tilt my head towards the sky, watching it drift in slow motion above me as two large fluffy grey clouds threaten to crash and burst with rain.

I don't like to admit that I'm angry, so I'll do what I always do to divert my mind. I'll close my eyes and I'll pluck a memory from the past, back to when we were love-struck teenagers without a care in the world between us. Back to when our eyes sparkled in sync at first sight in school, a sign of the magical bond that was just about to begin. Oh, how magic it really was, and how we did love so deeply.

But then love and magic are one and the same, really.

Remembering this, I tell myself that although it may be lonely and broken right now, my heart was made to love and be loved.

The human heart is as big as the ocean.

What a truly beautiful thing to know.

Grid Pic: A moody sky over Lough Neagh
Likes: 1,277
Comments: 118

1.

'Yes, yes don't worry Mr Stephenson. I'll have a word with Danny right now and make sure this never, ever happens again. I can only apologize. I'm very sorry.'

It's Friday evening and this phone call from my son's form teacher is the very last thing I need right now. I pinch the top of my nose to try to release some pressure, a tip I've picked up along the way on how to deal with my daily stressors that fill life as I know it.

'Yes, of course. I'm going to speak with Danny immediately and it won't be taken lightly. No, no, you haven't bothered me at all. Yes, you have a lovely weekend too. Thank you.'

I hang up the phone, take a deep breath and shout up the stairs.

'Danny!!' I roar from the pit of my stomach. 'Daniel James Madden come down here right now!'

The winding mahogany staircase that was once my pride and joy needs a makeover as much as I do but I park it in the back of my mind with a million other things around here that need my attention, including my very unhealthy bank balance that has the ability to break me out in a cold sweat every time I check it.

There's the chicken coop fence that needs repairing, the washing machine leak that is currently being soaked up with towels on the floor, the garden shed that needs painting and the faulty wiring in my bedroom that makes the light flicker. Our farmhouse is over a hundred years old and, just like I am, it's beginning to show its age – thanks to a lot of neglect and a lack of love and attention.

I know I'm still young at forty years old but I feel twice that age lately, as home life makes me gasp for air on a good day and makes me want to crawl back into bed on most others.

I catch my look in the hallway mirror which does nothing for my mood by reminding me I'm long overdue a hair appointment. I make an inner pledge to make more of an effort with my appearance one day very soon, but I try to look at the bright side. I may have dark roots to clash with my blonde but I've no grey yet, which is a bloody miracle, so that's a little ray of hope to hold on to.

'Danny, I said get down here now!'

My thirteen-year-old son saunters down the stairs in his usual zombie-like state, rubbing his eyes as he adjusts from too much time in front of his game console screen and looks at me as if I've just interrupted a very important moment of his life.

'Mr Stephenson just called,' I tell him with my hand on my hip, knowing I look and sound as bedraggled as I feel. 'I think you've some explaining to do? Again?'

'Who?'

'Your form teacher?'

'Oh, *that* Mr Stephenson.'

'Yes, *that* Mr Stephenson! He said you were smoking on school grounds. How many times have I had to speak to you about this? It's exhausting, not to mention unhealthy and not to mention against *all* the rules. Do you think I need this on top of everything else?'

Danny turns on his squeaking sock soles on the bottom stair and hunches up the stairs again, mumbling something under his breath.

'Speak properly!' I demand, but he just lets out a deep sigh.

'It wasn't me!' he says, turning to face me again. His cheeks are flushed and his fair hair is standing sticky on his head. 'Cabbage is always picking on me. He blames me for everything.'

'Cabbage?'

'Mr Stephenson,' he explains with a very staid expression. 'His breath smells like rotten cabbage, and I mean *really* bad. Maybe *he* should take up smoking and he'd smell a bit better.'

I shake my head not knowing whether to laugh or cry, which is more or less the theme of my life these days.

Cabbage! Thank God for my son's sense of humour, even if he does almost topple me over the edge with his school-time antics.

It really is my saving grace lately.

'You OK?'

Kelly closes my husband's ground-floor bedroom door ever so quietly, but it's enough to make me jump.

I realize I've been standing at the bottom of the stairs for much longer than I needed to now that Danny is long gone back up to his room. I can hear Meg singing a cheesy pop song in the shower, which is a welcoming sound and a contrast to her recent unpredictable bouts of silence, which are deafening in a different way. Instead of standing here in some sort of ongoing daydream I should be finishing dinner, which is exactly what I was doing before I got a phone call from a man I will forever now think of as Cabbage.

'Yes, yes I'm fine,' I say with a smile to Kelly, who follows me into the kitchen where I manage to salvage a shepherd's pie from the oven just in time. 'How is he?'

'Asleep. He couldn't keep his eyes open,' she says brightly. 'So at least you'll get to eat dinner before he wakes from his nap. He's had a good day. I think he enjoyed the fresh air this afternoon when you brought him to the lough. I got two hand squeezes when I mentioned it to him.'

I lean both my hands on the counter and bite my lip,

holding back how heart-breaking it is that my husband Peter's main way of communicating now is through a series of coded hand squeezes, even though I realize they are now only reflexes with his 'good side'. They don't mean what they used to – a firm squeeze would once mean 'no', two would mean 'yes' or 'happy', three would mean 'I love you', which is rare, and four squeezes, which was always a lot less frequent but sometimes funny, once meant something along the lines of 'you're really annoying right now'.

It used to be either a coded hand squeeze or a series of low roars that spilled out of his mouth and pierced my shattered heart, so two hand squeezes is a sign of a good day indeed. I'll take that, even if they mean nothing now, as Dr McCloskey constantly reminds me.

Peter doesn't communicate any more really, not like he did in the early days after the accident. His hand squeezes and the ringing of the bell attached to his chair and on his bed are now just reflexes. I should remove the bell from both places, I know I should.

'Stay for dinner?' I suggest to Kelly.

'Oh come on, Annie, this is becoming a habit. You're too kind.'

'I have wine?'

Her eyes widen and, before I know it, we're all tucking in to a steaming hot shepherd's pie washed down with the obligatory single glass of wine I allow myself each day as a tiny reward for making it through another twenty-four hours. Just having Kelly here a little while longer reminds me I'm not totally alone when it comes to adult company in my home. Her vibrant, bubbly ways, which reflect in her sparkling green eyes, always brighten me up if even just a little.

'So I was thinking of wearing a dress and heels, just for a change and to really shock Joel for his fortieth,' she discusses as I serve up some extras. 'I mean, there's only so many pairs of DM boots and skirts a girl can own. I like to keep it fresh, you know.'

Kelly's husband's forthcoming milestone birthday is her favourite subject these days and I find it a welcome distraction, even though my teenage daughter seems to have zoned out from the conversation already.

'Meg?' I say to her. 'Meg, where are you going?'

She lifts her plate and her cutlery from the table, the din of dance music ringing from the air pods she wears on an almost constant basis.

'Meg!'

'Just leave her, Annie.'

'No, that's rude,' I remind my friend. 'Meg, come back to the table with your plate right now.'

'I'm going to eat in my room,' she shouts, then at least has the grace to remove one bud from her ear. 'What's the problem?'

I glance in Kelly's direction and plead with my daughter via a stern look for her to have manners and sit down for dinner. She rolls her eyes, switches off her music and reluctantly plonks down at the table.

'Oh, that's right. Is our wee Danny in trouble at school again?' she asks, her eyes darting from me to her younger brother with a smirk on her face. She has Peter's mysterious brown eyes, his raven-black hair, and she even walks like he once used to, but these days she is just becoming more and more distant. Danny, who sits opposite me, is pale and fair like my side of the family, and even strangers often remark how two siblings can be so very different to look at.

'Our wee Danny is *never* in trouble at school,' Kelly chips in, as always the mediator at our dinner table when she is invited to stay on after her two-hour shift as Peter's day nurse.

I'm just glad that we managed to divert Meg's departure and that she is actually talking to us for once.

'It was a case of mistaken identity in the secret smoker gang,' I explain on Danny's behalf, as I can see he has his mouth full of dinner. 'Sure, look at that innocent face. Butter wouldn't melt in his mouth.'

Meg snorts in disbelief and Danny shoots her a warning look.

'It's true!' he says as he reaches for a second helping of shepherd's pie. 'It was Charlie Bell and his gang who were smoking this time! Cabbage blames me for everything, doesn't he, Mum?'

'Cabbage?'

'Mr Stephenson. His breath smells like rotten cabbage,' I chirp in, and Danny gives me a high-five across the table.

Once again, my son's humour makes me chuckle. While he looks nothing like Peter, Danny's joking ways always remind me of his father in days gone by. As he sprouts up so tall, the one other thing he does have is Peter's height and if I close my eyes, as I sometimes do as he speaks, I can almost pretend it's Peter talking.

I miss my husband's voice. I miss his laugh.

I just miss my husband.

'I hope I didn't pressurize you to stay,' I say to Kelly when we finish washing up after dinner. 'I don't want to ever guilt you into it if it doesn't suit, but boy it really does help keep our spirits up sometimes.'

Kelly throws her eyes to the heavens.

'Believe me. I enjoy it as much as you do, Annie,' she tells me. 'Joel and I are often like ships in the night between shifts, so it's lovely for me to have someone to eat with too. Plus, you're a wonderful cook, and the kids are a hoot when they're both on form.'

'They sure are,' I say, unable to hide my pride, even though Meg's moods and faraway stares these days are almost enough to just topple me over the edge.

'Now, tell me the truth. What's up with you today?' she asks, seeing right through me even though I feel a hundred times better now than I did earlier.

'Ah, nothing, it's just one of those days,' I say with a shrug. 'I'm perfectly fine.'

'*Another* one of those days, you mean?'

I pause.

'Sometimes . . . sometimes I'm glad my kids don't long for the way we all used to be as much as I do.'

Kelly tilts her head to the side and looks at me with such pity, and I feel pitiful too. Gone is the spark I once had when I'd work all week and look forward to Friday when Peter and I would go dancing in town, or when we'd snuggle on the sofa and watch a movie or when we'd do something as simple as grocery shopping together. Now I do everything alone. Every day of every week, I do everything alone.

'Have you thought any more on the respite proposal?' Kelly asks.

'No,' I reply quickly, shaking my head.

'You're exhausted, love. You need a break, and it won't do Peter any harm at all to be looked after by someone else, even for just a few days a month at first. Look at it as a weekend here and there just to catch up with yourself?'

'No.'

I feel hot tears prick my eyes at the very thought of leaving Peter in some sort of structured care, even on a temporary basis, but Kelly is right about one thing.

I am exhausted.

'OK. Then will you *please* at least ask Bernice to take over for the evening so you can come out for Joel's fortieth bash next Saturday?' she continues, brightening up a little. 'It's only dinner and a few drinks down at the Red Fox. No big fuss really, even if I have pledged to wear a dress for once?'

'Thank you, but I can't.'

'But you *can*,' she says, before I launch into excuses. 'You can but you don't! Bernice has offered so many times and she's Peter's mother, Annie! *You're* allowed to go on living, you know, even though Peter can't.'

I almost lose my breath.

'He's not dead, Kelly!' I say, my eyes blinking as seven years of hurt and loneliness overcomes me.

'Oh God, I'm sorry!' she says to me with her hand across her mouth. 'You know I didn't mean it like that. I'm so sorry!'

I look away, doing my best to keep it together, but I know that as soon as Kelly leaves I'll have my usual carefully timed daily cry in the bathroom before washing my face and getting on with my evening duties where I'll feed Peter his dinner, perhaps read some of my own writing or old diary ramblings to him for a while, then oversee Danny and Meg's homework and listen to whatever news they want to tell me about. I'll watch some TV in Peter's room with him and slip out when he falls asleep, and then I'll lie in my own bed and long for the way we were.

I'll dream of a life where one day I can be held closely again by a man who loves me, and I'll punish myself for even thinking of such a selfish thing by crying more until he wakes and it's time to face it all over again.

'Anyhow, who would want be around me on a night out?' I whisper to Kelly, looking down at my staple choice of wardrobe, which consists of denim dungarees and a worn-out T-shirt, or a cardigan and long dress on a Sunday. 'I'm a bit of a miserable mess these days.'

Even Kelly can't deny that. It's been a lifetime since I've worn make-up and when I look at old photos of us all together when I was smiling and happy, tanned and bleached blonde, laughing and smug, with absolutely no idea of what was around the corner for us, I hardly recognize the woman I used to be. In fact, the state of the farmhouse is a reflection of the state of myself. It really is crumbling around me; everywhere I look, something needs fixing. The pine kitchen is so outdated and worn, the paint is peeling off the walls in corners, my own bedroom is past vintage and is just old and musty, and I've been ignoring a damp patch on the ceiling in the dining area for far too long.

'I'll see you Monday,' says Kelly gently. 'Maybe you could relax in a nice bath later when Peter is down for the night? Or you could write?'

I physically shoo away her suggestion with the tea towel in my hand, trying to lighten the moment with a smile.

'I've no need to write. I'm absolutely fine,' I tell her, not mentioning to Kelly the anonymous Instagram account where I vent to strangers and remember better times in my life.

I don't mind ten thousand unknowns reading my rants, but I don't exactly want Mary from 'up the road' knowing my innermost fears and feelings, not to mention Kelly or my children.

'Try to relax, whatever you decide to do,' Kelly tells me. 'And please remember I'm here for you always.'

'Thanks, Kell,' I whisper. 'What would I do without you?'

I see her to the door just as Peter's buzzer rings loudly and on repeat. I close my eyes as the sound pierces my ears.

My husband may not be the man he used to be, but he is still here. He still needs me.

At least I think he does.

2.

Peter looks fresh, clean and comfortable when I go into the room, which always makes my heart rise. His silky dark hair, which I used to run my fingers through, is now cut tight and short for easy maintenance, and his handsome face, a little gaunter than it used to be, no longer lights up when he sees me, but I like to still think my being here makes him feel safer.

'Kelly was saying you enjoyed our walk today,' I say, leaning across to kiss his cheek and touch his face. I imagine he might still love for me to touch his face and I do it every day. His skin is warm and spongey and, for someone who only sees daylight for a very short time, he is tanned and healthy in his complexion.

I picture sometimes, if my mother still lived in the same country, what she'd say if she saw me on a daily basis here, acting out duties like a well-trained nurse, even though in my earlier career choices it would never have crossed my mind. I was always referred to as a dreamer during my childhood, someone who avoided reality at all costs with my poetic offerings and novel dreams.

I don't deny it. I was never naturally maternal, but instinct kicked in as soon as my own children were born, and I enjoyed every moment of their early years. Then, when the initial shock wore off, after Peter's tragic farm accident and the subsequent stroke that has left him in this state of paralysis and inhabiting this locked-in, lonely inner world, I had to step up to the plate and do the same for him too.

Apart from Kelly's contribution, it's up to me to make sure Peter has everything from food and drinks, to visits to the bathroom, from hygiene to medication, from conversation and entertainment, to – most of all – companionship, even if I know the words I speak don't go anywhere.

'You hungry?' I ask, knowing of course that he can't answer. Even though I jump to his attention when I hear the buzzer, it doesn't mean a thing.

'I'm sorry,' I tell him, lifting him up on the bed, trying not to make it sound like it's any trouble to do so. 'I'm here now. OK, give me two minutes and I'll get your dinner from the oven.'

His eyes don't move from mine and the pain I feel for him lands right into the pit of my stomach. I sometimes wonder if he would be better off dead, and I hate myself for even contemplating that.

Moments later I spoon-feed my husband slowly and tenderly as the evening news is broadcast on the television in his room and I don't speak until it's over. He always enjoyed the news bulletin every evening at six, and I like to think he still gets annoyed if he misses it, even though he can never show it.

Most mornings we go out for some fresh air, even if it takes me longer to get him ready to leave the house than we actually get to stay out for, but a walk in a park or just a stroll around the lough shore or the farm where I push him in his chair over lumps and bumps on the muddy ground, pointing out updates on the chickens we've always kept or the children's pet rabbits and guinea pigs, or our old lazy sheepdog Rex and the vegetable garden, which I do my best to keep in honour of his parents, from whom we bought our family home.

He swallows his dinner as I feed him, staring at me as if he is deeply concentrating. I watch his swallow so carefully these days, noticing how it's becoming so slow and deliberate. Any day soon I expect that might go as well as his memory.

'I can read to you for a while, or you know there's a great series on Netflix we could watch together?' I suggest, as if we're just a normal wife and a normal husband on a normal Friday night. 'It's one of those gritty crimes you love that I always suffer through on your behalf, but to be fair it *is* getting great reviews.'

I scrape the sides of the plate to make sure he gets as much nutrition as I can manage into him.

'Or we can watch some of our own family home movies, eh?' I say, my voice rising slightly. 'You're so talented with the camera, much more creative than me, even though you insist on telling me different.'

I smile as a memory flashes through my mind of us both, just young teenagers lying in a cornfield back in the late 1990s, as Peter snapped photos on a Polaroid camera of me blowing dandelions into the cool summer breeze. I can still smell his skin in the sticky heat and see his eyes dance as he waved the little squares of plastic in his hand until they popped with colour, bursting with memories.

I try to avoid phrases like 'we used to' or 'before' or 'when we could' when I talk to him now. Instead I keep everything in the present, as I can only imagine how lonely it is in his locked-in mind. We may not know how much he understands right now, and we probably never will know for sure, but as long as he is by my side, I will continue to talk to him with the respect he deserves.

I wipe his mouth clean and, with the help of a hoist that sits at the side of the bed, I fix him until he is cosy and comfortable. His eyes never leave mine the whole time. I smile in the knowledge he feels safe with me, even if in the early days I'd see a tear escape and fall down his cheek, especially when we'd watch home movies from days gone by. I still show him videos of the children as babies, of our wedding day, and of simple but magical moments around our home when we'd have made a big deal of anything worth celebrating with music and bubbly. We watch back on days when we'd jump on a plane and spend at least two weeks in the sun, with the kids at waterparks or on beaches, so carefree and so full of joy.

'Mum, can you *please* tell Danny to turn his bloody Xbox down? I'm trying to FaceTime Jodie and I can't hear what she is saying with that constant din! Either he is stone deaf or is totally ignoring me as usual! I'm so sick of him.'

Meg hangs on the doorframe, interrupting my trip down memory lane with her real-time issues about her younger brother. I subtly clear my throat and nod in her father's direction, even though I know I should be grateful she is talking to me at all.

She sighs.

'Hey Dad, what's the craic?' she says in monotone, remembering with my nudge to always acknowledge his presence. 'Oh, you're watching home movies again? Does he even like those any more? *Seriously?*'

I feel my lip tremble at the thought that I might be doing something wrong, and it stings how Meg talks about Peter as if he isn't there. It's a constant gripe of mine, but I guess to both our children he is just a shell of a person who shares a house with them. He just exists to them. She was only eight years old when the accident happened and Danny was six, so although they may have little snippets of fading memories, they've very little idea of what they're really missing out on. They've no idea of the man he used to be.

'Why don't we ask your dad as he is actually sitting here?'

I say, trying to keep my voice neutral and not the overly sensitive quivering wreck I feel inside today.

'What?'

'Ask your dad if it's bothering him that we're watching this again?'

Meg rolls her eyes and sighs from the pit of her stomach. Both of us know that as each day ticks by, our horns are locking together even tighter and, as much as I try to understand how she feels or doesn't feel, it's getting harder and harder to hide how much it hurts that she barely acknowledges his existence.

'Would you rather watch something else, Peter?' I ask my husband. 'What will we watch? Maybe we could—'

'He can't answer you, Mum!'

'Meg, don't say that!'

'Stop pretending! He can't answer you and he can't even hear you any more!'

I breathe in so sharply it hurts, then I watch for a blink of his eyes to prove our daughter wrong but I get nothing. I take Peter's hand and wait for a squeeze but still get nothing. I look at his mouth, hoping his lips might curl up into even a hint of a smile to give me a clue as to what is going on in his mind, but it doesn't move. I wait some more as Meg takes out her phone and texts her friend and my eyes sting as I ask the question again, but I don't get a response, not even a flicker of his eyes.

Then I feel his hand in mine and I get four lightning-fast

squeezes, which choke me up entirely and I can hardly breathe. Meg is still stuck in her phone.

'*You're really annoying me right now.*'

'I'll be right back,' I say, quickly flipping the channel to Sky Discovery, where plant life under the sea is being documented. 'Meg, just stay here a minute, will you? I really need the loo.'

I leave Peter's room past my daughter, who still hovers by the doorway, and I quicken my step down the hallway to the little downstairs bathroom off the kitchen. This tiny room is my usual haven, where I go undercover on a daily basis to allow myself a quick, quiet sob into my hands as I sit on the lid of the toilet, then I grab a few deep breaths to settle me before I dab round my eyes over the sink. I allow myself exactly three minutes every day to do this when I need to, but no more, and it's a routine I've grasped control of from years of practice.

'She doesn't mean it and neither does he,' I tell my reflection in the mirror, glad I no longer wear mascara or I'd be a constant spidery-faced mess. Maybe I took too long with dinner? Or is he mad at me being snappy with Meg? I wish he could tell me! 'It's not the real Peter any more. The real Peter loves you. He doesn't know what he's doing and he doesn't mean it.'

But no matter how many times I chant these words to myself, the hurt still fizzles in my veins and my heart pumps faster. I check the time. Its seven p.m. already and time for

Peter's medication, so I've no more time to feel sorry for myself, no matter how much I want to. I open the bathroom door, blow out a long breath and get on with it.

'Danny, turn down that bloody racket!' I shout as I pass the stairwell. 'Danny!'

He does it immediately which reinforces that he *can* actually hear and isn't stone deaf as his sister thought a few minutes ago.

'Meg, there you go, problem solved,' I say when I get back to Peter's room.

But of course, just as I should have predicted, she has already gone.

3.

The weekend rolls by and our daily weekly routine clicks in like clockwork once Monday comes. The children are back at school leaving Peter and I to our own devices, where I'll potter with him about the house on his motorized wheelchair, a skill we have managed to not only master but also embrace, after a rocky start when he refused to co-operate by slumping over at every given opportunity.

'I'm just going out to feed the chickens,' I tell him as I park him at the window like a waiting puppy. 'I won't be long and you can watch from here.'

He'll sit there by the window as usual, as I tiptoe through the gauntlet of our vast garden, down by the rusting green-house in which we once joked he would one day take up full-time residence, when he was older and more green-fingered just like his late father was. He'll watch me as I dodge the springtime puddles that fill the dips and gaps on the lawn, and as I duck under the cherry blossom tree, whose flowers come and go in the blink of an eye once a year for too short a time. I'll make my way through the garden until I reach the small space in the far corner known as the 'hen pen' – a tiny triangular home for our four chickens whose company I enjoy every day.

'Good morning, Hilary,' I say to the plump-breasted mother hen as she struts around my feet, waiting for her daily feed. 'Good morning, Rooster Henry! Look at you, all handsome and magnificent, just like a rooster should! And a very good morning to you young George and Molly! How's life today in your little corner of the world? I hope old Freddie the Fox hasn't been sniffing around again!'

I put my hands into the old navy bucket that came with this house when we first moved in, and I fill my palms full of golden grain pellets, then watch as they fly through the air and onto the soil, where the family of four get stuck into their morning feast. I can still see Peter in the distance by the window, but I wish he was able to properly share such a simple yet joyous daily moment where our chicken family – a mum, dad, son and daughter – share their morning breakfast, just like he used to. Any recent attempts to take him to feed the chickens were met with low moans the moment he saw me fill the bucket of grain.

I glance up to the window, hearing the buzzer attached to his chair ring in the distance, and I wave to let him know I haven't forgotten him.

'Just two minutes!' I say out loud, knowing there is nothing he needs urgently right now. I remind myself it's just a reflex of the fingers and not an actual call for help.

It rings again, burning in my ears, and I do my best to ignore it. I try to allow myself this moment in the morning air, alone with nature for only a few minutes. Even though I'm only a few steps away from the farm-house, in my mind I can ever so briefly drift into another make-believe world.

The buzzer sounds again.

Just two minutes, please.

I close my eyes, seeing him as he used to be, so tall and strong and proud of the life we'd made here on our farm, just like he told me we would on our wedding day.

Another ring of the buzzer.

'I'll be right with you, honey!' I call to him, waving fran-tically like a proud mum in the audience of a school play who wants their child to see them. 'I won't be long! I know you're there!'

But the buzzing continues.

'Please! Just two minutes to myself!'

I put my hand to my chest as a weight, like a thud or a thump, overcomes me, and before I know it I'm on my knees on the soil, heaving ugly sobs onto the ground below me as grief takes over just like it is known to in a huge suffo-cating wave when I least expect it. No, my husband isn't dead, but the life we once had is long gone. And then the flashbacks fill my head.

The accident wasn't meant to happen, but then that's the sneaky way of an accident, isn't it? An accident pounces

25

and in the flick of a switch, in the blink of an eye, with the tick of the clock, life as we know it no longer exists.

It was just an ordinary day and we were just an ordinary family. We were a young mother and father who only had eyes for each other, and we idolized our pigtailed eight-year-old daughter in her yellow welly boots and shorts, who held hands with her adoring little brother as they named their new pets here in the Irish countryside. We were safe, all of us, in this picturesque lough-side paradise so far away from harm and danger, or so we'd thought.

Peter had dreamed every piece of our very existence into life. He'd taken the house he grew up in so idyllically and together we'd made it our own. He'd built a double swing in the garden from old tyres, and a tree house that over-looked our small collection of animals which our children adored. A sheepdog called Rex, a ragdoll cat called Bluebell, an old-fashioned grumpy goat who had no name. She was more trouble than joy, but we loved her nonetheless, and there was also a cluster of sheep in the field over the fence. We painted the sheds forest green, we bought an old red tractor and fixed it up, we even transformed the barn into a bar where we'd have our friends round for drinks and music, or we'd host barbecues for neighbours who always left with their hearts full as well as their bellies.

We were known for our hospitality and our positive energy. I was an English teacher and a freelance features writer for newspapers and magazines, who could never shake off winning the first and only village beauty pageant here at the age of sixteen. Peter was the handsome Madden son who'd won my heart not too long after that, here in our homeland which is named after the green hills and valleys that look out onto the western sultry shores of Lough Neagh.

Now, instead of the golden couple we once were, we are looked upon by neighbours with heavy sighs and tilted heads, we are spoken to in shops in sorrowful whispers, and this farmhouse that once was so full of love and family laughter has now become a place where a medical support team comes and goes from daily, just so that Peter can live here still, rather than in a care home. Instead of a home bouncing with love and fun, it's now a place where we all tiptoe around reality in scenes of silence and frustration, no matter how hard I try to create this new 'normal'.

'I see you, Peter!' I call out again from where I crouch, on all fours now, as the chickens peck the seeds from the ground and the buzzer in the distance rings on. 'I see you! I'm coming back now!'

The unannounced sound of a car on our laneway makes me gather myself together, so I brush down the soil from my dungarees, fix my hair behind my ears, and dab under my eyes with the heel of my hand. I grab the bucket, fake a smile, and then make my way towards the house to see who our most unexpected visitor is.

'Bernice?' I whisper to myself as my mother-in-law's car comes into view. Peter's mum *never* arrives here unannounced, but as I get closer I realize she has company. 'Hang on. Is that . . . is that *Kelly?*'

I quicken my pace, my heart racing with dread as I wonder what on earth brings these two women together on this crisp spring Monday morning. My mother-in-law lives forty-plus miles away from here and her visits are always planned and carefully scheduled to fit around her busy new city lifestyle with her new husband. Why would she be here now and, more importantly, why would she be with Kelly?

'Go inside, we'll follow you in,' says Kelly, her voice soft and reassuring as always. 'Don't worry, nothing is wrong. Peter is calling you.'

'I'll see to him,' I hear Bernice mumble as she closes the car door, but I almost race to get to him before her. As much as I enjoy Bernice's ways, she can still push all the stereotypical mother-in-law buttons when she feels like it. When we clash, we go hard, and I've a feeling there is something brewing to coincide with her unannounced arrival.

I push the back door open, noticing how the handle is getting looser by the day, and make a mental note to put it on my to-do list, then I make my way across the slate-tiled floor to Peter, who stares out the window as if I'm still out there.

'What's wrong, my love?' I ask, slightly breathless. 'I wasn't very long, was I?'

The buzzer rings again and I put my hands to my face. The noise! That goddam noise! He doesn't know he is doing it any more. It's just a reflex. It's just a *reflex*!

I take his hand off the buzzer, and when I look up I see Kelly and Bernice watch on at us, their heads tilted and deep concern in their eyes.

'How about I take you out for some fresh air, Peter, while Annie and your mum have a catch-up?'

Kelly doesn't wait for me to respond to her suggestion, but swiftly takes over with my husband while my mother-in-law fills the kettle. Despite my initial reaction not to let her come in here and instantly take over, my inner distress makes me give in. I sit at the worn pine kitchen table when she nods towards it, indicating me to do as I'm told. My head spins a little, I'm dizzy with exhaustion, and the room is a swirl around me.

'We are worried,' she whispers.

'No, Bernice.'

'You need to make some changes and fast,' she says a little louder as soon as Kelly reaches the other side of the back door, her voice lilting and full of chat as she takes Peter out into the morning sunshine. 'Kelly and I are concerned and we wanted to come here together to tell you so. You cannot go on like this.'

Bernice is as firm as she is delicate in her looks. 'Delicate like a rose,' her late husband Bob Madden used say. 'And just as prickly too.' She is glamorous and slender in her face and figure, she is petite but she is fierce, and I know that when she means business, she means business. A blind man could see that this is one of those times. I sense my own defences rise.

'I'm fine!' I say, launching straight into denial mode as I always do. 'Peter may be your son but he is *my* husband and this is *our* life.'

And you have your own fancy life to get on with, I feel like saying. It's on the tip of my tongue but I refuse to sound bitter and resentful of how Bernice has moved on from the grieving widow she was all those years ago to a reinvention of life with Jake, a handsome banker from the north-east coast, who whisked her away from this rural village to his fancy apartment overlooking a harbour outside Belfast city. He even has his very own boat. She goes sailing again like she used to do with Bob on Lough Neagh, only now instead of fishing for eels it's for much more glamorous jaunts around Bangor Marina. She goes for lunch with her book-club friends and her library colleagues, and she is president of a wine-tasting club (a very expensive wine-tasting club).

She pushes a coffee cup into my hands and holds her cool nimble fingers on top of mine, looking into my eyes for a few seconds. I feel my throat close in and the swell of tears rise, trying to choke me. I swallow hard. I don't want to cry in front of her but my lips purse, fighting back the urge that overcomes me.

'You always were a stubborn little so-and-so,' she says,

tilting up her chin as she speaks. 'I tried to tell Peter that but he wouldn't listen.'

'I think that's a perfect example of the kettle calling the plot black,' I reply, as the tears subside, thank goodness, and my defiance matches hers. 'You're not exactly known for your easy-going ways either, Bernice, believe me.'

She raises an eyebrow and we both smile.

'Look, I'm negotiating with work to cut down my hours at the library, so I can come to you once a week,' she says, and again I open my mouth to protest but she keeps going. 'Perhaps every Friday, or I can do Saturdays if that's better?'

'But—'

'No, Annie, please listen! I want to do this and I think you need it, even for just a little while to give you some breathing space.'

'And do what?'

'Whatever you like!' she exclaims. 'Spend the day in bed if you want. Or read or write or do whatever it is that makes you feel like your old self again. Go down to that bookstore you love and browse, instead of scooting in and out like your life depends on it. Look around you! Smile again! Reconnect with some friends. Get out of this house and live a little, for goodness' sake!'

'I don't have any friends except—'

'Well, find some! Remember how you used to love—'

'I used to love being with Peter,' I whisper as my bottom

lip trembles. 'My old self doesn't exist any more, Bernice. It hasn't in a long time.'

'But you can find yourself again, love. You deserve to.'

'I can't! Now, thank you for your offer, but Peter is my husband and it's up to me to care for him, in sickness and in health. Remember our wedding vows? He'd have done the same for me.'

Bernice raises an eyebrow. I know what she is thinking because I'm thinking it too. *Would he?*

'Annie, it's time to get real when it comes to looking after everyone and everything!' she tells me, her voice rising again just a little. 'Of course you feel that's your duty, but it doesn't mean you can't do other things as well. Peter is the victim of a horrific, life-debilitating accident, but what would he say to you if he could? Would he like to see you like this? Not a chance! You can still find yourself again, Annie. It's important, darling. It's too sad watching you fade into this miserable existence.'

I sniffle and she takes a tissue from under her sleeve, and then hands it to me just like I'm her own child. This simple gesture sets me off and I'm back to how I was in the pen with the chickens again, sobbing like a baby.

'I don't know what else I should be doing,' I cry out loud, so glad my children are in school and far away from my meltdown. 'I don't know what I'm doing wrong!'

'You're doing nothing wrong,' she tells me. 'But you're doing this all on your own and it's horrible! It's absolutely awful what has happened to Peter, but you're suffering so badly too and it's incredibly sad.'

I shake my head.

'I'm not suggesting you hit the tiles on the weekend or anything,' she says.

I throw my eyes up and laugh out loud in protest.

'Go for dinner, go for lunch, even if it's on your own,' she suggests. 'Find a new hobby or interest.'

'I couldn't.'

'Write the way you used to. *Dream* the way you used to. Remember that article you wrote? The one that made that big magazine? Every editor in the business was calling you non-stop wanting more after that, and Peter was so proud!'

I roll my eyes. I had to turn down a lot of work after that one article, only because fate got in the way and my husband was almost killed.

'I can't dine out on that for ever,' I say, pushing my hair off my face. 'That was years ago for a start. And again, that was before . . . before all this.'

'When did you become so negative?'

I stand up and lean my hands on the table.

'When my whole fucking life fell apart seven years ago, that's when, Bernice!' I say, finally cracking now. 'It's all right for you with your fancy lifestyle and handsome new husband to distract you! I'm in a living wake here! I can't just brush myself down and start again! I'm doing my very best, and if I'm struggling then I'm struggling! I'm keeping my head above water as well as everyone else's around here!'

Bernice doesn't flinch at my change of stance in our conversation. In fact she barely blinks an eye. I sit down again and put my hands to my head, staring at the table, trying to control my breath.

'Meg and Danny need me to keep some sense of normality, not to go running the roads with new-found friends,' I say, feeling like she can't argue with that. 'It's important for them to have—'

'It's important for them to see their mother live a happy life, not for her to be an exhausted shell of the woman she used to be!' Bernice replies firmly. 'I wasn't going to tell you this at all, but it was Meg who called me to say you've been crying behind closed doors every day and in bed at night. Then I was told by someone at work in the library about an Instagram account, where you say how you really feel, and it made me realize you need more help than you've been admitting.'

'Oh God!'

'I know about your huge following, Annie,' she whispers. 'And that's OK. You have to let it out somehow. It's like therapy for you and that's good.'

My stomach churns.

'I didn't – I didn't think anyone . . . does Kelly know?'

Bernice shakes her head.

'No, she doesn't. Look, it was a busybody colleague at

my library who put two and two together after hearing me talk about you and Peter, but don't worry, I could never bring myself to read it and I know I never will,' she explains gently. 'But I'm afraid for Meg. She hears you, Annie. She is worried about you. Then Kelly contacted with the same concerns. We are all worried sick.'

I feel like a lump of lead has settled in my stomach and my eyes widen. Not only have my innermost thoughts been exposed to my mother-in-law, but now I'm being told my children hear my not-so-silent tears.

'Meg called me yesterday. And Danny says he tries so hard to make you laugh, but sometimes it's like your mind is a million miles away,' she whispers. 'He tries his best to put a smile on your face, Annie, and it's making him sad. Seeing you struggle so badly is not good for them, nor is it good for you.'

The tears spill out and I put my hand over my mouth. I've always tried desperately to put on a brave face in front of my kids, but all this time they've seen right through me.

'Accept some extra help for goodness' sake,' Bernice tells me, pushing her slender shoulders back. 'If you won't consider respite, then please let me help you in the small way that I can.'

'My children aren't meant to be worried about me,' I whisper. 'It's meant to be the other way round.'

'Exactly, so on that note,' she says, straightening up in her chair even more, 'I'm coming to stay with you all this weekend, so you can go out for dinner with Kelly and her friends at the Red Fox. End of story. No feedback required. Both Danny and Meg agree it's a good idea.'

I open my mouth to respond but she puts up a pointed finger, just as Kelly arrives back into the kitchen with Peter.

I look at my husband for some answers or support but he doesn't say a word.

Of course he doesn't say a word. He bloody well can't.

~ Meg ~

Dear Daddy,

What can we do to make her smile again? I don't mean to be so distant but I can barely look at her these days.

I know you can't hear me and you'll never, ever read this, but I keep writing to you in this diary until I can think of something to do to make me feel better.

I feel so guilty for what I said that day to make you fall and I know I'm about to tell Mum everything, even though I know it will upset her even more. I pretend I'm doing homework, I pretend I'm chatting on my phone, I pretend I'm sleeping and I spend my time writing to you just so I don't have to look at her too much, in case I tell her what I know.

It's making me so sad, Dad. I'm so confused, and I don't know how to talk to Mum about it.

I hate to hear her cry and then watch as she hides how sad she is too. I know she's going to be mad at me for running to Nan, but I just had to tell someone.

And why don't I cry like she does? Maybe I should be crying too? Maybe I don't deserve to cry because of what I said to distract you.

But I am crying on the inside, I really am, as if it was me who fell that day in the barn and not you.

Like a balloon that's floating away, I do my best to grasp on to happy memories of the way it used to be, but nothing seems to work any more. I reach and stand as tall as I can, but they are drifting away, out of reach and out of sight. I am forgetting you fast. So fast, and it scares me so much.

I can only remember what I said to you that day. I can only remember the look of horror on your face before you fell. I can only remember how it was my fault.

It was all my fault!

And I'm angry at you too, Daddy. And I'm sorry for you. But most of all I'm sorry for her, who has to live this life of misery, all because of me.

I don't want you to remember that day at all. Instead I want you to remember how you cheered when you taught me to ride on roller-skates without falling over. You did cheer on my efforts, didn't you? Or am I making that up in my own mixed-up mind?

I want you to remember the fishing trips on the lough with Grandad Bob by our side before he passed away. I only remember those in stills, like a flicker of black-and-white images in my head.

I try to hear your voice in real time so badly, but I can't find the words you might say to fifteen-year-old me now. I want to talk to you about my schoolwork and my so-called social life. I want to tell you so much of what I'm doing now,

I want to hear you tell me off for being more obsessed with boy bands instead of reality like Jodie's dad says to her. I want to tell you everything, but the words just won't come my way, no matter how hard I try to find them.

Most of all, I want to tell you that I'm sorry. Most of all, I want Mum to have something to smile about again.

Please let that happen one day soon, and maybe life will get better for all of us.

x

4.

The restaurant has six concrete steps that lead downwards from the main street, and as I teeter carefully in my black heels, the first thought that springs to mind is how the Red Fox, our local tavern-turned-bistro, is totally unequipped for wheelchair users, which is so unacceptable in this day and age. I feel like going back and forgetting the whole thing, despite Kelly and Bernice's insistence that I join in on this birthday dinner.

Why should I go to such a place when it doesn't cater for people like my husband? But when I look back, I see that Bernice has already left the kerbside where she dropped me off, probably knowing if she hung around in the car to make sure I'd made it inside that I'd be more inclined to change my mind.

I hold onto the railing that leads to the glass front door and push my way inside, scanning the dim lighting for Kelly and Joel's gathering. I don't have to look very hard to find them. A sea of balloons to the right guides me on the way, but my focus is interrupted by Kelly herself, who appears out of nowhere to greet me in a beautiful black dress that hugs her figure and makes her look more radiant than ever.

'Look at you!' she exclaims, holding my arms and leaning back to get a proper stare at my attire. 'You look like you've stepped out onto the red carpet in Hollywood, not downtown mid-Ulster! Come and meet everyone!'

'Wait Kelly, just wait,' I say, trying to catch my breath. My shoes are too tight and this stupid dress I found in my wardrobe is digging in around my shoulders. I feel like a total imposter just being here. I can't bloody afford it for a start, and I feel like everyone is staring and whispering in my direction, even though I've absolutely no evidence to back that up whatsoever. All I can see are happy couples, all I can hear is jolly background music and laughter over the usual clinking restaurant sounds. This is so not me any more.

Kelly hands me a glass of bubbly and I drink it in one go, right here in the middle of the restaurant where she's come to meet me.

'Breathe, Annie, for goodness' sake,' she says. 'You're safe. You're in your own home village, remember?'

'It feels like a different planet,' I confess. 'There's something about this place that . . . boy, those bubbles are good.'

I've known Kelly for seven years now, since a month after Peter's accident, to be precise, when she was assigned as his community nurse, and we couldn't believe that we both lived in this little lough-shore village where there's not much more than a small grocery store, a chapel, Corners bookshop, a school and this restaurant. She is what's known as a 'blow-in', since she moved here one summer from Belfast with her very beautiful Italian-American friend Lexi, who worked right here in the local pub. Lexi moved back to the States very suddenly after her first summer here, Kelly stayed on to be with Joel, who she'd met at the hospital; then just like us they got married, took over his family home, and the rest is history.

Lexi was never heard of, or indeed mentioned around here again, while Kelly became part of the community.

'Happy birthday, Joel,' I say gently to Kelly's husband, who takes the small gift I've brought with me for him when I slip into the seat beside him. Kelly sits opposite us, her bangles jangling as she speaks with her hands to the lady beside her. Thankfully, Joel doesn't make a fuss, nor does he open the modest gift in front of everyone. I've only met Joel a few times and he's always been quiet and humble, letting Kelly talk for him mostly, which is a soft relief as I really don't want to be made a fuss off.

'That's so kind of you,' he says, leaning across and giving me a friendly air-kiss, his cheek brushing against mine. 'I can't believe I'm forty, but it's when they say life begins, isn't that right?'

I freeze automatically at his manly smell, the brief sensation of his light stubble on my cheek and his slight touch. I look across the table at Kelly. She is grinning and nodding towards me, which thankfully washes away the pity-party

I was about to have inside for how Peter's fortieth, just a few months ago, was far from a 'life begins' milestone. My own had been just weeks after that, and was a non-event at my own insistence, even if the kids did their best with some gifts and a cake with my name on it.

'I'm going all out and having the finest fillet steak with a big fat glass of yummy Malbec to wash it down,' says Kelly, rubbing her hands. 'There's some live music afterwards too, so we can keep this table and maybe even have a dance once the food settles.'

She sees the fear in my face at the very thought of it.

'No pressure! Food first, of course,' she says with a wink. 'Now, Annie, before we eat, let me just quickly introduce you to Joel's sister Sharon and her husband Gary; then there's his cousin Ciara who joins us all the way from London with her partner Martha, and at the end it's the very quiet Dave who is here from Dublin. An extremely friendly bunch, but you'll find out for yourself in due course, I've no doubt about it.'

Everyone seems to think it's hilarious that Dave is described as quiet. I feel my face flush when they all look my way again, even though they really couldn't be nicer in their approach. I give them all a polite wave, but I'm so relieved to be at the far end of the table, close to Kelly and Joel, where I do my best to resist the urge to check my phone to see if Peter is all right at home before we've even ordered our food.

'Annie, you'll never believe, but look at what's on the specials this evening,' she says, pointing out the menu. 'Your absolute favourite! Seafood paella.'

My eyes meet Kelly's, and as always her warmth makes me totally at ease. I absolutely adore a good paella dish, especially in a restaurant when it's made by a proper chef, and my heart rises a little in excitement. It's been so long.

'You're doing great,' says Joel beside me. 'We'll look after you. Just be yourself.'

I feel better for his sentiment, even if I've no idea who myself really is any more.

The evening passes quite pleasantly, but it's when we are enjoying dessert – which for me is the most delightful panna cotta with pomegranate – that my ears really tune into what's going on around me, as Londoners Ciara and Martha are now the focus of everyone's attention.

'And the book was snapped up by an indie publisher and Martha has never looked back!' Ciara announces as her blushing partner tries to play the story all down. 'She now has the eyes and ears of some of the big guns and it's very thrilling indeed.'

'Ah, you're making it sound a lot more exciting than it really is,' says Martha, as she fans her face with a napkin. 'It's not as fancy as she says, believe me.'

'You're just being modest, darling,' says Ciara, touching her partner's arm as she talks. 'Martha is making quite a name for herself in the publishing world across the water now that she's sold her first book. Her client list is growing and I couldn't be prouder.'

My stomach twists and turns as I listen in awe about Ciara and Martha's busy life in London, where Martha, as we've now learned, works in publishing – a world that I used to dream of so badly.

'Are you a writer?' Kelly asks for clarification.

'Oh no, I'm a literary agent in a very small boutique organization in South London,' says Martha. 'I manage the writing careers of a few authors, ghost writers and poets. No one you'll have heard of yet, but I'm still building my list and taking it slowly. I'm always scouting for new talent.'

Kelly looks at me open-mouthed as the others chat over each other and I plead with my eyes that she won't mention my own humble writing efforts in days gone by.

'Annie writes amazing stuff!' she says out loud, and the entire table stop their conversation and look at me like I've just landed in from a different planet. 'She really does! One of her features was published in *Grazia* magazine a few years ago and it was totally ground-breaking! What was it called again, Annie? Something about—'

'Upsetting the Apple Cart,' I say, squirming in my seat.

'Wait a minute!' says Martha, and my stomach flips. 'I remember that piece! I took a clipping of it and I'm sure I still have it somewhere in a file back home. Gosh, please tell me you've written more since that, Annie! It was indeed ground-breaking!'

I feel beads of sweat form and a fizz of anxiety rush through me.

'Oh, no honestly, Martha, I think I peaked at that,' I say quickly, embarrassed as hell when I think of the stories I've made up lately about Henry and Hilary the chickens, or the Instagram that not even Kelly knows about yet. 'I'm a former features writer who once had a dream, but now I'm just a mum and a wife who lives in a rundown farmhouse out by the lough. I had high hopes once, but life had other plans.'

I want to kick myself for playing this all down, but it's been a very long time since I had eyes on me like this for my writing. For a brief moment, it looked like the world was at my feet. I always believed I had the ability to write so much more, but Peter's accident took me down a very different path, didn't it?

I don't want to be centre of attention like this and I'm glad when Dave takes over at the other end of the table with a claim that he should write his own life story. It would be an instant bestseller, even if he does say so himself.

'I'm sure it would,' says Martha with a wry smile and when all eyes divert Dave's way, I breathe a sigh of relief.

I've stayed much longer than I'd planned to. It's time I headed for home.

* * *

Martha is at the sink of the bathroom cubicle beside me almost twenty minutes later as my taxi waits outside. She has some mascara and lipstick out in front of her and I try not to stare as I wash my hands and dry them quickly.

'According to Dave, his life story would make *great* reading and would shoot right up the charts,' says Martha with a smile and roll of her eyes. 'If I had a pound for every time I heard that, I wouldn't have to worry about my bills.'

I smile in return, wishing the wine would loosen my tongue like it used to do and give me something witty to say in return.

'Between that and Kelly blowing *my* trumpet about a magazine article years ago, I'm sure your career is going to zoom into the stratosphere.'

'You're different,' she says, holding my gaze now before going to her handbag. 'And I mean that. Look, here's my business card if you ever feel like getting in touch for a chat. Despite my sarcasm about Dave, I am new and hungry for writers, so this is good timing that we've met. You're not in the Dave category at all, Annie. I'd love to hear your writing voice, I really would.'

I glance at her card and flip it in my hands, reading her London address as a shiver runs through me. There was once a day when I knew almost every literary agency in the UK and Ireland as I'd scour the internet searching for the right match for my dream career, yet here I am now, standing in my own home village in the middle of nowhere, with a real live agent offering to read my stuff. I seem to have lost all my vigour, just as Bernice reminded me recently, which pains me deeply.

'Thank you. That's very kind of you, but I really don't have much to show just now,' I tell her as my confidence stays rigid on the floor. 'My family keep me very busy these days so writing has taken a back seat and . . . '

I trail off before I say any more. Martha the literary agent does not need to hear my sob story on her night out.

'Oh, of course,' Martha says. 'I know how it can be. Well, I don't *know* yet but I can imagine how busy family life can be.'

'But thank you for showing some interest.'

She nods politely then goes back to the mirror to retouch her make-up while I stand there, kicking myself inside, knowing that an opportunity like this comes only once in a lifetime.

I go to walk away but then I stop and catch her eye in the mirror.

Say it. Just *say* it.

'I have an Instagram thing I do,' I blurt out from behind her. 'It's anonymous. Well, at least it is to most, but you could maybe read it if you want?'

'Really?' She stops and turns towards me, red lipstick poised mid-air.

'It's about us – me and my husband – and how we used to be and how I am feeling now,' I continue quickly. 'Which is mainly angry and feeling sorry for myself, I have to warn you, but my followers seem to like it a lot, even if they never see my face or know my true identity. Ten thousand of them. Just please don't tell anyone it's me. Please.'

My eyes are like saucers and Martha's are too now.

'Ten *thousand* followers?'

I swallow hard and nod. I don't think I've felt so vulnerable in a long time, but that younger Annie who once had a dream is now screaming inside for me to make this moment last, despite my lack of self-esteem and crucifying inner fears.

'That's something! What's it called?' asks Martha. She quickly takes her phone from her handbag.

'It's called *Mum of Two Missing You*,' I say, closing my eyes tight and hoping I won't regret this in the morning. 'But my husband isn't dead before you feel sorry for me. You can just – you can just read it and see. You can follow me.' I tell her the handle and she looks it up on her phone there and then.

'Amazing! I've just followed you,' she adds, looking very hip and cool with her bright lips and short caramel hair. 'I honestly *adored* that article in *Grazia*, Annie. And don't worry, your secret Insta is safe with me. I can't wait to have a scroll and I won't tell anyone, I promise.'

'Thank you.'

I take a deep breath and saunter out of the bathroom, feeling amidst my shock and fear a rush that comes from the very tips of my toes to the top of my head, like a sudden burst of electricity.

Wow. This is what I've tried to tell Meg and Danny to find in life in a 'feel the fear and do it anyway' type of attitude, even if I haven't exactly practised what I've been preaching to them until now.

I feel a spring in my step as I walk through the restaurant and say my final goodbyes to the birthday party revellers who are itching to dance, unable to hide the smile that creeps over my face and, when I go outside, I honestly feel like I could dance on the street, even if my feet are killing me.

For the first time in for ever I'm excited for something just for myself, and maybe it's the rush of the wine, maybe it's the safety and warmth of Joel and Kelly's company, maybe it's the opportunity Martha has just presented to me, even if it could be pie in the sky, but all in all tonight was unexpectedly enjoyable and I can't wait to go home and tell Peter all about it.

He will be so . . .

He will . . .

Even if I will never know if he understands me, I can still tell him all about it, and that's something, I suppose.

@mumoftwo_missingyou

It was a Saturday morning.

We were lying on a patch of grass by the
lough. The ground was still damp from the
morning dew despite the rare blast of hazy sun
during that rainy summer of 1999, and the
famous midges that swarmed the lough shore
were having a feast on my bare legs as we lay
there making daisy chains.

It was the day we'd said goodbye to my
father, and he'd had a send-off like no other, or
so my mother told on repeat to anyone who
would listen. According to her there hadn't been
a bigger funeral in the chapel since the old
schoolmaster had died. A lone piper led the
cortège, followed by me, Mum, my sister and
hundreds of mourners who knew my dad from
all walks of life. There were fishermen lining

the roadside, their heads bowed in sorrow as we walked past. There were rows of men and women of all ages who donned the local football colours, and there were men in suits I'd never seen before who whispered in low muffled voices and who smelled like warm tobacco. He slipped into the pew beside me in the front row of the chapel and I had never been so glad to see him as I was then.

I read a poem I'd written about my dad, then everyone cried, but I suppose that was to be expected.

And after all the fuss and chitchat as teacups clinked and mourners reminisced, he and I sneaked away together to our little place where we lay together hand in hand, trying to let the sound of the water soothe away my pain.

'You should be very proud of yourself,' he told me as he placed a daisy chain around my wrist, tying it so delicately with his nimble fingers. 'You read your poem so beautifully.'

'Thank you.'

'Imagine you wrote those words?' he said in awe. 'And everyone knew you meant every single one of them. You should be so proud, and your dad would be too of how you held your nerve together.'

'It was so hard,' I told him, remembering how being up on that pulpit felt like I was standing on a world stage.

'I know it was. I could see your lip wobbling at one point and I was urging you to get through it before you cried, and you did get through it.'

I sobbed like a baby in his arms when he said that, my black woollen funeral dress suffocating me, but I was glad of its warmth and of him as the whip of the wind from the lough blew in my hair. He cupped my face with his hands and I could see there were tears in his eyes too. I'd never seen him cry before. Boys from where we grew up never cried, but I saw such tenderness in him that I'd never seen before in any man I knew. Not even my own father, who I loved and adored more than anyone else until then.

'I love you,' he told me, and his eyes wrinkled and he smiled when he said it. 'I really love you.'

I couldn't speak as my throat was so dry, so all I could do was nod and cry into his shoulder until my voice eventually came back, what felt like five minutes later.

'I love you too,' I replied with such sincerity

that it came from my toes. 'I think I'm going to love you for a very long time.'

We lay back down on the grass and I wished right then for the world to stop spinning to let this moment freeze in time. My dad was gone, my pain was immeasurable, but he was here holding me.

And I knew right then that as long as we were together, I'd never be afraid or lonely again.

But now I am, you see.

He is still here but I am afraid and I am so terribly lonely.

My family and friends are telling me to find myself again but guess what, readers . . .?

For the first time, tonight, after seven long years, I think I caught a glimpse of who I really could be.

Tonight, at the restaurant, I think I caught a glimpse of who I really am, and deep down, I believe that my husband would want me to be that person too.

Grid Pic: A bunch of daisies from our garden on my windowsill
Likes: 2,111
Comments: 234

5.

Two weeks have passed since Joel's birthday bash, and for most of that time Kelly and I have a daily debate about why I'm refusing to come to some sort of regular arrangement for the weekends when the offer of help is there. The more she brings it up, the more I turn it down and I'm glad when she eventually gives it a rest and decides that risking our friendship over it isn't worth it, but Peter's neurologist at his next check-up isn't quite so willing to give in.

My handbag is full of leaflets and brochures on respite suggestions when we return home from the hospital, but there's nothing in there I haven't seen before. I say a sullen hello to Kelly who waits for us.

She takes Peter to his room and I make myself a coffee, which I sip as I prepare a curry for the kids coming in. Meg has cello practice today and Danny has football, so they're not due in just yet, and thankfully there's a late bus on a Thursday to get them this far without me having to race out to pick them up like I do on other days of the week.

I ignore the stack of laundry I could be doing right now

to flick through the brochures, stirring the pot of curry with my other hand. I do my best to actually read the words this time rather than skim over them nonchalantly like I have done so many times before.

The first place, Beechwood Manor, is nestled in a forest park and boasts an excellent 'home from home' environment (of course it does), as does the privately owned Maryvale House, which offers twenty-four-hour visitation and costs the equivalent of a vital organ for the privilege, or there's the much more modest Carndale Lodge, which I remember an old school friend's granny staying in. We used to hold our nose going in to visit her because it smelled like, as we once put it, 'old people'.

No matter where I look, though, they all cost a fortune, even for a weekend respite here and there.

I turn down the cooker and go to the table, where I sit down and lean my head onto my left hand. I look around in a daze, drifting off to another world as I often do when things are quiet at home. I must have sat for longer than I thought, as I have to jump up to save the curry just as Meg bursts through the back door, looking as if she has the weight of the world on her shoulders.

'Ah, there she is!' I say, taking the pot off the heat and trying not to look as though I have just clicked back to reality. 'Hungry?'

'Cello practice was horrendous as usual and I've *so* much homework,' she says, flopping herself down onto a beanbag where Rex normally sits, and as usual he sniffs her out and leaps onto her lap. At least for a change she hasn't gone straight to her room. Danny follows suit, with his school tie peeping out of his bag and his grubby football jersey still on after his football practice. I shudder at how his trousers are skimming his ankles.

'Dinner is almost ready,' I say, putting on my best Stepford Wife act as Danny searches in the cupboards for snacks.

I remember the brochures on the table and quickly gather them up before they notice them, shove them in a drawer and quickly serve up dinner to my two children who glance at me tentatively as I pick through my food.

'Is Kelly joining us for dinner?' Meg asks. 'Is she even here?'

'She's here at this time every day during the week,' I say with a smile.

'Of course she is,' Danny mutters, almost as if it's a complaint.

'Is something wrong? I'd imagine she has plans with Joel for dinner,' I say, 'but there's plenty of curry here if she wants some. Or I've some stew from yesterday I could offer her, though that's mostly for your dad after his nap. I still need to blend it, mind you.'

'This is just so weird,' Danny says, picking onions out of his curry and scraping them onto the side of his plate.

'What is?' I ask. 'Oh no, maybe I overdid it with the spices. I think I may have added too much chilli powder, sorry.'

'Not the curry, Mum. All of this,' he says.

'What?'

'Our life. It's a bit weird. Like, who else comes home every day to a nurse in their house, or a physio, or social worker, or that strange squealing music therapist Margo, who really can't sing? It's all a bit . . .'

'A bit what?' I ask, putting my knife and fork down and my hands under my chin as something invisible thumps me in the stomach. 'What is it, Danny? Elaborate on "weird" please, if you can. I'd really love to know what you're finding *weird*.'

Meg shifts in her seat and swallows her food then waves her fork around as she speaks.

'I think he means it's a bit *strange* that we have half a hospital here and no one else we know does,' she says.

'*Strange?*' I choke.

'I didn't say strange, I said weird,' Danny chirps in quickly. 'I'm just saying it's different. We are different, that's all. It's weird.'

I sit back in my chair, my appetite disintegrating at the wonder of what really does go through my children's minds when they are on the outside looking in, or when they are at school heading home to this.

We eat the rest of our meal in silence, and I'm glad when they eventually leave the table, lift their school bags and head to their rooms with full bellies. I gather up the dishes to wash up. I check the clock. It's almost five thirty, which means I've half an hour left before Kelly leaves.

I approach the laundry basket as my phone bleeps a message, but I ignore it at first as I sort darks from whites onto the floor then put the most urgent load into the machine, pour in the liquid and switch it on. I used to love this time of the evening, when dinner was over and Peter and I would chat while cleaning over the kitchen together as Meg and Danny watched cartoons. We'd catch up on each other's day. I'd bitch about some of my teaching colleagues and marvel at some of my favourite students, while he would listen intently – or as best he could – as I rambled on. He'd wash the pots and plates and I'd dry them. We'd do the children's homework, take turns in bathing them a night about, and then I'd pour us a glass of something when they were asleep and we'd snuggle on the sofa in front of the TV.

I lift my phone to see a notification for an email in my inbox, which is unusual at this time of the day, not that I'm exactly bombarded with correspondence on any day, unless it's from school or something medical. I sit down at the table and click on the Outlook icon, assuming that yes, it will either be something from the school about the forthcoming exam season, a follow-up from Dr McCloskey with more recommendations on respite options, or some disappointing junk mail that will tell me I've won something exotic.

But when I open it, I get a surprise.

It's from Martha Walton, Forest Hill Literary Agency. And the subject matter says, 'Quick chat?'

I drop the phone onto the kitchen table as if it's burning my hand, and I stare at it for a few moments, trying to let this sink in.

Thirty-year-old me is dancing a jig inside, while forty-year-old me is determined not to get my hopes up.

I open the email with one eye open and one eye closed, as if it's a scary movie and I'm afraid of what I might see.

'We absolutely adore your work, Annie,' Martha Walton tells me after I've digested the content of her email and called her immediately, as Kelly watches on in my kitchen some minutes later. My stomach flutters. 'I've read every single post online, your followers adore you, and I really think you've got a voice I can work with, so if you've got a few minutes I'd like to tell you about an opportunity you just might be interested in.'

I can barely speak, so I just nod and let her keep going.

'Have you ever thought about ghost-writing?' she asks.

My heart begins to thump, my eyes are wide, and my hands are physically shaking as I put Martha onto loud-speaker.

'Ghost-writing?'

I put the phone on the table. Kelly stares at it from one side and I stare from the other.

'Yes, writing someone's life story as if you are that person,' Martha continues. 'It would be in the person's own words as interpreted by you.'

'Oh, yes I know what ghost-writing is, of course I do,' I say quickly. I push my hair behind my ears, still watching the phone as if it's Martha herself on the table. 'But I've never thought of doing that, no.'

I grimace and shrug in Kelly's direction.

'Well, I've been chatting to a publishing house about you,' says Martha. 'They're looking for a ghost-writer to compile an actor's life story. You've heard of Senan Donnelly, I'm sure? He was very famous in the Nineties and more recently in a big US series called *Broken*?'

'Senan Donnelly?' I repeat.

Of course I've heard of Senan Donnelly. My friend Stacey from school had her bedroom walls plastered with posters of him. In fact, most girls my age did.

'Yes, yes I know exactly who he is,' I reply. 'But I haven't heard of him in years. Where is he now?'

'Right now? West Cork, to be precise,' says Martha. 'He was London- and LA-based for most of his career, but when things began to go, let's say a little bit pear-shaped for him, he moved to a holiday home outside a town called Clonakilty. He has quite a back story and we're wondering if you're up for the challenge, or at least – at this stage – hearing more?'

I do my best to digest what she is saying, but I fear there must be some sort of mistake. Since I stopped feature writing, all I've ever scribbled down is my own feelings on an Instagram post, or a diary I read to Peter, or some random poetry. There's no way I could write someone's life story, especially not someone like Senan Donnelly, who has lived much of his life in the glare of the media.

'Are you sure about this?' I ask her. 'Do you really think I could do that?'

'Of course I do,' laughs Martha. 'Look, I know it's not everyone's gig, but it's a book and it's work. I've told the publisher, Caroline, all about you, and she'd love to talk a bit more if you're up for it.'

My head begins to spin and when Meg comes into the kitchen, I make hand signals for her to be quiet. She rolls her eyes as if I've just sprouted horns and my stomach sinks from the ceiling to the floor. Kelly, meanwhile, is now pacing the room from one part to the next.

'It's a set fee,' Martha continues. 'They're offering decent money but I could probably squeeze them for more. The good news is there's a quick turnaround timewise so, although it's not huge, it's not a bad fee for your first job with us. Put it like this, it would be a published book on your CV and, in this game, that's a very big step on the ladder.'

I glance at Kelly who is now whispering to Meg by the kitchen sink a few feet away. Meg gasps and covers her mouth when Kelly fills her in, but I'm suddenly plunged back to reality as a million questions run through my head.

'So, how would it work?' I ask her, sitting down at the table to compose myself. 'Would Mr Donnelly be able to come here so I could interview him about his life, or would we just talk on the phone? Or we could FaceTime? Or Zoom?'

Martha's long pause says it all.

'Well – well, no, I'm not sure that would be an option, Annie,' she tells me. 'You see, normally the writer "ghosts" the subject. Not the other way around.'

Another pause.

'So I would have to go to him?'

'Yes,' she tells me. 'You would have to go to him. To Cork. Would that be a problem?'

Of course it's a problem, but I don't want to be as blunt as that. There's no point going any further. It's a non-runner. I shake my head and signal to Kelly and Meg to be quiet. There's no room for any more silly excitement. It's not going to happen.

'I'm afraid so, but thank you so much for thinking of me for this, Martha,' I say, looking around me at my kitchen as my excitement goes out the window. 'It sounds like a wonderful opportunity and the money would certainly be a great help, but it wouldn't suit my lifestyle, unfortunately. Thank you all the same, and please do keep me in mind if anything else closer to home comes up.'

Kelly raises an eyebrow, while Meg looks on, as if a million thoughts are running through her puzzled young mind.

'I've two teenagers at home who need me,' I explain further, diverting my eyes from my audience so they don't distract me further, 'and I'm a full-time carer for my husband, so I'm afraid it's not for me.'

'OK, of course. I understand,' says Martha, sounding a

lot more deflated than I thought she would. 'I should probably have explained at first that this is only the offer of an initial meeting with the publisher and with Mr Donnelly in London to discuss it, if that makes any difference. They just wanted to meet to chat it through, but if it's not for you, I totally understand.'

'Ah, so I'd also have to go to *London*?' I laugh, almost snorting at the very notion. 'There is absolutely no way I could go to London! I can barely make a quick trip to the shops never mind—'

'She'll do it!' says Meg, and my eyes dart in her direction. 'Meg?'

'You'll do it, Mum!' she says. 'Why wouldn't you?'

I try to find the words. It's perfectly obvious why!

'Because I can't do it, that's why! What about—'

Meg's reaction has really stumped me. She has tears in her eyes and Kelly stands behind her, biting her lip.

'But you can if you really want to!' says Meg. 'She'll be there! She'll go to London!'

Martha mutters a reply that I can't quite make out, while Kelly makes hand signals for me to speak.

'But—'

'It's only an initial meeting,' says Martha. 'No commitment after that whatsoever.'

I put my hand to my forehead and try to think straight about all of this, especially Meg's out-of-character encouragement. I think of the extra money and all I could use it for around our home. It's not a lottery win like I often pray for, but it would certainly take some heat off here. But mostly I think of my daughter's face just now and the tears in her eyes. She is only fifteen years old. She barely speaks to me these days, but maybe if I don't at least try this out and push my boundaries, she might never forget it? What would this tell her about following her own dreams and taking chances in future if I turned this down?

'We can make it work,' says Kelly, quickly. 'Just go to London and find out more, then we'll take it from there.'

My stomach whooshes at the thought but the weight of Meg's stare pushes me into saying yes.

'OK, OK I'll go to London! But no promises for more,' I say, sitting up straight in the chair as Kelly and Meg's mouths drop open in shock and delight. 'I hope I'm not wasting your time as I'm not sure if this will suit me at all, but I'll go and see what it's all about.'

'Fantastic!' says Martha. 'I'll get your flights sorted and we'll be in touch shortly with all the finer details. I can't wait to meet you again and I really hope you take on this wonderful opportunity. You deserve it!'

I hang up the phone and, as if time stands still, Kelly and I stare at each other for a moment before my hands go to my mouth and I stifle an excited scream. Kelly races towards me and wraps me in a hug, but when I look over her shoulder to see Meg, as usual my daughter has already made her escape.

Just when I thought we'd taken a step closer to each other, she has gone again. When it comes to Meg, I just don't know how to do right from wrong.

~ Meg ~

Dear Daddy,

You'll never believe what just happened, but it's almost like you made my last wish come true and I'm almost pinching myself here in shock and excitement.

I've no idea how, but all of a sudden Mum is going to London to meet a publisher and she might even be writing a book about someone famous, or who used to be famous! Imagine! I've never heard of him but I'll probably google the life out of him after I write to you.

Of course she was going to say no to even finding out more, which is so typical of what life is like here right now. She was going to just throw it all away, but I could see in her eyes she really wanted it. In fact she did say no, but I just looked at her for that split second and something told me to speak up quickly before she lost the opportunity all because of this stupid house and her never-ending commitments around here.

I saw photos of her earlier today when I was in the attic, and they almost made me cry, Dad. It takes a LOT to make me even think about crying these days. I didn't even cry *when Rex almost died after a tractor hit him and that's saying something.*

The photos I found were taken ages before your accident, and she really did look like a different person back then. She was younger, but that's not what I mean. She looked alive, much more alive than she does now, and to be honest it scared me a little how much she has changed.

It's like she's been here but she's not here. It's like she's been dead behind her eyes, just like – well, just like you are, I suppose, so when I saw Kelly's reaction and I heard her saying no because of us – and because of you and having to look after us all as usual – I don't know what came over me but I just blurted it out that she should go.

Then I ran to my room before she asked me any questions, considering I avoid her eye as much as I can now I'm old enough to realize what I did that day.

But I'm not talking about that now. . .

I just wanted to tell you about this because . . . well, for the first time in a long time I think I feel happy for Mum, even if I can't find the words to say that to her just yet.

I think she almost smiled again, just like she did in those old photographs.

x

6.

'Where on earth do you think you're going dressed like that?'

Ten days later, after a lot of deep breaths and numerous convincing pep talks from Kelly and everyone in my family, I'm getting ready to go to London for the day and I'm absolutely terrified.

I stand in the kitchen as they stare at me like I'm a rebellious teenage girl trying to sneak out the door behind my father's back in a skimpy outfit he wouldn't approve of, but it's Kelly's voice I hear just as I am about to head for the airport.

'I thought I looked like a writer,' I say, looking down at my grey pinstripe blazer, white blouse and below-the-knee pencil skirt, an outfit I used to wear to school or for important interviews. 'No?'

'You look like a very prudish, very stuffy English teacher, and that's not what we need to be showing Senan Donnelly today, is it?' she says. 'Let's go back upstairs. We still have time.'

Within minutes I'm changed into a plain white T-shirt, an indigo denim jacket and a flowing pale pink tulle skirt. I found it lying at the back of my wardrobe, but Kelly and Meg both insisted that it made me look much more Carrie Bradshaw than the previous outfit, which according to them resembled Mrs Trunchbull. My blonde bobbed hair is scrunched into rough curls and my make-up is touched up, but I'm not ready yet to go on my merry way of course. I need to run through absolutely everything again with Bernice, who is already bedazzled by the step-by-step daily instructions I've charted out and stuck to the fridge, and that's just for the children.

Kelly is here for the day as promised to look after Peter, even though it's a Saturday and is usually her day off from us. Though my flight back from London tonight will see me home before midnight, I'm a bag of nerves at the occasion that lies before me and all that weighs on it.

'I'll be honest with you, Annie, I'm not the only agent scouting for a writer for Senan's life story, so nothing is guaranteed,' Martha told me this morning on her call to double-check I knew exactly where I was going. 'I'm not sure what you know of him, but Senan has quite a reputation for being, let's say, difficult, but please don't let that put you off. It will be a very challenging yet a very rewarding job, should it all work out.'

Difficult?

I thought instantly of the battle I'd had that morning lifting Peter into and out of the shower chair, slipping on the tiles so that I bit my bottom lip when my chin hit the nearby sink. I'd washed him down only to have to do it all again moments later when he'd had a toilet accident before I'd dressed him properly, and while I puffed and panted my way through it, I could hear Meg and Danny having a full-blown argument in the kitchen over who was getting the last spoonful of Nutella, as if they were both going to starve to death.

'I can do difficult,' I told myself after that, almost tasting the much-needed pay cheque, as if I already had the job signed, sealed and delivered. 'I can definitely do difficult.'

'Don't think about this any further than what today brings,' Kelly tells me when I take a totally expected turn of cold feet just as I'm about to leave the house. 'Don't think about time-frames or commitment or how it might mean you have to leave here for a short while to do the job if you get it. We'll sort all that out. Just take today as it comes and be proud of yourself for getting this far. I will be right here with Peter until you come back tonight, and Bernice is here with Meg and Danny, so there's nothing for you to worry about, only finding your way from Belfast to London to meet Martha and of course the delectable Senan Donnelly. I'm trying to pretend I'm not jealous, but I am. I really am.'

I would pinch myself, but I think I'm too much in shock to pause for a moment to even do that.

*   *   *

'Annie! It's so good to see you!'

Martha's familiarity and open-armed welcome makes me feel slightly at ease when I eventually find myself at her offices in Forest Hill in leafy South London.

I spent most of the journey here, via Gatwick Airport, reading affirmations in a book Kelly bought especially for me in Corners and, if truth be told, I'd sneaked in a brandy on the plane to try and calm my nerve endings (again, a tip given to me by Kelly if I was finding it tough, so I can claim to have done so on purely medical grounds). I've been texting her constantly too as I manoeuvred my way through Tube stations to get this far, and her calming tones definitely helped immeasurably, no matter how many times I fell into a puddle of self-doubt or fear that this was all way too much for someone like me.

'What's Peter doing now?'

'Sleeping.'

'And now?'

'We are at the park.'

'Is all OK?'

'He's having a nap.'

No matter how many times I messaged her, like a frantic mother who'd left their baby for the first time, she indulged me with a short and swift answer which was enough to pacify me a little bit longer. But now that I'm standing on this rather attractive street in London on a beautiful May afternoon, I have to really fight with the imposter syndrome that floods my mind in order to get through this meeting.

'Senan is running a little bit behind, but come inside and I'll introduce you to Caroline, who will be publishing his memoir,' she tells me. 'She's a friend of mine, so please don't be nervous. We're all rooting for you here as it's important for all of us to find the perfect match for Mr Donnelly and his very intriguing life story.'

We climb a flight of stairs to a first-floor office, and Martha leads me inside to a smart but modest meeting area where I see a young red-haired lady who I assume is Caroline, scrolling through her phone. She looks not much older than my Meg, even though I've no doubt she is a fully formed adult and totally competent at her job, but it strikes me immediately how young everyone seems to be, even the receptionist, Jane, who met me with a dazzling smile on the way past.

'You must be Annie? It's so lovely to meet you,' Caroline says, extending her hand to mine. The room smells of coffee and perfume mixed together, and the table is strewn with various celebrity autobiographies, as well as literary magazines and newspapers. I honestly used to daydream of moments like this, spending hours of my life imagining what it might be like to go to London one day and be in this position. I just wish Peter was here to experience it with me.

Caroline leads the discussion, letting me know the background to the 'project' she refers to, outlining how they've allowed three months in total for a first draft to be delivered, which includes a two-week residential and research stint with Senan at his holiday home in West Cork.

I've never been to Cork before. In fact, I can barely remember the last time I was out of my home county until today.

'Two weeks in Cork?' I say, unable to hide my terror as the thought of leaving my family for so long engulfs me. Caroline pauses and Martha thankfully steps in.

'We can go over all of this after the meeting, can't we, Annie?'

'Of course,' I say, doing my best not to be totally overwhelmed when we've barely started.

As the subject changes to the word count and the overall feeling of the story they want to present, I feel a rush of adrenaline run through my veins as the prospect of writing a real book comes within arm's reach for the first time in my life. I salivate at the opportunity of a dream come true, wondering if this is really happening to someone like me. Plus, there's the not-so-small matter of some much-needed money. I think of the list of repairs I have lying in my kitchen drawer. I think of the new clothes I could buy the children. We could maybe even squeeze in a simple holiday by the sea in the summer time . . . oh, how good would it be to see them smiling in the sun like we used to do?

My imaginary spending spree is interrupted when all eyes go to the office door and the grand arrival of Senan Donnelly, whose very presence changes the mood like nothing I've ever experienced before.

Everyone, even Caroline, who so far has been so cool and sophisticated, gasps and shifts in her seat a little.

Despite my determination to play it cool, I have to admit that in the flesh he's even more of a dreamboat than I could ever have imagined.

He's taller than I thought, he works out a lot more than I thought, and he's a hell of a lot more attractive than he looks on screen, if that's even humanly possible.

'He truly is a thing of bad boy, delectable, lick-able beauty,' Kelly had drooled when we'd googled him at every given opportunity leading up to today. 'If he has a light stubble when he shows up, I'd have to be restrained from stroking it, and I'd be fired instantly if I was with you. Thank God it's you and not me going for this writing job.'

And he has a light stubble. Well, he has a *heavy* stubble, but when he says my name in his gravelly, distinctive voice, I don't even flinch.

I'm a professional. I've dealt with celebrities before, albeit minor local celebrities like the mayor or a lad picked to play national football, so there's no way I'm going to lose my cool on this occasion.

Through the glass doors, Jane in reception is reapplying her lipstick and fanning herself with a magazine at the same time as soon as he is out of her sight.

'I'm Senan,' he says, but instead of shaking my hand like Caroline did before him, he leans in and kisses my cheek. He smells of alcohol and cologne, which makes me automatically shift in my seat as if it's a reflexed reaction.

He doesn't apologize for being late, I notice, but instead just clasps his hands on the table and watches for Caroline to continue from where she left off, which she seems to do smoothly and calmly even though I can tell she fancies him just as much as, I'm guessing, most of the female population who meet him might do.

I look at his arms. I look away.

'So, I guess it's over to you two,' Caroline says moments later, fixing her notes into a neat bundle and looking our way now. 'Have either of you any questions for each other? From my end I'm more than happy with Annie's credentials, but I know that the final say is, as always, yours, Senan. And Annie's too, of course.'

'I've a question,' says Senan, staring my way. My stomach flips. You could hear a pin drop. He has the potential to be very intimidating, the way he looks at me like I'm the only person here. His green eyes suck me in. He is so very intense, and while he radiates energy and certainly knows how to command a room, I'm not going to fangirl him like everyone else here seems to, no matter how they try to disguise it.

'Go ahead.'

'What part of Ireland are you from?'

I feel my shoulders relax, relieved it's a very run-of-the-mill enquiry and not something from my ancient CV that sits on the table.

'I'm from a very little village in County Tyrone,' I say to him with just a hint of confidence. 'You won't have heard of it, I'm sure, but it's beside Lough Neagh and it's the most beautiful place in the world.'

His eyes widen.

'Well, maybe you'll show me around someday,' he says with a very, dare I say, endearing smile. 'My childhood was spent in the very south of Ireland. West Cork, where my dad is from.'

I nod, and tuck my hair behind my ear. Then, when I turn my head slightly, I notice how Caroline and Martha are both staring at us, taking this all in and totally agog.

There is a brief awkward silence. I look back at Senan and he's still looking at me, then as I'm searching for what to say next, it's as if he's snapped out of a trance.

'Look, ladies, I'm more than happy with Meg for the job,' Senan announces as he changes the mood quickly by getting up from his chair.

'It's Annie,' I correct him with a smile, hiding the fact my stomach is now in bits again with nerves.

'I'm so sorry!' he exclaims. 'You remind me of Meg Ryan. I was in a movie with her many years ago.'

'I know you were,' I respond, eyeballing him now just like he has been doing to me. 'My daughter is actually called Meg, but not after Meg Ryan. I just liked the name.'

'Sorry,' he says, looking at me now like he really means it. He puts his hand very briefly on my shoulder, his eyes meeting mine again. 'I have a lunch date, but I'll see you soon, I hope. I look forward to working with you.'

Martha stands up quickly to match him and speaks on my behalf, as if she's my lawyer in a court of law.

'Obviously – well, obviously Annie and I have some discussing to do, but if she's agreeable with all she's heard today, we'll be in touch very soon with a plan going forward. It was nice to meet you, Senan.'

'And you all too. Have a good day.'

He shoots me one last glance and a friendly dimpled smile before he leaves through the glass doors, out past Jane in reception and, when we all know he is safely out of sight, we all start talking over each other.

I'm shaking now he's gone, and I don't think I'm the only one.

'Well,' says Caroline, shuffling her papers together again. 'It looks like you've got the spark he was after, Annie Madden!'

I've no idea what to think and it's going to take me every second of the next two days to digest this all. I'm not even sure what just happened but I feel like I'm drunk or high – it's something out of control and I'm not sure I like it. I don't know anything about West Cork, nor do I know how I could honestly settle away from home for two weeks, nor do I know if I could cope with being around someone like Senan Donnelly alone for two whole weeks. But Caroline isn't finished yet.

'We've been searching for the right candidate for this project for quite a while now,' she says directly to me, 'and when Martha told me about you, I'd no doubt that you'd be exactly what we are looking for. It looks like Senan felt that too.

'I won't lie to you,' she continues. 'Dealing with someone like Senan Donnelly isn't always for the faint-hearted but this is a professional role which will involve digging deep into his heart and soul to get the story the public wants – not from a journalistic or a scandalous point of view. We considered that route, but it was a big no from him. He wants a very human approach and you showed him you're the very person we're after. He's had enough of people kissing his ass. He wants someone who will simply get the job done.'

I am totally astounded. I know this is going to be very hard to turn down.

In fact, I can already imagine what Kelly, Bernice and maybe even Meg's reaction is going to be. They'll be chasing me to Cork.

I excuse myself to have a think about things and step outside for a moment. I look at the sign on the doorway: Forest Hill Literary Agency.

I watch as a London bus whizzes by me, and I inhale the opportunity of a dream come true that is right under my nose.

'I want to do this, so badly,' I say out loud. The bus leaves a gust of wind that blows my hair back from my face and almost knocks me off my feet. I close my eyes and I smile.

There's no denying it. I really do want this.

For the first time in forever, I think I might feel like I'm alive and I just know, from deep in my heart, that Peter is cheering me on right now.

7.

I believe there's a mood of escapism here by the lough and it always gives me the headspace to think and make my biggest decisions in life, including the decision that I would marry Peter all those years ago.

There's a magical pull of the water here and I've marvelled all through my childhood at how – no matter how scary life's problems became – by just sitting here and looking out at the shape of the Mourne mountains, so far away in the distance on the other side of the water, I could always solve any of my inner dilemmas.

Legend has it that Lough Neagh was created by the footprint of a giant, and I love to believe that even the biggest problems can be answered by taking a few moments on this water's edge.

This secluded little haven is only a stone's throw away from our home. We can see it from the front of the farm-house, and I take nothing for granted about its sandy bays and skyward views that never cease to take my breath away. Sometimes it's dark, rugged and moody. Other days it's light, still, blue and so uplifting. There's a breeze that would often cut you in two down here and in summer the midges make you itch so badly, but on this crisp spring morning I try to ignore the cold by taking in every lush shade of green that surrounds me, every colour of navy and blue on the water. I inhale every welcome breath of fresh air.

'You always said you felt at home anywhere you could see this lough,' I remind my husband as I park his wheelchair just inches from a small patch of sand. 'I loved how we'd pretend we were at our very own beach here, remember? And on a summer's day it really was the next best thing – right at home yet so far away from reality.'

I kneel down in front of him and fix a tartan blanket around his knees and tuck his scarf in around his neck, before sitting on a fold-up chair beside him, taking in our surroundings. I allow myself some time beside him just to think, away from the hustle and bustle of our home where Meg and Bernice are making pancakes for breakfast, convinced I need time out to make my decision on whether or not to take on Senan Donnelly's autobiography. In the meantime Danny, who now suddenly fancies himself as in charge of DIY in our family, is attempting to patch up the chicken coop, having felt inspired after Bernice paid for some local handyman to fix our back door.

It was a spur-of-the-moment decision to come here, but I just had to get away from Bernice's excessive questioning

about London and Meg's sultry avoidance of me. I sometimes think she hates me, but my own mother tries to
convince me it's just her age.

'Are you're taking Peter to the lough at this time of the
morning?' Bernice asked as I packed him into the car a little
earlier. 'It's a bit cold out, especially by the water? Are you
sure you wouldn't rather take the good of some rest when
you can while I'm here?'

'I want to go to the lough,' I said, feeling an unexpected
magnetic pull towards one of my favourite places in the
world. 'I need to talk to my husband.'

Bernice's face looked crestfallen. 'But I'm making
pancakes?' she said, pointing to the spatula in her hand as
if I needed evidence.

'I won't be long. I just need to talk to my *husband*,' I said
to her as I defiantly strapped Peter into our modified car.

I don't think I imagined that she slammed the back door
as she went back inside, but I know what she was thinking.
Just like everyone else in my life, she was thinking I was
wasting my time by talking to Peter, which always makes
me want to do it even more.

'So, do you still think I have what it takes?' I ask Peter as
we listen to the lapping sound of the water and the whistle
of the wind around us. 'You know, to write? You used to
believe I could, so much, and I could really be doing with
your positivity right now.'

I lean across and rest my hand on his. It's cold, and I wonder if my last-minute spin out in the car was actually too much for him on this hazy Sunday morning.

I look at the side of his face from where I sit, and I long for an answer that will never come from the man I talk to long into the night. He more often than not always had the answers, and if he didn't have them straight away, he'd help me find them within myself.

His profile from where I sit is so angular and strong, with his short hair that peeks out ever so slightly from beneath his grey woollen hat, his straight nose and his full mouth. His thin stature is probably unrecognizable now to those who see him when we are out for our walks, but to me, or so I like to tell myself, he is still the man I fell in love with.

How many times have I kissed those lips in my lifetime? How many times have I stared at this face? I know every curve, every corner, every crease, and I feel a grip of loneliness overcome me again with the knowledge that – even though he is right here beside me – he is still so very far away and has been for such a long time now.

And I try to let it all sink in.

He will never kiss me again. He will never caress my body like he used to. He will never hold me tight when I need him so badly. He will never ease my fears when I lie alone in the dark of night. He will never speak the words I need to hear so badly.

But still I keep hoping and waiting for a miracle.

'It's just . . . it's just, you see, I've been offered a writing job. A proper one, would you believe? And . . . well, it will involve me leaving you all for two weeks but . . . can you hear me, Peter?' I ask him. 'Can you hear anything I say? Do you understand anything any more?'

My lip trembles now. I look at his face, his eyes that dart around as if they're swatting flies sometimes, when at other times, like now, they just stare into space and seem to be in some state of oblivion.

I wring my hands together, hearing my words echo into nothing, bouncing back and mocking me like they always do when I try to have a proper conversation with someone who simply cannot speak back.

'Please just give me a sign,' I beg of him. 'I'll take anything, Peter. Can you hear me? Do you know what I'm saying? Please, just give me something! Oh God, if you can hear me just give me something!'

A huge grey heron swoops past, almost clipping me with its wings.

'You're freezing, Peter! My God, I'm so stupid for taking you here,' I mutter as I get up and manoeuvre the wheelchair across the bumpy grass towards the car, leaving the moody lough and all its promise of tranquillity behind. 'I'm obviously not thinking straight! Let's get you home and warmed up and I'll get any silly notions of writing dreams out of my muddled-up head once and for all. I'm sorry.'

Bernice meets us at the back door of the farmhouse,

holding a plate with a stack of home-made pancakes, her own face matching my look of despair.

'What happened? You weren't very long at all,' she says, puzzled.

She puts the plate down on the sideboard and makes her way outside, where I wave my hands when she tries to help me get Peter out of the car. This is the one thing in life I definitely don't need help with. I paid a lot of money, the last of our savings, for this car; the height of the seats makes it very easy to move Peter in and out in just a few choreographed movements. The chair is lighter than it looks and folds perfectly to fit in the boot, so anyone who tries to interfere in the process is only ever going to be in the way.

'You were right. It was colder down there than I thought, plus maybe you *are* right about everything. Maybe I *am* slowly losing my mind,' I say, swiftly pushing the chair along the smooth tarmac and up the specially built ramp that leads to our back door and into the kitchen. 'I mean, why did I even go there? Did I think that by taking Peter to the bloody lough that it was going to make some miracle fall out of the sky, that he might suddenly be able to tell me to follow my dreams and reach for the stars? It's pointless, Bernice. You are right. I don't have a husband any more. He's here but he's gone. I don't have a husband!'

I stop in my tracks when I see Meg and Danny at the kitchen table, their mouths full of pancakes and strawberries with fresh cream and chocolate spread, a signature breakfast when their grandmother is here. I put my hand to my own mouth as if I'm gasping for air.

'Mum, are you OK?' asks Danny, pushing his chair back so that it scrapes along the tiles.

'Of course I'm OK! I'm fine!' I say quickly, snapping myself back into the only role I know as I try to deflect any fuss. I really want to soften my tone but, no matter what I do, I still sound hysterical when the words come out. 'You have absolutely nothing to worry about. In fact, the next time either of you *are* worried about something, how about you talk to me directly instead of running to your nana or Kelly, do you hear?'

'But Nana just—'

'I'm the mother around here,' I continue. 'I'm the one who calls the shots. I'm the one who needs to know if my children are worried. No one else is!'

'Annie, please, there's no need,' Bernice says in a hurried whisper. 'Let me get you a cup of tea.'

'I don't want tea!' I plead, almost stamping my feet in frustration.

Meg gets up from the table.

'Meg, sit down right now and listen,' I interrupt my daughter before she runs away from me as usual. 'You don't need to think about anything else, only your friends and your schoolwork, what to watch next on TV. You need to think of the songs you like to sing or the make-up you want to try and Harry what's-his-name or whatever boyband member you fancy these days.'

'I don't fancy anyone.'

'And Danny, I'm delighted you want to help around the house, but only do it if *you* want to,' I say to my son. He sits back down. 'You don't have to do it to make me happy. Do it for yourself only. Not for me.'

I feel the energy suck out of the room, and I'm instantly sorry when I look at the despair on my children's faces, but I need to say this. My mother-in-law, who has brought so much distraction since she arrived yesterday, with her cooking, cleaning, her treats and her movies, and whatever else she could think of, was just that – a welcome distraction. But it's not our reality.

She can pay to fix the back door but she can't fix us. No one can.

'You have to stop. You have to do something, Mum. Take the job, Mum!' says Danny, and I freeze on the spot. 'Do anything! You can't stop living just because he has.'

I put my hands over my face. I can't hear this out loud, least of all from my children.

'Meg thinks so too!' he blurts out as tears stream down his beautiful face. 'Just go and do something for yourself for once, something that makes you happy, please! We will all be OK here. Just go, OK!'

He storms out of the kitchen and I'm left there with Meg and Bernice staring at me, their eyes pushing me to reply, but I can't get the image of my son's face out of my mind. He was actually in tears. And now so is Meg.

'I agree, Mum,' she whispers, before she too leaves me standing here. 'You have to do this. Please! For all of us.'

I look at Bernice, waiting for her to tell me, *I told you so*, but she just boils the kettle.

'Do you want pancakes?' she asks me, as if it's business as usual. 'I can make a fresh batch if you're hungry?'

8.

One week later, just around teatime on a crisp Sunday evening, I tentatively pull up in Bernice's VW car outside Seaview B&B in a small town in West Cork. I borrowed her vehicle for the journey in case they wanted to take Peter out in mine while I was away. As much as I'd planned to explore my surroundings on arrival, I'm thoroughly exhausted after my epic journey, which I've calculated took over six hours since I left home.

Leaving was emotional, but not as bad as I expected, which was mainly due to a group effort by my family to make sure I couldn't for one second change my mind. Kelly will stay to look after Peter, which is way beyond her paid commitments, while Bernice moves in to supervise Danny and Meg. I had run out of excuses not to go and, now that I'm here, I can't deny it's as exciting as it is daunting.

'Annie Madden, all the way from County Tyrone!' says Bob, my host at the B&B, who is a friendly, fussy Englishman who definitely loves the sound of his own voice. 'Let me show you around and please make yourself at home. My

Liam and I will look after you like an egg, I promise, so you can take that look of fear off your face immediately. It's not the Hammer House of Horrors, you know.'

Bob laughs at his own joke and gives me a very quick tour of the three-storey townhouse I'll call home for the next two weeks. He chats flamboyantly, swiftly running through some basic house rules, and when he shows me to my room, a sudden outburst of homesickness is quickly zapped away when I'm met with a heart-warming welcome pack from Martha and Caroline, which sits on a small table next to a shuttered window with a view of the sea in the distance.

There's a bottle of red wine, some fresh fruit, a selection of local artisan cheeses with crackers and some tea, scones and jam.

'You're going to rock this, Annie!' the accompanying note says. 'Work hard but enjoy every moment!'

'So what brings a beautiful young lady like you here?' Bob asks, as if he just can't resist knowing before he leaves me to my own devices. 'Work or pleasure?'

'Work,' I say, letting out a very deep breath. 'Sorry if I look like a rabbit in headlights, but it's a long time since I've travelled alone. I'm here to work with the actor, Senan Donnelly, who lives further down the coast. Maybe you know him?'

Bob mutters something untoward about the likes of Senan Donnelly and other 'so-called celebrities', who holiday in West Cork like 'dandelions in a breeze.' My eyes widen at the irony from the man with the Geordie accent who, despite his constant commentary, is really quite endearing, with his over-exaggerated eye-rolling and animated hand gestures.

'I know *of* him, anyhow. Most people do. He was in that TV series, the big one in America where everyone is ridiculously good-looking, which made him very rich and very arrogant,' he says with a pout. 'My husband, on the other hand, is a huge fan, but that's just because Senan's parents used to holiday here. Well, that and his good looks, I suppose. Anyhow, maybe he's a nicer person in real life than his media profile would suggest. I'm sure you'll soon find out.'

'That I will,' I reply, seeing him off.

I'm sure he doesn't even reach the bottom of the stairs before I make a quick phone call home to let everyone know I've arrived safely, then my head hits the pillow and I fall fast asleep.

The next morning, with my leather satchel-style shoulder bag packed with enough pens and notebooks to last the average student a full school year, I set off on foot to find Senan Donnelly's beach house, where I've been instructed to meet him at 10 a.m. to begin our first session.

I walk along the sea front with a breeze in my face.

'Remember, you're a professional writer and you're there to do a job, not to take any nonsense,' Kelly texts me on the way. 'Earn respect from the start and make sure he ditches the ego. Oh, and send me a sneaky pic when you can (joking, not joking!).'

My mother-in-law has a much more subtle approach when she checks in.

'I'm sure Senan will be a lovely lad and that he'll be honoured to work with you,' she tells me, and I hope she is right. 'Just be yourself. That will keep him on his toes!'

I manage, despite my nerves, to chuckle at Bernice's hint at my former reputation at home and at school of being a bit of a bossy boots, a trait that Peter both loved and loathed at the same time.

'I'll go easy . . . well, I'll try,' I reply, to which she sends me a laughing emoji. My face crumples into a smile when I think of how hip Bernice has become, considering she had no clue how to switch on a smart phone until she met her new husband, Jake. I marvel for a moment at how much people can grow in so many ways with each chapter that life brings them.

Just ten minutes later, I find myself on the sand looking up at Senan's magnificent home. I'm met firstly by its modern appearance, its breathtaking location overlooking the magnificent Atlantic Ocean, and secondly by a very angry, very flustered lady, who almost takes the door off the hinges on her way out of it, shouting expletives in her wake. Not exactly the welcome I'd visualized, which was more along the lines of starting off with some coffee on a sun-drenched patio followed by cool mocktails and an easy-going chat with Senan.

'Find someone else to clean up your mess!' the lady shouts in a high-pitched voice as she makes her way down the wooden steps towards me. 'I'm too old for this, Senan! I quit!'

I freeze on the spot, wondering if I should make myself scarce in case I'm seen watching on, but it's too late. I'm too close.

Senan opens the door his housekeeper has just slammed and follows her out, wearing only a pair of rather fitted black boxer shorts which leave very little to the imagination. I feel my face flush and I look away. His caramel skin and super-toned physique make my skin flush, and I blink my eyes to try, as Meg might say, 'un-see' him.

'Sorry, Silva, I'd lost track of the days! Please come back.'

But Silva is long gone in her yellow car, leaving quite a sandstorm behind. Senan spots me standing below and his eyes widen.

'Oh no, Meg? I totally forgot!' he says, putting his hands to his just-out-of-bed dark-brown hair. 'Is it Monday already? Of course it's Monday! Shit! Give me ten minutes. Actually . . . look, can you come back in half an hour so I can shower and clean up a bit? This place is a tip and my—'

'It's Annie,' I say, feeling my blood boil. After all this build-up, he'd forgotten I was coming here. 'My name is Annie Madden. Not Meg.'

He isn't listening as he rummages around on the deck, rearranging fancy chairs and cushions like a headless chicken.

I drop my bag onto the golden sand and watch as he

flusters around, lifting out bags of rubbish to the outdoor bins, swearing as he does so. He is still only in his boxers, and I take a moment to absorb my surroundings to try to distract my mind from all the effort it took for me to get here, only for him to casually forget what day of the bloody week it was.

Difficult. Yes, I'm beginning to get the picture already . . .

'I'm so sorry!' he shouts on repeat, and I can't help but answer, 'And so you should be! I won't hang around for long, you know,' I tell him. 'I'll follow Silva like a bat out of hell.'

He peeps over the deck, down onto the sand, and tilts his head, flashing a superior smile. 'Please, I'm begging you. Don't.'

The West Cork beach house where Senan has been living for the past few months is even more exquisite than I'd imagined it would be, with its white wooden-slatted exterior, perched on an elevated site that has steps from an extensive deck down to a small beach shared by just three other houses of varied stature. Some are much older in design, one is particularly ramshackle but charming nonetheless, but Senan's place is the one that stands out as a place of beauty and modern architecture that is truly breathtaking.

I can hear the waves gently lap from only metres away, and the sound of silence, apart from the seagulls squawking as they circle above me, a sound that takes me back to holidays with Peter by the coast when the children were small.

I gaze up to see that there are floor-to-ceiling sliding windows all along the front of the house and, overlooking the bay, a large deck with grey furniture that would look as good indoors as it does outdoors, a giant hot tub, two sunloungers, a fire pit and a top-of-the-range gas barbecue. I notice a silver Jaguar in the garage that sits to the right-hand side of this very luxurious villa. Bob was right. It looks like money is definitely no problem where Senan Donnelly is concerned. He must be very rich, but he also seems to be very messy.

I take a seat on the steps while I wait for him to clean up and get organized, trying my best not to overthink our awkward start, but then I hear him muttering more expletives after a crash of what sounds like tin cans falling onto a floor. I wince when I hear this and, judging by his reaction, he does too.

'Fuck!'

'Senan?' I call, standing up again.

'Five more minutes,' he shouts, before there's another crash.

'I could come up and give you a hand?' I shout to him, realizing this clean-up could take a very long time. I go up a few steps. 'I really don't mind if it speeds things up?'

He comes out to the deck and looks down at me with desperation. 'You really wouldn't want to do that. It's a disaster.'

I think I've gathered that.

'Well, I've two teenagers at home who can make quite a mess, so I'm sure it can't be anything I've never seen before?' I shrug.

'Seriously? Well, that would be utterly humiliating but also very kind of you,' he says in his very sultry tone. 'I'll make it up to you, Meg, I promise.'

I shake my head. 'It's Annie, OK? Annie. Not Meg. I think I've told you that before?'

'Sorry, sorry, sorry . . .'

I make my way up the wooden steps which are crumbed with grains of sand, and Senan holds the glass door open for me with his head down. He has a robe on now to cover up his toned, tattooed chest, which makes things just a little less awkward, but when I step inside his eclectic open-plan home, I do a double-take as I see that Silva wasn't exaggerating when she turned on her heels and fled.

'You really are very, *very* messy,' I tell him, as if I'm talking to Danny at home or one of my former students at school.

'Not usually,' he replies. 'Please don't judge a book by its cover. Actually, why don't you just go back and wait for me to—'

'We have a lot of work to do, Senan. I don't have time to sit and take in the glorious surroundings alone, as much as I'd like to.'

His eye catches mine and he breaks into a smile with a look of surprise at the same time. He shakes his head in bewilderment.

'Go and shower and I'll try to make head of this,' I say, scurrying him along. 'I'll get stuck in. Now, go, before I change my mind.'

He looks like he isn't used to being told off, and reluctantly saunters off in the opposite direction.

When he is out of sight and I hear the shower run, I tiptoe around at first, lifting sticky glasses of all shapes and sizes and filling the dishwasher, taking in the villa as I do so. I throw out numerous empty bottles of champagne and beer, countless pizza boxes and other takeaway containers. Once I get into a rhythm I take great pleasure in blitzing the granite worktops to make them shine. It really is a magnificent home. I open all the windows and I brush and mop the white tiles on the floor, strangely delighted to use up some of the pent-up adrenaline and nerves that have flooded my body since I first arrived here, a place that is so much more than a world away from what I'm used to.

When the place is clean, I can see just how absolutely exquisite it really is; I stand back to admire my quick clean-up which has made such a difference. The expansive glass lets in an abundance of natural light; sliding doors lead out onto the wooden deck, which looks as if it is touching the sea. Tasteful art – all original pieces, of course – grace the whitewashed walls, which are lined with green plants to perfectly complement the muted-hues vibe. A well-worn tan-coloured Chesterfield, and a large cream velvet sofa which wouldn't last a second in my house, sit face to face; the spectacular brick fireplace is home to an eye-level modern stove. There are scattered bookshelves and framed photos of Senan and some friends and family, but the true *pièce de résistance* is a polished black baby-grand piano, which sits by the huge window that overlooks the beautiful bay right on its doorstep. Whoever designed this house had a spark of genius to create such an intriguing home.

'Wow,' I hear myself say out loud.

'Wow indeed,' says Senan, who I didn't realize was now standing behind me. 'You did all of this already?'

I try not to look surprised when I turn to face him. He is wearing a white linen shirt which emphasizes his deep tan, long light-coloured denim shorts and sandals, and he smells like a dream.

'Don't make a habit of it,' I say, doing my best to set boundaries from here on. 'And for the record, you're worse than my teenagers, and that's saying something.'

He eyes up my bag, sitting on the floor by a coffee table, and arches an eyebrow.

'You used to be an English teacher, isn't that right?' he says with just a little look of trepidation in his eyes, and he signals to me to have a seat. I lift my bag and sit down on the Chesterfield while he goes to the opposite cream sofa and leans his elbows on his knees.

'I did,' I reply. 'I loved it, most of the time.'

He looks me up and down. I suddenly feel very like Mary Poppins in my choice of attire, which is the grey calf-length pinstripe pencil skirt and buttoned-up blouse I almost wore to London. I had no idea how to look today without Kelly's advice, so I played it safe – another indication of how sheltered my life has been for the past seven years.

'You look like an English teacher,' he says.

'Meaning?'

He looks genuinely surprised now at the challenge in my voice. I tug at my skirt and brush off imaginary crumbs.

'You sound like one too,' he continues. 'Right, off you go. Get your pen ready and ask me anything.'

He rubs his forehead which, just like the last time we met, and judging by the recent carnage in his home, is obviously sore from a hangover.

'I beg your pardon?' I tell him quickly. 'Get your pen?' I raise an eyebrow in his direction.

'To write the story?' he says. 'Isn't that what you're here to do?'

We eyeball each other like two opponents in a ring, instead of a man and woman who are meant to 'dig deep', as Caroline had instructed. My mind flies back to that day in London when he kissed my cheek to say hello and charmed everyone in the room to the point of no return. Right now, the man in front of me seems like a very different person, but then I have been warned about his tendency to be difficult, and perhaps arrogant, as Bob suggested.

'No, no. You see, I intend to find out about you a bit more organically,' I say to him, determined not to be intimidated in the slightest by his nonchalance.

'Organically?'

'Yes, organically,' I repeat, doing my best to stay calm. I have dealt with a lot of spoilt teenagers in my earlier career, so I won't tolerate bullshit from Senan Donnelly, no matter who he thinks he is. 'Caroline has suggested a few things to warm us up before I put pen to paper, to try and ease the process along. We need to—'

I scroll quickly through my phone and find her email. Then I clear my throat and read aloud, doing my best to ignore the blank look on his face as he tries to follow what I'm saying.

'For example, Caroline says, *Maybe you could cook something together first, or walk the beach and chat about music and movies? Break the ice to let the conversation flow.*'

I don't tell him how she feels this will loosen his inhibitions and make him open up a lot more. Instead I stop there and glance his way for a reaction. He arches an eyebrow now, and then widens his eyes, looking very confused.

'*Just get talking!*' I continue, quoting Caroline. '*Do something to relax and get to know each other. That's so important before you write even one word.*'

Senan sits forward on the cream sofa opposite me, hands clasped together, and laughs out loud, rolling his eyes at the same time.

'What's so funny?' I ask him, very seriously. 'I'm simply reading out Caroline's suggestions. She's the one who hired me for this job.'

He looks totally perplexed. 'Does Caroline work at a

publishing house, or is it an amateur dating agency she's trying to run?' he says, stifling a yawn. 'I mean, walk the beach? Cook together? I'm surprised she didn't say Netflix and chill.'

I stutter out a response in a fluster. I may have lived a very sheltered life lately, but I do know what 'Netflix and chill' indicates.

'I-I don't think a dating agency is her vision, as she is very aware that I'm a married mother of two and you are . . .'

I can't finish. Again, he laughs. Again, he rubs his head. 'I'm joking, Annie. Jesus!'

At least he got my name right this time. 'Plus, as I'm sure you've noticed by all the takeaway crap, I don't cook, so we can rule that one out.'

I put my phone down and tug at my skirt again, feeling very much like an English teacher, very stiff in my long straight grey skirt, and very like I've absolutely no sense of humour, but I won't be beaten yet.

I look around the now pristine beach house, eyeing up the black ornamental eight-ring cooker that doesn't look like it's ever been switched on, and my mind goes into overdrive.

'OK then. Let's cook lunch – something from scratch, Senan,' I suggest, standing up with vigour. He won't belittle me, no bloody way. 'If you never cook, now is as good a time as any. I'm sure it would be good for your health – as well as for the environment, going by your trash – not to mention your book in the long run.'

His eyes widen and his jaw drops, then he stands up and walks across the tiled floor to grab a beer from the fridge. I shudder at the fact it's not even eleven in the morning yet.

'Hold on, please! Is this your way of getting back at me for such a bumpy start?' he asks with a nip in his voice. 'Look, I don't even know how to switch the cooker on, and I'm not joking about that.'

'Or we could barbecue?' I say, not letting him off the hook totally. 'Please tell me you at least know how to switch on and cook on your barbecue? It's a beautiful day outside.'

He stares at me intently, and then shrugs. 'I'm too hungover for food right now, Annie, plus I've dinner tonight with friends,' he smarts. 'I'm not cooking.'

'Fine then, maybe we could—'

I was going to suggest we take a walk somewhere, but I'm rudely interrupted.

'Look, seriously. I'm a busy person, as I'm sure you are too, and this is not what I was expecting,' he says, in between slugging his beer. 'I'd rather you just fire out the questions and write down the answers like the others did, so we can get this over and done with.'

'The others?'

He looks back with a raised eyebrow. 'The other writers who tried this before,' he says, enjoying my look of shock. 'The others who fled, just like Silva did, and just like everyone else who comes my way does.'

I'm not sure if he's trying to test my strength or if he's

trying to unnerve me, but as well as his bluntness there's also a little bit of bitterness and a pinch of smugness too. Hearing that other writers have tried to work with him before is something I wasn't aware of. I knew the team had done a bit of scouting around, but I didn't know anyone else had made it this far and changed their mind.

'I had no idea about the others, no.'

I can't help but sound deflated. Senan, on the other hand, is unconcerned.

Think of the money, I tell myself firmly. I can do this. I'm not like the others. I've interviewed people before, I've worked with very boisterous teenagers down the years in the classroom, I've managed Peter's early frightening mood swings on his darkest days, and I've dealt with Danny and Meg's pubescent hormones at home. Someone like Senan Donnelly will not unnerve me, no matter how hard he tries.

'Well, Mr Donnelly, if that's the case, maybe that's why Caroline is taking a *new* approach with her ice-breakers to see if that works?' I suggest. 'Maybe she doesn't want a repeat of what happened with "the others"?'

But instead of biting, he leans back on the sofa, looks up at the ceiling, and then blows out a long breath.

'Ah, I'm this close to giving up on this whole damn thing!' he says, shutting his eyes tightly. 'I don't have time for any other bullshit, seriously. Just ask me the questions, write down your answers, and let's just get this goddam book done, once and for all.'

9.

'So?' Bob asks me when I bump into him on the stairwell back at Seaside View B&B later that afternoon. 'How did your first day on the job go?'

I need a shower, my head is frazzled, and I feel like I've been squeezed through a mangle after a few hours of stilted answers and defensive deflecting from Senan, but I'm not going to tell Bob that.

I'm a professional, just as Kelly reminded me, and professionals don't talk out of school, plus as much as I like Bob so far, I sense he may be the 'I told you so' type.

'I've a lot of work to do and not a lot of time to do it, so I'm glad to get started,' I say, putting on a fake smile. My eyes start to glisten, though, when I think of the utterly hellish morning I've just been through.

I'm so tired and I'm absolutely starving; even though it's only three p.m. I'm exhausted and feel like I've done ten rounds in a boxing ring.

'So he's an asshole, just like I predicted,' Bob says as he pushes his black glasses back on his nose and gives a dramatic flick of the tea towel that sits permanently on his shoulder. 'All that man knows is how to spend money, how to look hot at the same time, and how to piss people off. I knew it.'

'I didn't say he was an asshole, Bob!' I call to him as he walks down the stairs, very aware of the confidentiality clause I signed when I took on the job. 'I'm tired. It's been a long day.'

I walk to my room, my tummy grumbling, and when I get inside I fling myself onto the bed and wonder if I'm kidding no one but myself.

Today was absolutely dreadful.

I had to suggest we had coffee mid-conversation, as Senan didn't so much as offer. He didn't even suggest a glass of water. I left with my mind in a muddle and a notebook full of scribbles that I know won't make sense when I go back to them.

So far, Senan Donnelly seems like a selfish, arrogant asshole indeed, and a very spoilt, rich one at that, but the most frightening thing of all is that he has totally lost touch with reality. I doubt if that's what Caroline will want to read about when I go back to her with my initial feedback. I've never met anyone so rude and up his own ass, and I honestly don't know if I can be bothered to get into his messed-up mind.

'Just keep firing out those questions and I'll answer more tomorrow,' he said, while slugging on his fourth beer as I was leaving, but I didn't even have the energy to respond to his parting words. Tomorrow is something I don't even want to think about yet.

Now, despite my hunger, I drift off into a restless nap in the B&B, until I'm wakened by my phone ringing just under an hour later. It's Bernice, full of anticipation and excitement to hear all about my first big day.

'It went really great!' I say, putting on my chirpiest voice. I even sit up on the bed to brighten myself up. 'It's going to be a bit of a challenge, but that's just what I needed. My brain hasn't had this much exercise in one day in a very long time!'

She quizzes me about Senan's beach house, which I 'ooh' and 'aah' over, just like she wants to hear me do. She asks me about the B&B and I tell her about the lovely welcome from Bob here at Seaview, and the surprise gift from Caroline and Martha. I stifle a gasping sob when she wants to know if Senan is as nice as she'd hoped he would be, and not the erratic, brash drunk she'd found when she'd googled him that morning.

'He's lovely, really lovely, and you've nothing to worry about,' I lie to her. 'As they say, don't believe everything you read in the papers! Now, tell me all about what's going on at home. How're my babies? And Peter? And old Rex and the chickens?'

I bite my lip as she tells me how Meg came first in a 'cook-off' demonstration at school today, how Danny's old nemesis 'Cabbage' apologized at last for wrongly accusing him, and how Peter was away for a spin with Kelly to pick up some dry cleaning in town. She wanted to get him out of the house, but I'm sure she just wanted to give Mum and the kids some space for a while at the same time.

'Do you think he misses me at all?' I ask her, gripping the duvet cover from where I lie in this strange bed, so far away from all my home comforts and the life I know.

Bernice pauses, and I know she isn't sure which would be the right answer. Would I rather he did seem to be missing me, or would I rather he was totally oblivious?

Even I don't know the answer to that one.

'He's being very well looked after and that's all you need to know,' she says, forever the diplomat. 'Now what's your plan for this evening? Isn't it so, so heavenly to be by the ocean? It will do you the world of good to get some fresh sea air into your lungs, Annie.'

I perk up at the idea of exploring the area, and my mouth waters when I think of sampling some local seafood, washed down with a cold glass of white wine. I can almost taste it already, even if the idea of dining alone will be very different to what I'm used to.

'I'm going to freshen up and then go and find a nice restaurant,' I tell my mother-in-law. 'It's my first proper day here, so as nervous as I am about exploring the place on my own, I'm going to treat myself and do my best to enjoy it.'

* * *

Bob and his husband Liam, who I have the pleasure of meeting before I head out to eat and explore, highly recommend I try a seafood restaurant on the seafront for dinner.

Where Bob is a funny, flamboyant and opinionated pocket-rocket, Liam is taller, a little less dramatic, but equally colourful. Together they come alive like a harmony and a melody, full of colour and joie de vivre like I've never seen before.

'The mussels are to die for, the prawns are mouth-watering,' says Bob, swallowing as he speaks as if he really is salivating at the thought. 'And the wine is heavenly! But the Spanish-inspired dish called marisco paella . . .'

'Ah, the dish called the marisco paella,' echoes Liam in his delightful Cork accent. 'How can I describe it? Well, it is like your favourite fish got married to each other and are having their after-party just for you! They dance with your tastebuds while flirting with the rest of your senses at the very same time! Oh, you've got to try it, Annie! I'll book you a table and tell Maria we sent you!'

Liam talks with his eyes and his hands, and I like him immediately – plus they both had me at 'paella'. As I leave them I feel full of energy, and wear a smile that wipes away any of my initial trepidation after my day with Senan.

The Spanish restaurant they chose for me overlooks the bay, and has a relaxing and warm ambience. The first thing I notice, apart from the deep red walls and cosy snugs, is the giant string of onions and another of garlic that hangs over the wine bar, plus a range of quotes in Spanish on little wooden slats.

The second thing I notice is that the place seems totally empty initially, but then my heart stops when I spot a very familiar figure, sitting on his own at a table nestled in a little booth at the very back corner of the restaurant.

It's Senan.

He doesn't notice me, thank goodness, as he is superglued to his phone and isn't facing my direction, so I take my own seat a few places behind his, which I'm shown to by a teenage waiter who introduces himself as Johnny. I try my best not to stare.

'Our specials this evening, madam, are a marinated seafood skewer or, if you feel like sampling our chef's favourite, the panko-coated cod tapas on offer,' Johnny explains. 'Can I get you a drink? Our wine list is on the blackboard.'

'Thank you,' I reply, trying to hide my face with the oversized menu, even though I know exactly what I want after Bob and Liam's gushing description. 'Can I get a large white wine please? House wine is fine. And I'll have this to eat please – the marisco paella, which I'm told is delicious.'

Johnny nods, seeming pleased at not having to run back and forth while I browse the select but superb menu, and returns with my wine within seconds, along with some complimentary cheese breads and a tapenade.

'Wow, thank you,' I tell him, 'I haven't eaten all day so this is most welcome.'

I butter the bread slowly, still watching Senan in the near distance, and feeling like a spy. It looks as if he may have just got here for dinner minutes before I did. I know of course from earlier that he's waiting on some company. Maybe he's meeting with some of his party friends, or could it be a date tonight with a girlfriend? We didn't cover much today, apart from a quick rundown of his very early childhood memories which I recorded, which is just as well as to be honest I zoned out when I shouldn't have, as he was not putting in any effort and every second was like pulling teeth. But I did remember he said he didn't want food as he was having dinner with friends this evening.

The very thought of saying hello to Senan makes my stomach lurch, and again a nauseating feeling grips my stomach when I think of home and of Kelly, sitting in my cosy kitchen, across the table from Bernice, probably both with glasses of wine and putting the world to rights.

Johnny the waiter comes back and clears his throat to get my attention, just as Senan's guests arrive.

'Compliments of Maria,' he says, holding up a bottle of wine before he tops up my already almost empty glass as soon as I give my approval. 'On her behalf, I'd like to wish you a very warm welcome to West Cork. Bob and Liam from Seaview B&B are two of our best customers, so please don't be a stranger.'

He sets the bottle down on my table and does a little bow as I put my hand to my chest in surprise.

'Ah, thank you so much,' I exclaim, feeling so much better already. 'How lovely! Thank you, Johnny. And of course, pass on my appreciation to the lovely Maria. I'm sure you have many regulars in such a wonderful place.'

'We do, though Bob and Liam are two of our favourites,' he tells me with a smile.

I spot an opportunity to find out some information. 'I've heard there are some famous people living here in West Cork. I can imagine they like it here a lot too?'

'Ah,' he says, shooting a glance behind him where Senan sits. 'You've spotted our number one customer, I see.'

'I have,' I reply, knowing I can't deny I noticed the famous actor in our midst.

Johnny looks around again and then his voice drops to a whisper. 'He eats in here every Monday evening with the same people,' Johnny whispers. 'Maybe I should have seated you closer and you could have joined each other's company.'

He is joking, of course.

'Oh gosh, no!' I say a little too eagerly, feeling all flushed at the idea of Senan knowing I'm here.

So he eats here every Monday night with the same people? I can't wait for Johnny to move on so I can observe more. He is blocking my view big time, and I can't see who these people he regularly dines with might be. I allow my mind to picture his expected company. Actors no doubt, young and lithe and full of themselves. Or maybe a harem of women who like to hang off his fame and good looks.

Models probably. Exceptionally good-looking people who ooh and aah over his very existence, just like he has always been used to.

'Now, more importantly,' I say, lifting my freshly filled glass of wine, 'please remember to thank Maria for her wonderful hospitality and welcome this evening, Johnny. It's so kind of her. And as someone visiting for the very first time, her personal touch would certainly encourage me to come back again. I can't wait to taste the paella!'

He walks away at last. Now I have a proper view of Senan from behind, and I see his companions have arrived.

I do a double-take.

They are nothing like what I had expected. Instead of a flurry of supermodels, Senan has been joined by a very cute-looking elderly couple, who shuffle around as he fusses over them before they sit down opposite him. The lady, who is at least in her late seventies, is rouge-cheeked, with fluffy lilac permed hair, and is dressed in a pale grey twinset, while her very dashing white-haired husband is dressed in a navy jumper with a crisp pink shirt underneath. They remind me of my late grandparents, very traditional and oh so sweet as she links into his arm. Senan has put away his phone now and is giving them his full attention, much to their delight as they coo and laugh at his every word.

'Everything OK for you, madam?' Johnny asks, hovering around a little too much for my liking.

'Yes, yes of course, thank you,' I say to him, before trying to distract myself from Senan's company across the room and focusing on enjoying the sumptuous breads and tapenades before me, not to mention the cool, crisp wine which tickles my palate like a taste of heaven.

My paella arrives and, even though it's strange first to relax and eat with no interruptions or without having to cook, I'm so hungry and I'm going to bloody well enjoy this.

For the next while I savour every mouthful of my long-awaited dinner as Senan Donnelly does something similar in the near distance, laughing and holding court with his elderly friends. I try to switch off from him and soon I'm swept away by the delicious food in front of me. I totally understand Liam's description of the food flirting and dancing in my mouth, where I can taste every burst of flavour popping on my tongue, awakening my tastebuds with every single mouthful.

This is a side of life I haven't experienced in so long. A beautiful sunny evening, a magnificent sea view, the most delectable food and wine, and the indescribable privilege of doing nothing, only savouring each moment and letting my mind run free without distraction. I allow myself to feel awakened and alive by something as simple as eating alone in a new place, where everything is there to be explored. I take a moment to remember that even though I've had a rough start to my stay in Cork, I can still appreciate how I've already experienced the kindness of so many people – Caroline and Martha with their thoughtful gift that really perked me up no end, Bob and Liam with their joyous way of life and colourful personalities, and now young Johnny and his boss Maria, who have made me feel so warmly welcomed here at their seaside restaurant.

I'd forgotten the joy of what it's like to experience new people and beautiful new places. I'd forgotten how it feels to do something just for me. Then, just as I'm really drifting off into a blissful state of wonder, a dreaded sense of guilt creeps up like a thick blanket covering my eyes.

I picture Peter on his chair beside his bed in our home, struggling with his swallow as Kelly feeds him right now. I picture the neglect to the farmhouse I call home, with all that needs to be repaired and fixed up, and I feel the heavy weight of worry about how the children are coping in their surroundings, both with and without me.

No, I'm not going to even go there. I pause, I compose myself and then I start again.

I deserve this moment. It's perfectly simple. I'm at work earning some money. I'm away from home for a reason that will benefit not only my family financially but will also help me on so many levels. I have the full support of my friend Kelly, as well as my wonderful mother-in-law and my children. I have no reason to feel guilty, none whatsoever. I should be proud of myself, they all said so. I *am* proud of myself, and I will continue to repeat that mantra for as long as it takes for these next two weeks to pass by.

Senan can be 'difficult' if he wants, but he won't break

me, no way. When you've found your husband – the man you grew up with, and the one person you love more than anyone else in the world – on the ground, unconscious and lifeless . . . when you've cared for him with every ounce of your being, only to be told you've hit a dead end and he doesn't even know who you are any more, when you experience the grip of loneliness and grief with no closure, you're a bloody strong person.

'He really does spoil us here, doesn't he!' I hear the old lady sing when the waiter goes to their table. 'Honestly, it's the highlight of our week and he never lets us down. Our darling Senan!'

Our darling Senan? Darling? Oh, they must be his grandparents, but even if they are close relations, I can't help but think I've now got a bird's-eye view of a very different side to the man I witnessed today with his 'get on with the job' attitude and 'get your pen out' swagger.

'Please give Maria my compliments as always,' I hear him say in a very humble voice as he gets up now that they have finished. I duck into the side of the booth where I sit and bury my face into my phone, doing my best to hide from his eyeline as he has to walk past me to leave. 'See you same time next week, Johnny?'

He stands up and reaches for his wallet in his pocket, as his grandparents (I assume) shuffle to gather their belongings at the table. Senan is much smarter now in his appearance, his earlier hangover seemingly forgotten, and no evidence visible of his having been topping up on beer. He wears a navy T-shirt and jeans, and he doesn't look so arrogant from here at all. He isn't as tough or cocky right now, and he certainly wasn't meeting a group of party types as I'd so casually assumed he was.

I watch him pay his bill and tip Johnny, it seems generously, and then I bury my head to the side as he walks past me to leave the restaurant. Thank goodness he doesn't as much as look my way as he is too busy chatting to his guests and, when they leave, I realise I've seen Senan Donnelly in a totally different light.

How many sides to him are there, I wonder? I think, on our first day together, I may have only scratched the surface.

10.

I stroll alone to the beach house the following morning, after a restful sleep that was undoubtedly aided by the delicious meal and complimentary wine. An early morning conversation with Kelly has me firing on all cylinders, and I'm ready to call the shots so I can do the job I'm here to do.

'He was testing you, I would bet my house on it,' she says to me as I take in the breathtaking scenery. West Cork may only be on the far end of the island I grew up on, but it's a very different vibe to the rural lough-shore village I know so well. Old men tip their hats here, just as the fishermen at home still do, but there's a slightly cosmopolitan vibe beneath the surface, a quirky feel that takes tourists by surprise when they peel back the layers of this wonderful region.

'Can you imagine how many people he has in his life who bow and beg to please him? It must be so tiresome. I mean it, Annie,' she says to me. 'You're better than this and he knows it. Don't be afraid to tell him exactly how he made you feel and that you won't tolerate such bullshit any further, even if he is a gentle soul to his elderly grandparents every Monday night!'

At breakfast earlier, Bob and Liam had also taken great delight in giving me their alternative views on my client.

'I'm dying to know if it's true he spent time in a famous clinic after his last marriage break-up to that actress, what's her name again?' Bob asked me with his arms folded. 'Agnes Patrice, that's her! Booze, of course, but probably drugs as well. He was very messed up, and that's when his career went down the river.'

'Babe, you're such a gossip!' said Liam, throwing his eyes to the heavens. 'Honestly, you need to spend less time reading those trashy magazines. Well, I saw him once in Maria's restaurant not that long ago and he was very polite and charming. He held the door open for me and not many people do that any more.'

'You just like him because he looks hot!' spat Bob.

'You know I only have eyes for you, my darling. But yes, he is very hot! I may be hopelessly devoted to you, but I'm not blind either.'

I bade them farewell, laughing as they argued with each other, while knowing that most of their antics were merely to entertain me and make me relax into the immense job at hand.

As I walk along the bay now, without Kelly's words of encouragement in my ear, I quickly begin to dread there may be another 'morning after the night before' scene of carnage in Senan's house, with beer bottles or whatever else he has left strewn around, matched with a bedraggled just-out-of-bed look, the stink of alcohol and a weary attitude again. I fear the lack of hospitality or even manners, and I go over and over in my head how I can't and won't be treated like that ever again. Yesterday was an induction, if you like; today is the start of me meaning business, and I will refuse to tolerate anything less than the respect I deserve after leaving my family to be here for two weeks.

But when I get there, I stop in my tracks, just as I did yesterday morning.

This time it's not because of a disgruntled housekeeper. This time, it's two young women leaving Senan's home. They giggle and gush as they leave via the deck and they do a double-take when they see me.

'It's the *English* teacher he's working with,' I hear one of them say under her breath. 'It has to be her.'

They look like they haven't slept much, and my stomach churns as my confidence leaves me after all my pep-talking along the shoreline.

I force a smile in their direction as they walk past me, linking arms and throwing their hair back at something I'm unaware of but, whatever it is, it must be hilarious. Are they laughing at me? They look back at me when they're a few steps away and giggle again.

'Everything OK, girls?' I ask, fixing my sun hat into position on my head. I've gone for a much more casual look today, matching the weather with a naval-style knee-length dress and a straw hat in the hope of taking the good of the sunshine, but maybe I look silly to them. 'Something funny?'

'It's nothing!' one of them calls back towards me. 'We're probably still a bit pissed. Sorry!'

I swallow hard, take off my hat, then take a deep breath and make my way up the steps, where I knock the glass door to let Senan know I'm here.

'Senan!' I call, as I knock again. 'Senan, it's Annie. Are you there?'

I do this at least three times but to no avail.

'Senan, can you answer the door please?'

I blow out a long breath and rub my temples, then take a seat on the deck furniture to contemplate my next move. He is obviously either sleeping or ignoring me, and I don't know how to react. I don't even have his number, so it's not like I can call him to try and wake him up and, in fact, I'm a bit exhausted already with his antics. My gut instinct tells me to pack my bags and head for home, back to the farm and the lough where I belong, instead of hanging around here and being made a fool of. How dare he treat me with such disrespect? How am I supposed to work with someone who blatantly ignores me and who chooses to party away his nights and sleep off a hangover during the day?

I get up again and go to the door, only this time I peer through the glass to see if there's any sign of life. The place looks relatively tidy, a far cry from the way it was yesterday morning, which surprises me after seeing his overnight guests, but when I knock again, I still get no answer.

I take out my phone and scroll to find Martha's number.

I need to let off some steam to someone, and get some advice – if possible – on what I should do. As my agent, I'm guessing Martha might be the best person to consult, even though I suspect she is likely to try to convince me to stay a bit longer.

'Hi Martha, sorry to bother you but—'

I've just begun to compose a text message when I hear a voice calling my name.

'Annie! You're here! Sorry!'

It's Senan – a very sweaty-looking Senan who, in shorts and a vest top, looks as if he has just finished a run on the beach.

'Oh!'

I jump up and stuff my phone into my bag again.

'Hi,' he says again when he reaches the top of the stairs and steps onto the wooden deck to meet me. He leans on the fence post to catch his breath.

'I've only just got here. Well, ten minutes ago I suppose,' I tell him. 'Your guests have just left.'

He puffs and pants as I speak, then takes a long drink of water from a reusable bottle and dabs his forehead with a towel.

'The two young ladies,' I say, trying not to sound like I'm his mother. 'Anyhow, it doesn't matter. It's none of my business really.'

He looks me in the eye, still waiting until his breathing steadies. Beads of sweat form on his forehead and he wipes them with the back of his hand, still holding my eyes with magnetic force.

'Ah, Sue and Rachel! At least I think that's their names,' he says between puffing and panting. 'Yeah, they're just some people who hang out around here. They turned up at mine last night looking for a party, but I left them to it and let them crash on the sofa. I hope they didn't leave a mess. There's no way you're helping to clean up today again.'

'Oh.'

'Listen, before we start,' he says, taking a drink of water, 'I need to go check in on some neighbours if you don't mind? Maybe you could come with me? It will only take a few minutes.'

I fix the straps of my bag onto my shoulder, and he puts his hand out to take it from me.

'Neighbours?'

'If you don't mind? You can leave your schoolbag here until we get back,' he says with a smile. 'Come on. Sid and Ivy will be delighted to meet you.'

Without having time to think much about it, I find myself trundling slightly behind Senan along the sand as we make our way past two other houses before he stops and nods towards an older beach house. The couple from last night are outside it, painting their fence, but in the lady's case there's much more paint on her than there is on her paintbrush.

'I told you a million times, I'm a lover not a fighter,' I hear her cackle. 'You don't have to keep telling me how to do this, Sid. I can turn my hand to anything.'

It's the couple from the restaurant.

Sid turns to greet us, wiping his hands on his overalls as he makes his way across their patio which, like Senan's property, has stunning views of the Atlantic Ocean.

'Aha! You must be the angel sent from heaven to work with our golden boy and tell his story to the world?' says Sid with a hearty smile. Then he whispers. 'Ivy will be jealous. I know she's only using me until I pop my clogs, and then she'll be moving in with Senan.'

I laugh and reach out to meet his hand.

'Annie Madden.'

'Sid Donnelly, no relation to the man himself but a close family friend,' the old man explains. I'm instantly smitten. 'Pleased to meet you, Annie.'

I can't help but notice how Senan looks on, beaming with pride.

'Ivy!' calls Sid to his wife, who is still talking to herself as she paints everything but the fence, it seems. 'Come and say hello to Annie. She's going to be here for two whole weeks to work with Senan and she's a writer. Imagine! Ivy?'

He and Senan exchange knowing glances and Senan makes his way toward Ivy, gently taking the paintbrush from her hand and setting it down across the pot. She takes his hand and places it on her waist, and Senan begins to dance with her as she throws her head back and looks up at him with adoring eyes. She is like a little fairy in Senan's strong arms, and I find my eyes filling up when I see how proudly Sid watches on.

'I told you, she's a real flirt!' Sid whispers to me. 'Now, can I get you two young ones anything to drink? Tea or coffee? If it was later in the day I'd offer something stronger, but I don't want to encourage Ivy to crack open the brandy just yet. It doesn't take much to entice her these days!'

Senan gently guides Ivy towards us and her bright eyes dart around her, then she gasps when it seems she has noticed me for the very first time.

'What a beauty!' she says, taking my hand in both of hers. 'I haven't seen you around here before. Do you work in the movies too? You really should if you don't! And you're much prettier than Agnes ever—'

'Ivy, this is Annie,' says Senan, interrupting her with a light laugh before she goes any further. 'Annie is here to write my book, remember?'

But she just looks at him like she's never heard of any of this before.

'Anyhow, I'm just checking in with you two as always,' he continues. 'Annie and I will be working most of the morning, but I can still grab some groceries for you later, so don't worry about that. And I haven't forgotten about the leaking tap in the bathroom. There's a plumber due around two p.m. today.'

'What would we do without you, eh?' asks Sid as he walks us back towards the gate, a hand on each of our shoulders as he does so. 'I think that's everything for now, but I know where to go if I need you. Relax and look after this lovely lady, Senan. You deserve some company around your own age for a change, instead of always looking after us old crocks.'

Senan rolls his eyes and laughs when Sid gives him a wink and a nod.

'Yes, we'd better get stuck in,' he tells his older friend. 'I have a bit of making up to do after yesterday, but it's never too late to make a fresh start, is it Sid?'

'If you aren't happy with yesterday, it isn't too late to do something different today,' says Sid with a hearty smile. 'Now off you go and explain yourself, my boy.'

Senan blushes just a little and gently puts his hand on my shoulder to guide me back towards his house.

'Nice to meet you, Sid, and you too, Ivy!' I call as we make our way onto the sand. 'Wow they're adorable.'

'Ah, they really are,' Senan agrees.

He walks slowly in time with me now along the beach, unlike before when he more or less stomped along to get to Sid and Ivy after his run.

'Are they related to you in any way, or really just family friends?' I ask. 'It's mad they have the same surname.'

'Ah yes, it is, isn't it? They're just friends but exceptionally close friends,' he tells me as we fall into step together. 'I like to check in with them most mornings and make sure they've got everything they need. Sid is amazing but Ivy . . . look, Annie, I really need to apologize for yesterday before we go any further.'

He stops at that and I do too.

'OK,' I reply, 'but before you do . . .'

I have rehearsed what I am going to say to him many times in my head all morning and, now the time has come to say it out loud, I feel my heart rate speed up a little. This is not what I was expecting this morning, but I must remain professional and polite. Firm, but honest.

'Yesterday is a bit of a disastrous blur,' I tell him, determined not to totally let it go, despite how charmed I was by our visit to Sid and Ivy just now. 'There's no point beating around the bush. We need to start again. Yesterday was a car crash.'

He has the grace to look a little bit embarrassed in return.

'Let's get this clear,' I continue, straightening my shoulders. 'I'm not an English teacher, or a teacher of any sort to you.'

'Ah . . .'

'Neither am I interested in merely firing out interview-style questions when it comes to writing your life story, so it's not just a matter of throwing them at you like you suggested yesterday. We need to give this book the respect it deserves. Respect to your life story, and my time in investing in it. I've interviewed a lot of difficult people in my former career and, not only is it tiring, but it's also a pile of bullshit which I'm not interested in any more. I'm here to do a job, and I'd appreciate it if you treated my time here with respect, just as I intend to do for you.'

That's it. I'm done.

I thought I'd be shaking inside, but I'm far from it. I think of Peter at home, and my children who I've left for two weeks while I took precious time out to come here; it makes me all the more certain that I should tell him exactly how it needs to be.

I expect him to respond vigorously, arrogantly, maybe to tell me where to stuff it, but to my surprise Senan doesn't look quite so smug now. He doesn't look so cocky at all. In fact, he looks sheepish, as he stands in front of me with his hands in his pockets and his eyes facing the sand as the waves lap in the distance.

'I . . . I had hoped it wasn't that bad, but I'll take your word for it.' He looks at the sea, then right back at me. 'But as I said, I need to apologize and explain. I'm sorry. I'm really sorry, Annie.'

He takes a deep breath.

'You are totally right. I was a proper dickhead, but I can explain. Can I get you a coffee back at the house?' he asks.

I push my shoulders back. 'That would be lovely,' I manage to stutter.

'And guess what?' he says, as we stroll along. 'Before we go any further, I think we're doing just what Caroline asked us to do. We're walking the beach. Imagine.'

I look back at him, feeling the wind in my hair as I do so, and I catch his smile.

'Imagine that,' I say, turning away from him again. 'I think we are.'

Back at the beach house, Senan goes to the kitchen, and I search for something to say in fear of a post-apology awkward silence, but I needn't bother as he jumps right in.

'So, before we close the subject about yesterday,' he says as he moves around the kitchen. 'I spoke to my sister this morning, and she gave me a right bollocking, which was very well deserved. I could give you a million excuses, but I'm almost forty years old and I should know better than to take my frustrations out on you.'

'Go on,' I say to him. 'Give me the excuses.'

He busies himself about the kitchen, finding cups and milk from the fridge, and within seconds he presents me with a steaming cup of filtered coffee from a very high-tech machine, and then sits in the same place as he did yesterday on the cream sofa.

'I've developed quite the habit of burying my head in the sand when life gets a bit shit,' he explains, avoiding my eye at the start but then he looks right at me again. 'I got bad news on Friday, so I did what I usually do. I went on a bender all weekend to try and forget about it all.'

I shift in my seat a little.

'I'm very sorry to hear that,' I whisper. 'I guess we never

know what's going on in someone else's world unless we are told. I'm not psychic, Senan.'

He lets out a deep breath, holding his coffee cup like he is gripping onto it for dear life as he tries to find the words he is looking for.

'It's Ivy . . .'

'Oh.'

He rubs his forehead.

'It's like this . . . for the past few months we've noticed little things,' he says, his distinctively low voice struggling as he speaks. 'Like forgetting where she put stuff at first. Then forgetting what she came into a room for. She started forgetting names of everyday things like a fork or a spoon. Anyhow, you know where I'm going with this. On Friday Sid called to confirm what we all feared. Even though we were expecting it, the diagnosis really knocked the wind from our sails. She's been like a mother to me, Annie.'

He clears his throat and stares at the floor. My heart is thumping in my chest as I feel his pain radiate across the short distance between us.

'I can – I can relate, of course,' I say to him gently.

'I thought so, and that's why I'm so sorry for being such an asshole.'

'It's not going to be easy,' I warn him. 'Watching someone you love slip so far out of reach is heart-breaking. I'm so sorry to hear this.'

He looks at me again with his thoughtfully intense stare.

'She's seventy-three years old and was always so sharp and sassy,' he says, his face crumpling. 'I know that's not exactly young, and I feel like a fraud even complaining to someone like you, but she was so young at heart and I never thought this would happen to her.'

I can only nod my head. 'It's tough.'

He puts his coffee cup down and puts his head in his hands, then looks back at me.

'I'm so sorry,' he says. 'I know you have your own troubles, and your husband is so much younger than seventy-three. You probably think I'm selfish to even think we are being robbed in this way.'

'We all have our own definition of "only",' I say to him with a light smile. 'My husband is only forty, your friend is only seventy-three. It means the exact same thing to each of us, and it sucks, big time. There is no "only" when it comes to missing someone. My only is the same as your only. Grief and pain are totally subjective and utterly incomparable.'

He crunches his eyes.

'I guess that's true,' he whispers. 'So that's my excuse. I hope you can forgive me.'

I need to stretch my legs, so I walk towards the floor-to-ceiling window and take in the view.

'I forgive you, Senan,' I say to him. 'We can start again.'

*   *   *

'So you live by the water too?' Senan asks, now that we've decided to move on and change the subject.

'That's right,' I reply, surprised that he remembered how I'd told him so at our first meeting in London. 'Though my lough-shore home is a lot more blustery than the sea breeze you have here. This view is breathtaking.'

'I guess I take it for granted some days, but it beats the smog and manic ways of London hands down,' he tells me when I take a seat back on the Chesterfield across from him. 'West Cork is a very different pace of life from London or LA, obviously, yet typically I still manage to fall down the rabbit hole of boozing it up with strangers on occasion.'

'Strangers?' I ask.

'Strangers who call themselves friends,' he says with a shrug.

We sit in silence for a few seconds, as if deliberately clearing the air. The coffee is aromatic and expensive. He may not know how to switch on the cooker, but he can serve up a mean cup of coffee. I search again to try and find something to say to ease the pressure, and to firmly put yesterday's episode in the past, but I don't need to as he is about to drop a tiny bombshell.

'I saw you at the restaurant last night,' I tell him.

He swallows. He puts his coffee cup down. 'What? You did?'

'I was too uncomfortable to say hello, or approach you, after yesterday,' I admit, to which he bows his head. 'I also knew you were meeting friends for dinner, so I didn't want to interrupt.'

'You should have said hello. I don't bite,' he says, his eyes avoiding me right now. 'Look, I'm sure Caroline – or whoever briefed you – has given you all the warnings you need about how I tend to go off the rails or how my bad-boy reputation follows me wherever I go, but there's a lot more to me than that.'

'Yes, well, to be honest yesterday more or less matched that reputation.'

'I know it did,' he says, 'and I was probably just trying to live up to that, but I really wish you'd said hello last night. Sid and Ivy don't take any shit from me either, which is why I like them so much.'

'Tell me more?' I say, intrigued.

He lights up at the very idea.

'Well, Sid is an old workmate of my grandad's,' he tells me. 'They've been together for over forty years, but just got married last year, right on the beach here, which was great fun. I try to visit them every day and run some errands or fix up things around the house when they need me. They are amazing. I've known them pretty much all my life.'

I do a double-take. Never in my wildest dreams did I imagine Senan Donnelly to be the type to run errands or fix things for anyone, never mind an elderly couple who live nearby. He has totally stumped me with this one.

I take a deep breath, wait a few seconds, and can't help myself from letting out a nervous laugh.

'Some of the suggestions you made yesterday,' he continues

to fill the gap, 'or that Caroline suggested, like cooking . . . Since we've already started by walking the beach, maybe we could do more?'

'Oh really?' I say to him with a smile. 'So, the amateur dating agency is open after all?'

He puts his head in his hands. 'I can't believe I said that! I'm such an ass,' he says, shaking his head. 'OK, give me ten minutes to shower and then we'll go to the supermarket and give this cooker a test run. Maybe, while I'm gone, you can think of a nice dish for a late lunch that won't make me look like an even bigger fool when I try to help you cook it.'

I lift my coffee cup in my hands and take a sip as I watch him walk away towards the bathroom. When he's out of sight, I find my phone and text Kelly, who I know is probably worried sick that I'm stuck in some form of writing hell again.

'Lesson one – nothing is ever all it seems,' I type, still delighted at how wrong I was earlier and how today is so much brighter already. 'Just want you to know that I'm already off to a much better start today. Senan explained, then apologized profusely, so we're starting afresh today. Give everyone a hug from me. Miss you all. Annie x'

11.

Senan and I walk around the cool interior of the town's only supermarket, and I'm fully aware of how people are staring in our direction. Some make no bones about it, nudging each other as we walk past, while others do a double-take before letting their jaw drop a little when they recognize him.

He doesn't seem to notice, but I do.

'Keep me right, Annie,' he jokes as we manoeuvre our way around the aisles with a trolley trying to find ingredients. 'Food shopping isn't exactly a daily habit of mine, unless I'm grabbing a few things from a list for Sid and Ivy, and even then it takes me ages to find everything.'

Senan pushes the trolley while I choose some cupboard ingredients after having checked in his kitchen for basics before we left. Unsurprisingly, I found that apart from some ketchup, some salt, pepper, vinegar, and an old tub of mustard which was well past its sell-by date, we really are starting from the very beginning with this grocery shop.

I've decided we'll cook an easy dish to begin with.

'Spaghetti bolognese?' I suggested, and he was in full agreement. 'I'm no domestic goddess, but I've managed to raise my children thus far without poisoning anyone, so I'm fairly confident I can teach you at least that.'

I choose some minced beef, oregano, garlic, basil, onions, tomato paste, tins of tomatoes, Parmesan to top it off and honey to sweeten it a little. As we walk and I choose, he talks and I listen. I don't put my brain under any pressure to absorb anything too deeply as it's just casual conversation, but I can see exactly what Caroline was up to when she suggested this. Our shoulders have dropped, our defences are down, and we are actually falling into each other's company very easily so far.

'How about some wine?' he asks me as we pass the alcohol section in the supermarket. 'I imagine a nice red would complement your lunch choice? What's your favourite?'

'Yes, I do love a good glass of Malbec,' I reply, but then I remember the number of bottles I helped to dispose of during my big clean-up yesterday, and fear any alcohol might be a bad idea. 'Though please don't feel obliged at all. I'm happy with some sparkling water.'

He stops at that to have a photo taken with an eager fan who has politely interrupted us, and I step back to watch his reaction as he does so. Just as Liam at the B&B told me, Senan actually is quite gentle and mannerly in his demeanour with people he doesn't know.

The man in question is a very excited husband, who

claims his wife won't believe he saw Senan in a super-market; he's apparently been chased out there to get some holiday essentials.

'What's your wife's name?' Senan asks as he poses for a selfie.

'Diane. She is such a huge fan of yours. We all are!'

'Tell Diane I said hi,' says Senan, and the man goes away like the cat that got the cream, already forwarding the photo to poor Diane, who will be kicking herself for staying at home. Senan turns to me again. 'Now where were we? Oh, wine?'

'Yes, wine,' I reply, marvelling a little bit at what I've just witnessed. Having strangers stop me for selfies is of course totally alien to my own life, but I'm fascinated to see how he handled it with such patience and care. I've so many questions for him about how he handles being stopped in everyday situations by people who feel like they know him, but I'll save them for later.

'I'm not an alcoholic, Annie, despite what the media likes to say about me,' he whispers, then pushes the trolley forward again. 'Yes, I can party like a teenager, and I have a tendency to go a bit crazy when I'm lonely or feeling down, but I can also behave like an adult when I'm in the right company. I have many vices and weaknesses, but I can hand on heart say that alcoholism is not my problem.'

'OK.'

'So we can have some wine,' he says with a smile that could stop traffic. 'In fact, I look forward to sharing a bottle with you after we've christened my cooker. Now, if Malbec is your thing, let's choose something nice to mark the first day of our work together, totally in your honour and as a proper welcome to West Cork. We may as well do it in style.'

I feel a rush inside – not only at the suggestion, but also how at how much I'd forgotten how good it feels to do something so simple as to go food-and-wine shopping with someone who is looking forward to cooking together as much as I am. It may not be Senan's usual way of living, but I've a funny feeling that – despite his initial refusal to take up any of Caroline's suggestions – there's something about this simple moment that warms something within him too.

'So, do you see her at all now? Have you managed to stay friends or is it all too painful?'

Our conversation over lunch, which we're enjoying in a blissful breeze out on the deck at Senan's beach house, has turned quite serious, in contrast to the very light-hearted chat we had while cooking. As he chopped up onions, I fried off the mince, and we covered everything from our varied musical taste to which box set we enjoyed more, *Luther* or *Breaking Bad*. After much debate, we agreed to disagree.

Now though, we're getting into the nitty gritty, as Senan opens up to me about his early first marriage to Catherine Day, a law student who was working on a film set to pay the bills in her early twenties, and then the more recent break-up with Agnes Patrice, a Swedish actress, who it appears broke his heart. The divorce spiralled into his stint in rehab for depression, and not alcoholism as the tabloids suggested.

I'm very discreetly taking notes as I eat, but only in a way that doesn't disrupt the flow of conversation.

'I don't see Agnes any more, no,' he says as he casually tears off some garlic bread from a sharing plate in the middle of the table. We managed to work the cooker very simply after all, and Senan joked that I'd witnessed history by watching him switch it on and by putting this tasty but simple dish together. 'We are, how can I put it? We are very aware of the pain we caused each other, and we've acknowledged that the damage is irreparable on both sides. There's no point pouring salt on an open wound by keeping in touch, is there?'

I put my pen down, and then twirl some spaghetti onto my fork, my eyes not leaving his.

'Irreconcilable differences,' he mumbles. 'Two words that cost a lot of money.'

'Do you still love her?'

'Woah,' he says with a nervous laugh, then his expression neutralizes. 'Do I still love her?'

I wait for his answer, not wanting to break his train of thought.

'I don't even know that we ever really did love each other properly, and that's the truth,' he says, shrugging his shoulders. 'I was besotted with her, yes, there's no doubt about that, and for a while that was mutual. I found her enigmatic, totally mesmerizing and I was wowed by her talent. I mean, she's a very beautiful lady who I liked being around, but I don't think we ever really got past the first layer of getting to know each other properly, the way a husband and wife should.'

'And how do you think a husband and wife should be?'

'My parents had a fantastic relationship,' he tells me, lighting up a little bit more. 'I can see that now through the eyes of an adult, and I've always assumed marriage would be what they had. I had a slight chance of that with Catherine, perhaps, but I would never have found that with Agnes. Our relationship was, as they say nowadays, toxic.'

'I'm very sorry to hear that,' I tell him. 'I guess living in the media spotlight and public eye wouldn't help anyone lead a normal life, in any shape or form.'

'It was intrusive, to say the least, but then we courted it too when it suited,' he says with a shrug. 'It was very easy to become swept away by the idea of a wedding that attracted a lot of media profile, including a very impressive magazine deal. Soon, our marriage became a lot more about profile and less about us. In fact, looking back, I think as far as Agnes was concerned, the whole relationship was much more about profile and much less about us as real people. I'm probably guilty of taking that approach too.'

I take a sip of my wine, knowing this is exactly what readers will want to know. I may not be recording Senan's life chronologically as I'd planned to, but chapters like this are exactly what I'm after, and I'm taking in every word, jotting down phrases when I can.

'But the wound is still open, you say?' I ask, trying to dig a little deeper. 'You don't love her, perhaps you never did, but you are still cut up about your split?'

Senan looks out on to the bay for a moment, then lets out a long, deep breath.

'I guess I'm always going to be cut up by how we both got sucked into something that was only ever going to hurt in the end,' he says to me, glancing around as if he's unsure he should confess all of this. 'The wound is still open in terms of the way I reacted afterwards, and how I let the whole marriage failure affect me. I'm not cut up about our split though, no. When it came to the crunch, that was definitely for the best, but the months afterwards were a living nightmare. I don't totally blame Agnes for that. Most of it was self-inflicted, and I've learned to own my mistakes as well as admit to them. I should have been a lot stronger than I was in my reaction. I shouldn't have let myself take the blame and feel like such a failure.'

'You mean by getting help? You're not a failure for getting help for feeling low, Senan.'

His pain is tangible. He nods and looks away.

While cooking earlier, he'd hinted at his stint in rehab,

brought on by a worried family member who'd found him drunk and suicidal and, even though I need to find out more, I also want to gain Senan's trust on such a harrowing part of his life. I need to take that particular chapter very slowly and, since this is our first proper day, I don't want to exhaust him too much by diving straight in.

'Look, Senan. We all react to situations in the only way we can at the time,' I say, offering my tuppence of advice. 'You reacted in a way that, although perhaps destructive to yourself, reflected the way you felt right there and then.'

'I was in a very bad way emotionally, Annie,' he tells me. He looks right at me now. 'I was totally lost, I was deeply depressed, and I mightn't be here now if I hadn't reached out and admitted I needed help. I hope you never feel that way, or even come close.'

We both put down our cutlery and share a moment of deep understanding.

'I've been close, yes,' I answer him. 'Yes, I have. But I've never told anyone how low I felt before. Like you, I should have asked for help a long time ago, but instead I tend to write my feelings down. "Journaling", isn't that what they call it now? It's great, but it's no substitute for a real-life conversation, like we're having now.'

He licks his lips and dabs his mouth with a napkin, still holding my gaze.

'Tell me more,' he says. And, to my surprise, I do. I don't know what it is about Senan Donnelly, but beneath the bad-boy exterior I think I'm slowly finding a very wounded, very lonely and very lost man, who also happens to be a very good listener.

'You sure?'

'Of course I'm sure,' he says, staring right into my soul. 'Go on. Let's talk about it.'

'Well, when Peter had his accident,' I confess to him, 'my initial reaction was to run away from it all for ever, and I honestly contemplated doing just that. Things had . . . well, every relationship hits the odd bump in the road, and at that time I feared ours had hit a pothole.' I laugh unapologetically at my choice of description.

'I was terrified of raising two children on my own, hopeless and alone,' I continue. 'Looking back, I honestly don't know how I muddled through those first few years. Now here I am at a very different stage, still finding it hard to cope with it all. Life is tough sometimes.'

'It really is, but I imagine you're a very strong person, Annie,' Senan says to me. 'And I don't mean that anything has been easy for you, because no one could imagine what it's like to come through what you have. I mean it as a compliment. A lot of other people would crumble under pressure. You haven't.'

'Yet,' I say, feeling a shiver run down my spine.

I've been called 'strong' many times before. In fact, if I had a pound for every time I'd been called strong, I wouldn't have a house that's falling down around me.

'Sometimes being strong isn't really a choice, but a necessity,' I whisper with a light shrug.

'Of course,' he whispers, drinking in my every word. 'I suppose I'm trying to say that I see something special in you, but go on. Tell me about your husband. Tell me about the good times.'

He smiles and I'm startled by his interest in me, but I welcome it all the same. I adore talking about Peter to anyone who will listen, and I'm humbled that he wants to know.

'He was . . . I mean, he is . . . well, we met at high school,' I say, feeling choked already as I try to explain Peter from days gone by without sounding like he has gone for ever. 'He caught my attention with his cheeky ways and an answer for everything. I liked that. He loved Springsteen and would gladly have followed him around the world if we could have afforded it, but he really came into his own when our children came along. They were his whole life. So was I for a long time until . . .'

Senan bites his lip as I speak. His forehead is creased in a frown and he seems genuinely interested, which makes me feel a little bit more at ease.

'They seem to have forgotten him, even though he is still physically here, which totally breaks my heart,' I say quickly.

I gasp, feeling a gush of emotion fill my veins.

'We had so many good years together. I mean, it wasn't always perfect. I'm not perfect and neither was he, but I think overall we were mostly very happy, and that's all I could have ever wanted.'

'You miss him,' says Senan. 'That must be so hard when physically he is still here.'

I nod, pursing my lips as I feel my eyes sting. 'I really do,' I say, closing my eyes for a second.

I stop myself before I go any further. I shouldn't be opening up to Senan like this. It's meant to be the other way around, so I quickly turn the conversation back to where it should be. 'But enough about that,' I say, 'we're supposed to be talking about you.'

'No, it's OK,' he tells me. 'I'd like to know about your life, too, if you don't mind. I'd like to get to know you better, since you're getting to know everything about me.'

He sits back in his seat now, so at ease, with a light smile as if he is bargaining with me. It makes my heart rate settle after thinking of Peter and how life once was.

'So, do you ever see yourself getting married again, or have you ruled that out completely?' I ask him, trying to do a complete U-turn.

He laughs a little at my direct question and the complete change of subject away from my own life and back to his.

'Marriage? You mean third-time lucky? No. I've certainly never met anyone to make me think that way,' he tells me. 'But I'll let you know if I do.' He holds my gaze.

'And do you ever feel lonely?'

He shrugs and looks away for a moment.

'I suppose I do,' he admits, clasping his hands together. 'Don't we all? Yes, I can say I'm sometimes lonely, which is a very hard thing to admit, especially when on the surface everyone you meet wants to hang out with you. It seems a strange kind of lonely, a selfish kind perhaps, but lonely nonetheless.'

I admire his honesty. I was expecting a flat 'no', but I'm beginning to discover that Senan Donnelly might be full of little surprises.

'Looking back,' he continues. 'I don't think Agnes and I had a proper marriage at all, not like what you had with Peter. I mean, not like you *have* with Peter, sorry.'

'No need to apologize,' I reply quickly. 'I know what you mean and I'm guilty of using the past tense too. In fact, I think I just may have.'

'For example, we never did anything like this,' he says, nodding at the food on the table in front of us.

'Like?'

'We never cooked together and then sat down to eat and enjoy the moment like we are now,' he explains. 'We never talked as much or as naturally or openly as you and I are doing now. In fact, we never really did any everyday normal stuff, and that's probably where we went terribly wrong. I suppose, in our defence and as you touched on, life in the public eye can be all-consuming. Egos are huge, profile is everything when it comes to getting the next big job, and I guess with Agnes and me, we were both too self-absorbed to press pause from all that and actually get to know each other by doing simple things together with no other agenda.'

I totally understand where he is coming from.

Not that I've any idea what it's like to be famous, but I do know that once a couple ignores or neglects the little things in life, it's when cracks begin to show, and there are going to be problems if those little things were never attended to in the first place.

'So, go on, tell me. What really is the secret?' he asks me in earnest. 'I've got it terribly wrong not once, but twice, so I'd love to hear your view on long-term relationship success. I ask Sid and Ivy this all the time, and they only ever reply with a joke, something about if they'd murdered each other they'd have been out of jail by now.'

I put down my knife and fork and sit back on my chair, totally lost in thought. I search deeply for an answer. The afternoon breeze blows my hair in the wind and I push it off my face as Senan, who sits opposite me in this little sheltered part of the deck, awaits my answer.

'I wish I knew, but I can only tell you that love comes in many shapes and forms,' I say to him eventually. 'I actually scribbled down a bit of a poem one day recently when I was feeling a bit reflective.'

He perks up instantly.

'I'd love to hear it,' he says, and I shake my head.

'Oh God, no.'

'Really. I'd love to hear some of your work. Go on, tell me.'

'I couldn't,' I say, tucking my hair behind my ear. 'I really couldn't.'

'Why not?' he asks, his face etching into a frown. 'I'll show you mine if you show me yours.'

I arch an eyebrow. 'You write poetry?'

'No, I don't, but I've always wanted to, and I'm very envious of those who can and do,' he says as he sits forward in his chair. 'Go on, Annie. Let me hear your poetic words of wisdom. Please.'

I run the words over in my head quickly and then push myself to recite them aloud without getting cold feet. Senan is all ears.

'OK, here goes,' I say, looking out onto the sea so I can concentrate. 'This is a bit embarrassing. Please don't judge me.'

'No, it isn't embarrassing. It's wonderful,' he tells me. 'I'm listening. I'm totally listening. Go.'

I take a deep breath and close my eyes as the words I shared on a recent Instagram post come flooding back to me. I remember the reaction it got, how so many people could relate to it and how it made me feel that somewhere inside of me was a real writer just bursting to find the confidence to seek out a real-life opportunity.

'Love is about the little moments in life as much as it is the big moments,' I recite softly to Senan. 'So, fall in love with someone who remembers how you like your coffee in the morning.'

I catch his eye and he is smiling from ear to ear, his eyes wide with anticipation.

'Fall in love with someone who knows when you need to talk and when you need to be quiet,' I continue. 'Fall in love with someone who holds you tight when the world you're in is a scary place to be, and who sets you free when you need some space.'

I glance at him again very quickly. He really is listening, so I continue.

'Fall in love with someone who makes you see the world a little bit brighter when things seem dark; with someone who reaches for your hand at just the right time. Fall in love with someone who sees you "ugly cry" but still thinks you're beautiful. Fall in love with someone who you will go that extra mile for you, and you for them too. Fall in love with someone who makes you want to be a better person. Most of all, fall in love knowing you can never, ever take it for granted or assume it will be yours for ever. Chances are, it will never be, but fall in love with all your heart, knowing that – at least for now – it's yours and yours alone.'

A brief silence hangs in the air as I open my eyes and come back to the moment. I feel naked, like I've just exposed a few layers of my true self in one short moment to someone I don't yet know an awful lot about.

'Wow, Annie Madden,' says Senan, blinking in response when I look back in his direction. 'That's – that's really beautiful. Thank you. Seriously, wow. I love that!'

'Thank you,' I reply, feeling my heart rate slow down, surprised at how I remembered it. 'I read it over so many times that I've more or less learned it by heart.'

I bite my lip, knowing that I still have his full attention, and I haven't quite finished yet.

'It was perhaps a note to myself in case I forget all the good times I had with my husband,' I tell him. 'But who knows what way Peter and I would be now if he hadn't had the accident.'

'What do you mean?'

A brief flashback comes to mind, something I'd pushed into the very back of my memory and I quickly shoo it away.

'No relationship is perfect,' I quickly explain. 'No one knows what lies ahead. I gave up on planning or assuming a long time ago, so all I can do now is hold on to the precious memories we had together and hope that one day I might even find . . .'

I stop.

Senan watches me trail off, and it's like a haze has covered my eyes as I wonder where I was going with that thought. Well, I know where I was going and it caught me unawares.

'You hope that one day you might love again?' whispers Senan. 'That's OK, Annie. That's really OK, you know.'

My stomach leaps and I lose my breath. I stare at the table.

'I'm still married,' I remind him. 'I still love my husband.'

'Of course you do.'

'But there are many different kinds of love. They are many layers to how we love, so I . . . God, I don't even know what I mean any more.'

I see my own pain reflecting in his eyes as he looks on with such concern. My heart begins to race again and I have a strange feeling he is going to reach across the table and touch my hand.

But he doesn't. Thank goodness. I feel so vulnerable right now that I might explode with pent-up emotion if he did. I imagine how it might feel to be touched again . . .

Senan doesn't physically touch me, but the way he listened just now and the way he speaks in response means he is still reaching out in a way that makes me feel totally out of control.

'You deserve to be loved again, Annie. You really do.'

We pause in a silence that lasts only a few seconds but my God it's like the world has frozen in time. I stumble over finding any kind of reply to this statement. I've been told by many people how I deserve to learn to live again, but no one has ever suggested how I might desire to one day be loved again.

For one more split second I briefly allow myself to just imagine being held again by a man who loves me, but before I go too far I shake myself out of my trance and take a sip of my wine.

'*Que sera, sera*, and all that jazz,' I whisper, doing my best to move the conversation on. 'No one knows what the future holds, that's my motto. A bit heavy for a lunchtime chat, perhaps, but that's how I see it anyhow.'

I shrug, trying to lighten the tension that lingers between us, but he leans forward and rests his elbows on the table.

'It's OK, Annie,' he says so gently, and this time he does put his hand on mine. 'I shouldn't have probed so much so soon. I'm sorry if it's painful for you to reflect on the way things used to be.'

'Sometimes it's good to let it all out,' I tell him with a shrug. 'It surely beats putting it on Instagram to total strangers, for sure.'

I look up at him with glistening eyes, slip my hand away from his touch and go back to my lunch, knowing that I could say so much more.

I could say how much food shopping with him today brought me back to the carefree, happier times with Peter, when we'd plan our Saturday night steak dinner and we'd choose a nice bottle of red to go with it.

I could say to him how much I loved listening to music as we cooked together this afternoon, how he brushed passed me as he chopped up vegetables and I called out instructions, laughing at his efforts and praising him when he got it right.

I could say to him how much it filled me up when I watched him set the table for us outside with such care and attention, how he lit a candle and fought with the breeze to stop it from blowing out, moving it around the table to find a place for it that worked. I liked that.

I could say to him how just eating with someone like this – just the two of us, away from the chores and pressures of reality – swept me away to times gone by, when I'd do the same with my husband as the children slept upstairs.

But most of all I could tell him how I know that later on, when I'm back at the B&B with only my thoughts for company, I'll feel guilty for so unexpectedly enjoying my time with him today. I'll toss and turn, and picture Peter so helpless and lifeless, and I'll beat myself up for being the one who is enjoying just a little glimmer of life as it should be when he can't.

'You sure you're OK?' Senan asks me. 'I didn't mean to upset you.'

'No, no, you haven't upset me at all,' I say quickly, knowing it's time to change the subject entirely. 'Now, what do you think of our joint culinary effort here? We'll be competing on *MasterChef* soon.'

'I have to say I'm surprised and impressed in equal measure at how good it's turned out,' he says, bowing his head and raising his glass. 'In fact, even though it's only lunchtime, how about I treat you to dinner tonight?'

'Here?'

'No, in a restaurant,' he laughs. 'We could call it a busman's holiday and do some work at the same time?'

I do a double-take. It's only gone two in the afternoon and the very thought of more food is the last thing on my mind, but I suppose the more time I spend with Senan, the better I'll get to know him. I do have a job to do.

'That would be nice, yes,' I reply, trying desperately to ignore the sound of my pulse in my ears and the butterflies that dance around inside me.

I put my wine glass to the side and replace it with a glass of water when I see him smiling in my direction. I could enjoy more wine, yes, but it's only lunchtime and I must do my best to stay focused, even though I feel we are slipping into a very relaxed and friendly mode together.

'We could go around seven?' he suggests. I can feel my face go pink at his undivided attention. 'I could pick you up or meet you there if you want to go and write up whatever else we do this afternoon in between times?'

'What's so funny?' I ask him. 'Are you laughing or smiling?'

His eyes glimmer and he rubs his chin as he takes me in, right in front of him.

'I'm not laughing, no. I'm smiling because I'm happy and I'm just thinking of how grateful I am. Thank you,' he says, interrupting my runaway mind, and I am utterly puzzled.

'What for?'

'You,' he replies. 'Thank you for this lovely lunch and conversation, but most of all thank you for pushing me in the right direction and for giving me a second chance after yesterday. It's been a long time since I've had such a satisfying conversation. I really enjoyed it.'

Our eyes meet and I can't help but match his smile. I

also can't help noticing his dimples, which I don't think I've paid any attention to until now.

'I really enjoyed it too,' I say to him. 'OK then! I suppose we should start clearing up and then get back to work properly, now that we're fed. I'd like to talk a bit more about your childhood?'

He stands up and gathers up the plates and cutlery, fumbling a little as he does.

'Sure,' he says. 'I'll pack up the dishwasher and we'll get stuck in.'

@mumoftwo_missingyou
It was the summer of 2004. We always loved cooking together, so I suppose looking back it makes sense.

He always said he should have planned it all for somewhere more exotic, but to me it was absolutely perfect. We'd just graduated the week before, and it was the last week of our lease in the student house in Belfast, a time when we were both high from the prospect of a whole new chapter of life and the hunt for a real job had begun in earnest. He was hoping for a job at an engineering firm on the outskirts of the city, while I was applying for teaching posts anywhere I could find one.

'I'm going to miss this place and all the memories we've made here,' he said as he slipped in a CD and played the song

'Somewhere Only We Know' by the band
Keane, a firm favourite of ours and one that
always reminds me of that little one-bedroom
apartment with the battered sofa, our plants
that we'd given names to and a stack of
magazines on which he used to set his coffee
cup when it got to a certain height. 'Sometimes
I love change, sometimes I hate it, and I'm
feeling really nostalgic right now.'

'I suppose we all have to grow up one day,' I
said to him as I looked around with teary eyes
to match his. He was right. We'd made so many
memories there. We'd celebrated our twenty-first
birthdays the year before, we'd partied as much
as we'd studied and, even though we were living
off student loans and part-time jobs, we
managed to make it feel like our own.

I was stirring a pot of chilli con carne,
laughing at his loud singing along to the music
he'd chosen, but I'd no idea that when I turned
around, there he'd be in his trusty old apron, a
wooden spoon in one hand and down on one
knee on our tiny kitchen floor with his arms
outspread and his eyes closed tight as he sang.

'What on earth are you doing?'

'Will you marry me, Annie Nolan?' he
shouted over the music.

'What?' I shook my head in disbelief, not knowing whether to help him up or push him over. 'Get up, you eejit!'

My heart was pumping, and inside I knew that – if he'd been joking – I'd probably have murdered him for playing such a prank.

'I'm serious!' he said, and when he opened his eyes and looked at me I could tell that he really was. 'Come on, don't leave me kneeling here for much longer. I'm carrying some football injuries, in case you forgot! Will you marry me?'

Of course I said yes. The chilli con carne was burnt amidst the excitement, and we ordered in some pizza to celebrate.

As far as proposals went, he always said it was a bit meek and spontaneous, but to me it was absolutely perfect.

The sense of joy, the safety, the togetherness we had, the 'us against the world' bubble that we lived in was the only place I wanted to be.

I never thought I'd ever feel that sense of place again with anyone else.

Until now.

I can't help this desire to love and be loved again. I can't help but long to be held, to be touched, to be kissed and caressed, to lie with

someone and talk and laugh and feel safe and
secure like I used to with him.

I still love my husband, I really do, but there
are many different kinds of love. There are
many layers of love.

To love and be loved . . . that's all we ever
want in life, isn't it? Am I wrong to want to be
loved like that again?

Grid Pic: A West Cork sunset
Likes: 2,303
Comments: 543

12.

'You're off early! Sea swimming and surfing, I believe?' Liam is on breakfast duty this morning, and I just knew he wouldn't let me slip away without hearing the latest on my progress with his favourite local celebrity. I yawn and excuse myself for doing so, hoping the caffeine from my morning coffee will kick in to prepare me for the day ahead. It's too early to eat, but I forced myself to have a banana and some toast to keep the blood sugars on the right side, as I'm going to need my energy this morning.

'Yes, I know that cold-water swimming is a bit of a hip craze right now, but Senan reckons I'm going to love it. I'm not so sure,' I tell Liam, who eagerly awaits more information. 'I think I love lying in bed more at this time of the morning, when I'm not on parent or Peter duty, but I'm sure it will be great fun. Bob kindly lent me a wetsuit, so at least I won't freeze to death. Any other tips for me?'

Liam shakes his head quickly, as if there are way too many thoughts going on in there, which I imagine involve seeing Senan Donnelly in swimming shorts and the sun glistening on his tanned, toned torso as he runs his hands through his damp hair . . .

'Hmm, I can't say that jumping into the Atlantic Ocean in May is something I'm a big fan of, but each to their own,' he tells me. 'I'm not sure if I'd be more torn between the sheer terror of the cold water and the sheer joy of being close to Senan Donnelly wearing a tight wetsuit! Or if you're lucky, even less! Phew! The images in my mind right now would shame my mother!'

I knew it.

He fans his face with a breakfast menu which makes me giggle. I had a fair idea he might be thinking along those lines, and I can't deny that the image hasn't crossed my mind as well this morning.

'Now, now, you're only human, but don't let Bob hear you come out with that or you'll be in trouble,' I tell him, patting his arm playfully as I make my way to leave. 'Wish me luck! I grew up by a lough where we spent summers messing around, but never did I think I'd be up and out at the crack of dawn to take a dip in the Atlantic Ocean. I'll fill you in later. Have a great day.'

As I walk down the main road which runs along the shoreline to Senan's beach house, I check in with Kelly to see how Peter got on during the night. He's been sleeping well and for longer periods lately, but I know it can still be quite hard trying to find some rest around his schedule. I'm only on day three of my trip away, but I'm sure Kelly is already exhausted.

161

'I had awful dreams last night, Kelly,' I tell her. 'Are you sure he's OK?'

'I can assure you that he is just the same, except for sleeping a lot more. I'm looking after him for you, please don't worry. The kids loved chatting to you last night,' she says, changing the subject. 'Meg might not say it, but I think she is secretly delighted for you, Annie. So is Dan. They said you looked so refreshed already. It really looks like this stint in West Cork is suiting you so far. Now, go and enjoy your morning swim. All is good here. No need to worry at all!'

I almost hug the phone when I finish speaking with her, wanting to show my appreciation so badly to both her and Bernice for letting me take this opportunity, even if – the truth be told – I had a horrible night where I kept dreaming of Peter who was telling me I'd abandoned him. I was glad to have an early start as I couldn't bear to lie in bed alone. Now that I'm up and out, and that I've spoken to Kelly, I'm determined not to get caught up in bad dreams that are only my subconscious playing tricks on me.

Back in the real world, I'm hoping Senan and I will fall into a bit of a routine where we will spend the morning doing something casual together, just like we did yesterday. While doing so we can chat through various aspects of his life, and I can make mental notes to remember elements I need to highlight later. Then for a couple of hours we'll knuckle down after lunch into the real nitty gritty, I'll go and write up some notes before we pick up again in the evening if we've anything more to give. If we can keep going like this, we will get on, pardon the pun, swimmingly.

Last night's supper at Maria's restaurant had been very worthwhile too, and I think I've made a really good stab at the early chapters, outlining his junior years in North London, charting how his Irish father Harry was working for an engineering firm out there when he met Sally, his English mum. We joked about the whole *When Harry Met Sally* line that of course they hear all the time, but that part should make for a fun, light-hearted read before the heavier stuff kicks in.

I've lots to patch in on so many levels, but for only one day in, we've made a great start.

'There you are!' he says from where he leans on the elevated deck, watching me make my way across the sand. 'Stay right there. I'll come and help with your bags.'

He races down the steps and takes my straw bag and light rucksack, which he really doesn't have to, but I've a feeling he's still trying to make up for Monday's faux start, even though he has no need to. I've taken a bright pink wetsuit supplied by Bob at the B&B, a swimsuit and towel and some toiletries to freshen up afterwards, so I'm all good to go.

'You're going to be buzzing after this, Annie, believe me,' Senan tells me. 'Cold-water swimming really is addictive. It's like pressing a reset button inside of you, like a deep cleanse on the inside. I bet you'll be swimming here in the sea every morning after this.'

I've discovered very quickly that Senan has a magical way of making you want to believe everything he says, so I follow his lead and, before I know it, we're changed and I make my way towards the water, just metres away from the beach house. But there's one rule he didn't tell me, which takes me aback slightly.

'Hang on, you need to lose the wetsuit for this part, Annie,' he chuckles. 'Yes, wear it for surfing later, but not for our swim. The whole point is to feel the water on your skin.'

He stands with one hand on his hip, wearing only his navy swimming shorts, and I try not to stare. I also try not to let my chin hit the sand when I think of exposing my very pale, very Irish and very ordinary body to him, but I do what he says.

'That's more like it!' he says. 'Now you'll get the full experience!'

I ignore his very quick glance at my shape in my black one-piece, and I head for the water as quickly as I can. Seconds later, when the cool turquoise water hits my skin, I see exactly what he means and, once the shock of the cold subsides a little, I find myself breaking away from all the noise that consumed my mind through the night.

'This is amazing!' I call to him, but he is too lost in his own thoughts to hear me. In moments I switch off from absolutely everything. For once in a very long time I focus only on the here and now, on my breathing, on this instant, and the stresses that have kept me awake for years seem to evaporate, if only temporarily. It's like a bolt of lightning at first, but when the initial shock subsides it's just me and the vast, crystal-clear water. It's like I've found a place where I can take back control when everything else in my life is out of my hands.

When I eventually leave the water, I feel an immense accomplishment and pride. It feels like some of my troubles were – for just those few moments – completely washed away.

Senan was right. I am buzzing. I am refreshed. I feel like I am cleansed inside and out, and I can't wait to do it again.

'You look really happy!' he says as he towel-dries his face and hair at the water's edge, the sun beaming down on his skin. 'You'll be craving for it from now on, wait and see!'

'I believe you! I'm speechless,' I reply, feeling like I'm on top of the world. 'That was something else; I'll definitely be back for more!'

'I knew it,' he says, and his eyes catch mine. 'That smile . . . it suits you, Annie.'

'You think so?'

'I do!'

I am totally glowing inside and outside, and I imagine so is he.

*   *   *

'Now the first tip for surfing is that it's all about rhythm, and of course, balance,' he tells me later when he carries two matching red surfboards across the sand to demonstrate a few basic moves and poses. I watch him carefully and dutifully imitate as best I can. 'The next tip is don't be scared, which I know is easier said than done. Not many people catch a wave on their first go, but the waves are good this morning, so you never know, you might get lucky.'

Senan lies, taut belly down on the board, then shows me how to pounce up. I copy him, which takes a few attempts at first. I graze my knee more than once through my wetsuit but, after a couple of goes, I'm able to do it fairly easily. I practise putting my left leg forward, my right leg behind, and I bend my knees slightly, not taking my eyes off his the whole time as I fully concentrate on the task at hand. Senan has an intense stare, I've come to notice, and it's very easy to get lost in those eyes.

I smile a little when I remember Liam earlier and his comment about being with Senan in a tight wetsuit and how distracting that might be. I'm doing my best not to look too much, but since his wetsuit still hasn't entered the scene, it's very hard not to glance at his tanned naked torso and muscular physique, covered only by a loose pair of now wet navy swimming shorts that cling to his legs in all the right places. His hair, still slightly damp from the seawater, glimmers under the morning sun, and when he comes to me and puts his hand on my back to adjust my position, I

try to ignore the flutter I feel from the warmth of his physical touch.

'You took dancing lessons, I bet?' he says, his right hand
still resting on the small of my back. He reaches out, skimming his fingers from his left hand down my arm as he
lightly takes my hand and stretches it out into a graceful
point forward. 'You've got excellent posture and balance,
Annie.'

His face is only inches from mine now. I feel his breath
on my face and I almost lose my own.

'Irish dancing,' I tell him, swallowing hard. 'I spent my
younger days running around the country taking part in
festivals. It was a lot of fun.'

'Maybe you could teach me a few steps,' he says with a
wink before letting go of my hand, but his touch lingers on
my fingertips.

'So, what's next?' I ask, shaking it off. 'Have you any more
words of advice before we hit the waves?'

He laughs and goes back to his own board, where he
mimics my stance and again holds my eye to concentrate.
My legs are like jelly when I think of what's ahead. At least
I think that's the reason why they're like jelly. I'm not afraid
of the water and I'm a decent swimmer, but trying to control
a board in the waves is a far cry from anything I've ever
done before.

'Don't ever let go of your board,' Senan tells me a little
more seriously. 'Don't bend your upper body forward too

much, and remember your head is your steering wheel, not your feet so always watch where you're going. Now . . . are you OK?'

'Yes!' I say, a little bit high-pitched as a surge of adrenaline fills me from my toes. Senan expertly pulls on his wetsuit as I do a last-minute practice. 'I'm absolutely terrified but also raring to go at the same time!'

'You're going to love it, Annie, I promise!' Senan tells me. 'Right, let's get you in the water and give it a go!'

He lifts his board so easily under his muscular arm, waits for me to fumble a bit as I do the same, and then he races me along the sand. We run towards the water and I laugh heartily when we hit the sea and wade out to meet the foam.

'Wait for me!' I call to him as he waves me on to catch up.

I really wish my children could see me now. They wouldn't recognize their mum being so bold and adventurous, in a bright pink wetsuit, trying out something so brand-new and totally out of my comfort zone. I allow myself a little moment of pride as I catch up with Senan and take in his every word over the rush of the sea. Then I lean down on the board and drift along, finding the rhythm he mentioned earlier.

I feel like I'm flying. I feel so flushed and energized, from the tips of my toes to the hairs that tingle on my scalp.

'That's it, now up on your feet and remember your head is in charge!' he calls to me.

I lean onto the board, then spring up onto my feet, and he gives out a cheer from behind me.

'Wow!' I call out as I sail across the water, and even when I fall off and hit the waves with a splash, still clinging to the board, I realize this is absolutely thrilling.

Between swimming earlier and now surfing the waves, I haven't been so exhilarated in a very long time.

In fact, I've been reminded once more how I'm totally alive and it feels so good.

After a hot shower and a change of clothes back at the beach house, Senan has surprised me with a delicious Mediterranean breakfast hamper, all prepared by Maria from the restaurant. My eyes nearly pop out of my head when I see the effort he has gone to by arranging it all. Every day he is opening up to me more and, as he does, I feel like I'm peeling back layers to find the real Senan Donnelly, who is a much kinder, a much more giving and much more attentive soul than the man I came across just a few days ago.

We seem to have clicked, even though it's early days, and I find it incredibly sweet how patient he was with me in the water, and how kind he is to have ordered this amazing hamper for lunch.

A white linen tablecloth covers the table outside where we ate lunch together yesterday. Freshly squeezed orange juice is poured from a long thin glass bottle, baskets of croissants and crusty breads sit in the centre, along with an array of cheeses and cold meats, with a mouth-watering variety of chutneys to dress it up.

A lot of my favourite things, in fact, and I can't complain much about the company either. Liam at the B&B would have had a heart attack if he'd seen Senan in action today, but no matter how much I continue to be impressed by him, he seems to always give me something to feel good about in return.

'You were amazing! Honestly, a star pupil!' he tells me. 'Are you sure you haven't done that before?'

'Bet you say that to all the girls,' I tease, and his eyes widen at my cheeky response.

'Touché!' he jokes in return. 'I don't really, but I'm not sure you believe that.'

He pours us both a coffee after insisting I take a seat, and we sit in comfortable silence, tucking into the feast before us.

'Surfing sure does work up quite an appetite,' I say to him eventually, even though I don't really feel the need to break the silence.

'Do you always do that?' he asks me, smiling as he speaks with his mouth full.

'What?'

'Hum while you're eating,' he says. 'It's cute.'

I feel my cheeks flush.

'Was I humming? My goodness I haven't done that since I was a child!' I exclaim, totally astounded that I hadn't even noticed. 'My mum used to say that I'd hum and swing my legs when I was eating and lost in some happy thoughts.'

I stop, not needing to elaborate any further as he adds a dollop of chutney to his plate.

'You're bringing out the happy in me too, that's for sure,' he tells me, with a glisten in his eyes. 'I feel very relaxed with you, if you don't mind me saying. It's very – well, without feeling cheesy, I find it very natural to want to do stuff and spend time with you, and I don't say that easily to anyone. In fact, as you saw on Monday, I usually try to push people away.'

I switch back into work mode.

'Why is that? Do you realize you're doing it? Like, it's a conscious thing?'

He talks freely as he butters some bread.

'I just don't let people in any more,' he tells me with a light shrug. 'After the car crash that my life was after two failed marriages, I chose not to. I still choose not to, so that I don't get hurt again . . . yet here I am, knowing you have a job to do, so really I've got no other option than to open up to you. And I suppose I'm doing so because I can justify it to myself. We have to be open. At least, I do, otherwise you can't write about me, can you?'

I don't know why, but even though he has been totally honest, I feel a little bit disappointed in his answer. He is open with me, he is letting me in, but only because we have a job to do.

'You're safe with me, Senan,' I tell him. 'Honestly, I know

we've a book to write, but if there's anything that's ever off the record, you know you've got my ear while I'm here.'

'I know,' he says. 'Thank you. You can talk to me too, you know. Use me as a sounding board, or for whatever you need me for.'

My stomach does a somersault and I blush again. In fact he does too.

'Within reason,' he says quickly.

'Good save,' I respond, relaxing a little more again. I catch him smiling at me again.

'This morning's surfing lesson was great fun,' he says, 'plus it was my turn to show you something new after your cooking session for me yesterday. I really enjoyed it. I'm looking forward to what we get up to next.'

He leans his left arm on the table as he eats some bread and cheese, and my hand bumps into his fleetingly from the opposite side of the table.

'So what you're trying to tell me is that it's my move?' I suggest to him, unable to hide my own smile. I like this game. My stomach flips again with excitement, and I feel a fizzy sensation rush through my veins.

If my mother could see me now, she'd say I was flirting, as I tuck my hair gently behind my ear and bite into some bread, holding Senan's eye contact all the while. Oh God, I'm embarrassing myself. I need to snap out of this. I haven't flirted with anyone since I first met Peter when I was a teenager, and a searing guilt rips through my veins.

'I look forward to hearing your plan,' he says, looking at me with those very intense eyes.

'Work first, though!' I say, snapping us out of our bubble.

'Do we have to?' he asks, with a hint of a twinkle in his eyes. 'I like our chats.'

'So do I,' I respond, standing up quickly. 'But some of our chats have to go towards a book. Come on. Let's get down to work.'

He lets out an exaggerated moan as he gets up from the table and follows me into the beach house.

Being with him can be quite riveting, and I agree we make easy company together, but I refuse to lose focus on the job at hand. It would be very, very easy to do so.

~ Meg ~

Dear Daddy,

The house feels different without Mum here calling the shots and, although I miss her, something feels different already in a good way.

Being around Nana so much is different. Nana takes no shit, but then you already would know that, having grown up with her! Like, yesterday she made both me and Danny get up really early to help her around the house. Mum never does that, ever. She just stomps around with a frown doing everything herself. By lunchtime Danny had sorted out the airing cupboard upstairs, weeded the back yard, and I'd hung out washing on the line as well as vacuumed the whole house from top to bottom. I swear there were cobwebs on our ceilings that were almost as old as I am.

Kelly and Nana talk a lot, but then when I come near their voices drop to a whisper, and if I even try to take my dinner to my bedroom Nana gives me a glare that warns me not to, and if we even try to sneak off without loading the dishwasher, there'll be hell to pay.

One More Day

We've been chatting a lot too over dinner, mostly about you and Mum when you were younger. Both Danny and I have loved hearing stories about how you used to sneak out late at night to see each other. You'd meet by the lough and be home in time for breakfast, but Grandad Bob followed you one night and pretended he was a ghost, which scared you so much you didn't ever do it again. Bob told that story on your wedding day and, even though we have it all on video and we've heard it many times, it was so funny to hear Nana's version, as well as tales of how you even skipped school on occasion to be together. One day you got the bus to Belfast but didn't realize one of the older classes were there too on a school trip, which led to a lot of explaining when you both bumped into your history teacher outside the Ulster Museum!

Hearing her stories has brought laughter and almost tears for both Danny and me, Dad. Even though Danny tries to hide his emotion so badly, I saw his eyes glisten when Nana told us about you saying goodbye to your first pet and how sad you were for months and months afterwards. Or when you were seventeen and you'd just learned to drive, how you'd brought strange little old man called Gerry back home after finding him wandering the country roads alone – the old man was so confused but you wouldn't give up until you made sure he'd had had a hot meal, then you found out his exact address and brought him back home to his tearful wife and children who had been searching for him all evening.

It may only be days since Mum left for Cork, but I'm

learning so much about both of you already, as well as seeing you in a totally different light.

Listening to Nana makes me realize that you aren't just my parents. You are real people with real feelings, faults and needs, just like my brother and I are. Real people mess up, they break the rules, just like me and Danny do from time to time. They are human. All of us can only do our best in life, a motto that Nana has been preaching to us since she got here.

Oh and Daddy . . . I managed to go to your bedroom door this morning. I didn't allow myself to think about it too much. I just walked down the hallway towards the room, I opened the door quietly and I took three steps inside.

The room wasn't silent as I'd expected it to be. Kelly had left some music on, Bruce Springsteen of course, on a very low level, and it made me so sad for you. I actually felt sad, and it felt so good. Does that even make sense? Does it feel good to feel sad sometimes?

Maybe I'm glad just to be able to feel anything at all at last.

But anyhow, I managed to say just a few words to you, right from the heart, for the first time in forever, which I still can't believe I did. I stood there frozen to the spot, watching you lie in your bed, staring into space, and I made myself say something.

I just knew I had to, so I whispered.

'Thanks for helping Gerry find his way home all those years ago, Dad,' I said to you. 'You were a very good man. You were a kind man. Thank you.'

I felt my eyes sting, but I didn't cry of course. Instead I just scarpered back upstairs to the cocoon of my own bedroom before I allowed myself to shed a tear.

I know it's hardly the conversation I've been meaning to have with you, but it's a step in the right direction I suppose. I can't explain it very well, but I feel different inside after today – like something ever so tiny has shifted inside of me.

I suppose I should sign off now.

Nana is calling me again from the kitchen, no doubt with another list of chores to do before dinnertime when once more we'll chat around the table and even, dare I say it, play a board game before bedtime.

I hate board games.

But I kind of like it though.

I really hope Mum is enjoying her time away from here too.

What I've learned most of all from her absence is that she does far too much, and she has been carrying such a heavy load for far too long. I now realize, thanks to Nana and her bossy rules, that we all need to help out a lot more.

Maybe if we did, we all might have the time and space to live again together, instead of just existing like we have been doing for so long.

I'm so fed up with us all just existing.

I bet Mum is too.

x

13.

By the time the weekend comes, Senan and I have spent a lot more time together than we have apart, and late every afternoon, before we join up again in the evening for dinner or supper, the words flow onto the page at my desk at the B&B.

In between our meetings, I also manage some downtime with the delectable Bob and Liam, who I discovered have a liking for a game of Scrabble over an afternoon coffee in what they call 'the good room', which is a drawing room-cum-library on the bottom floor, just across from where we have breakfast. Bob wins every time, thanks to his fine collection of rude and naughty words, which somehow earn him maximum points.

Their company is like a warm hug after an afternoon locked away writing, and we share stories and anecdotes, not noticing the hours tick go by. But soon my time with Senan takes over everything and my conversations with Bob and Liam are either snippets over breakfast, or just before I race out for the evening for dinner.

As our first week together comes to a close, I've made excellent progress on the book. Caroline is very pleased so far.

'It sounds like you and Senan are getting on like a house on fire,' she says to me on the phone on day seven of my stay. 'Everything is reading well so far for a first draft, Annie, but more than that I'm so thrilled he has found a match in you. It took a while to find you, but now we couldn't be happier.'

And it's true, Senan and I are getting on exceptionally well. We spend all our time discussing what we're going to do next for fun, as well as how we'll break up the day working. He brightens up when he sees me and I can tell he finds it hard to say goodbye. In turn, when I lie in bed at night and he texts me for the silliest reasons just as another excuse to say goodnight, I feel an inner glow I'd forgotten had existed.

He pushes me to read my writing to him, he revels in my words and he encourages me to follow my dreams, asking me what's next for my career and offering to introduce me to people who might offer me some work down the line.

He makes me feel worthy inside in ways I never have before, while his words of encouragement never fail to put a spring in my step. He has demons, which he spills out to me so I can put them on paper, but he is as strong as he is vulnerable.

I see myself in him, and he gives me strength with his

words of wisdom, as well as with his confessions of his deepest, darkest feelings.

'I feel we can tell each other anything,' he said to me this morning, mid-writing flow. 'I love how you trust me, Annie. I trust you too, and your stories are always safe with me, you know.'

We swim every morning in the sea, we have breakfast on the deck, we work and talk and then we either barbecue in the evening or grab a quick bite in one of the restaurants along the bay. As much as we both love Maria's delicious restaurant, I have managed to convince him to try other places too, to make sure our days don't ever feel tiresome or the same.

Not that they have so far. We've watched movies together during downtime, we've added a few more 'easy cook' dishes to our repertoire, for which I've written out the recipes so he can save on takeaways when I'm gone. Now, even though it's only seven days since I got here, I realize that everything in my real life back at the farm sometimes seems so far away, and that scares the hell out of me, even more than my deepening bond with Senan.

My mind races between moments of blissful companionship and laughter with him, times when I'm so happy, to night sweats of panic that I'm leaving my real world behind.

'Stop panicking, please, Annie,' Bernice tells me when I FaceTime on Sunday afternoon to talk to her and the children. I feel an overwhelming sense of missing them when I see their faces, but they've so much to tell me and they genuinely don't seem to mind that I'm away at all.

'Danny is even folding his boxer shorts,' Meg tells me with a giggle. 'He is on his best behaviour, but he's just showing off in front of Nana.'

'She's just showing off in front of Nana!' Danny pipes in. 'Meg has turned into a domestic goddess, Mum. You should see her bedroom. You wouldn't recognize it.'

I'm both startled and impressed. Not only do my children sound as if they've learned about housework in my absence, but they also seem to be enjoying it. In fact, dare I say it, Meg actually sounds happy? This is both relieving and terrifying at the same time.

Bernice takes over and rolls her eyes. 'I'm keeping them on their toes,' she tells me. 'Nana takes no shit and they know it.'

My stomach sinks, even though I know I should be delighted that no one is pining for my speedy return, or that the whole house isn't falling down without me there to oversee everything.

'And I do?' I mumble, knowing how ungrateful I must sound. 'I *do* take shit?'

'That's not what I mean and you know it,' my mother-in-law replies sharply. She lets out a deep sigh and I know a lecture is coming.

'It sounds like you've swept in and made everything better for them already,' I say.

She laughs now and I genuinely feel like hanging up.

'Annie, this is your home and you make the rules,' she says as she steps out of earshot of Danny and Meg, 'but I think you'll find some changes for the better now that you've taken a tiny step back from it all. I mean that in a good way. Danny and Meg are very capable young teenagers. They aren't babies any more.'

'They'll always be my babies,' I say to Bernice. 'And Peter used to call you a slave-driver, don't forget.'

In spite of my mood, I start to laugh, and she does too.

'Ha! So he did, you're right! But it's not all work and no play, my darling. We've been eel fishing with Jake on the lough this morning, which was a real hoot,' she tells me. 'He and Danny have painted the shed and it looks magnificent, all shiny and red under the sunshine.'

I lighten up, reminding myself that I have to shake off my sense of control, and that Nana Bernice does mean well.

'Fantastic, that's so good for Danny,' I say to her. 'I love how he and Jake get on so well.'

'Yes, it's so sweet to watch them together. Now, the weather is pretty fine, so today, after a hearty Sunday lunch,' she continues, 'we're going to find a nice forest park to go for a walk and then we're going to the cinema this evening before back to school tomorrow. So not all Cinderella-type slavery around here, I can assure you!'

'You're wonderful, Bernice, thank you,' I say to her as my

defences simmer. 'Kelly is too. She keeps telling me everything is fine with Peter, but I know she must be finding it tough now that she's almost a week on duty. I'd rather she told me the truth if she's struggling?'

I can hear Meg singing in the background, and my hand goes to my chest as my heart pangs for my children. Meg only ever sings in the shower when she thinks no one can hear her, yet now she is singing aloud around the kitchen. Was I really such a bag of misery that she was afraid to sing or sound happy in front of me?

'Darling, Kelly is a trained nurse,' Bernice reminds me. 'She knows Peter and his needs just as much, if not more than you do. Yes, it's tiring, but just like you do every day, she is getting through it. The difference, as she says, is that for her this is temporary, plus it's not her own husband she's caring for. We both don't know how you do this long term, but let's not discuss that now.'

A sense of dread overcomes me when I think of the decisions that still face me when I go home. The longer I stay here, the worse facing up to reality becomes. Also, the longer I stay here, the more I realize that I've been clinging on to a false hope for too long and for all the wrong reasons. I was a shadow of my own self, I was a worry to my children. I was going to get worse, a whole lot worse, if I kept walking towards the darkness that I felt I deserved to be in. I was depressed. I was a mess. I was on the verge of a very dangerous breakdown, and this trip away has made me see just how vulnerable I was becoming and how desperate and lonely I truly felt.

'So, what are you up to this evening?' she asks me. 'Please tell me you're having a little bit of time off and doing something nice in your glorious surroundings!'

I do my best to bounce out of the plunge of grief I just felt.

'Well, not time off exactly, as I've some writing to do right now. But I'm skipping Sunday lunch and saving myself for dinner later in a favourite restaurant of Senan's a bit further down the road in Clonakilty,' I tell her.

'Sounds divine! Are you looking forward to it?' she asks me.

I obviously don't look as if I am on the phone camera.

'Well yes, I was, but . . . oh, I feel so torn, I really do. I feel like I'm neglecting all of my responsibilities by having a nice time here.'

'Annie, that's not true! I'm sure you're working hard too!'

'Yes, I am, but still.'

'But still, nothing,' she scolds. 'Stop beating yourself up for having some joy in your life. Come on. Snap out of that. Tell me more.'

I manage to smile a little.

'I'm hoping to go to hear some live music later tonight,' I whisper, quickly avoiding using the term 'we' to my mother-in-law, which just might sound a little bit too cosy. 'There's a pub in town that has a two-piece band on Sunday nights and Senan says, since I've worked so hard, and to mark the first week as done, I deserve to celebrate.'

'Wonderful!'

Guilt grabs my insides as I overthink what's ahead, and how it must sound to Bernice while she is there looking after my family.

'Tell me the truth. Do you think it's a bit much?' I ask her. 'Me going for dinner out of town? With him? Be honest, please. I fear I'm doing something wrong by accepting his invitation.'

Bernice takes the phone outside into the sunshine, where she looks away for a few seconds, and then her voice drops down to a whisper.

'I only fear you'll forget you're allowed to enjoy yourself,' she tells me as her eyes fill up. 'I really mean that, Annie. Go out and enjoy every single moment of your time there while you can. As long as Senan is being nice to you and treating you with respect, you deserve to use this as a well-earned working break. You'll be back here feeding the chickens in your dungarees in no time, so go and work for the afternoon, then get dressed up for dinner and have the most wonderful day and night with your friend.'

I feel my throat choke up and my eyes fill at my mother-in-law's reaction.

'But what would Peter say?' I ask her, feeling my lip tremble. 'It's not like I'm going on a date, of course, but what do you think he would say if he could?'

185

Bernice pushes her hair out of her eyes in the afternoon breeze, and I can see the lough in the distance behind her, which makes me briefly long for home.

'Peter would only ever want you to be happy,' she tells me, smiling through the tears that fill her eyes. 'Now, I'd better go and get the troops ready. You only live once, so enjoy the ride, Annie. That's my motto.'

I manage a smile. Bernice and her never-ending mottos can be both endearing and eye-rolling at the same time.

'I will,' I tell her before we say our goodbyes. 'Give everyone a hug from me. And thank you again for everything.'

I put down my phone and open my laptop at my desk in the B&B as a million thoughts flood my mind. Would Peter really just want me to be happy? I know deep down he would, but thinking of him always catches my breath. Are the children really feeling lighter now I'm not there? Should I really allow myself to enjoy this time with Senan?

My phone bleeps and I see his name pop up on my screen, which makes my heart skip a beat.

'Table booked for 7.30 p.m. I'll pick you up at 7?' he says. 'Looking forward to it! In the meantime, stop daydreaming and get writing. See you later x'

I spring right back into reality and shudder at the 'x' at the end of the message. It's not something either of us has ever added before in a text, and it jerks me inside as a fizz of energy runs through my veins. Did he mean to send me a kiss? Was it just in a friendly manner, or does it mean more than that? We have grown exceptionally close in a very short time and, no matter how much I deny it, I know we are dancing around an urge and desire that is threatening to explode at any given moment.

Maybe I should cancel.

Or am I totally overthinking as usual?

'It's a term of friendship,' I say out loud, as I find the latest chapter of his life story on my laptop in front of me. 'I have total control and so does Senan. Just stop over-thinking and stop jumping ahead!'

Also, stop daydreaming and get writing, like Senan just said. How did he know I was lost in a daydream when he messaged?

It's sometimes as though he is watching me, or that he can read my mind. It both thrills and excites me at the same time.

I *am* looking forward to tonight, even if all my feelings are matched with equal moments of remorse about having a good time. My biggest fear is that we are both looking forward to it just a little bit too much.

I'd better get writing.

14.

Without having said a word, I think both Senan and I knew what could potentially happen when we both shut off from our professional side, when we both got dressed up and when we both got out of town together.

It has been simmering under the surface, and as the days have passed by and the weekend has come hurtling towards us, the tension has bubbled until it seems about to boil over and reach the point of no return.

We've become almost inseparable in such a short time, in what feels like a blissfully platonic holiday romance and, as I dig deeper and deeper into his life story, he digs deeper and deeper into mine too. We share secrets and fears as if we've been friends for ever.

'This is like getting to know someone in fast forward,' he jokes, as we share a five-star dinner in the magnificent Gulfstream Restaurant, which overlooks the breathtaking Inchydoney Beach. 'I don't think I've ever got to know someone so quickly, or felt so comfortable in their presence. It's all a bit of a whirlwind, isn't it?'

'And we've to do it all over again for another week,' I remind him. Not even the huge windows with their epic views can distract me from Senan and every word he speaks. 'Imagine if we fell out and had a huge bust-up row just as we hit our peak, and the whole thing went pear-shaped at the eleventh hour.'

'I can't see that happening. Can you?'

I shake my head. The truth is I can't see that happening at all, and when I look back on the version of Senan Donnelly I was first presented with early last week, I know now that – just like me – he was filling the void of loneliness with whatever he could find, even if it was self-destructive. While he chooses to go on a bender to ease his pain when life gets tough, I've been choosing to run myself into the ground, physically and mentally, by ignoring medical advice and keeping Peter at home full time just to ease my own fears of letting go.

Now, just a week out of my usual routine, I feel like the future doesn't have to be that bleak, and inside I'm a whole lot stronger. On the outside, I'm barely recognizable. I take pride in my appearance with my red lipstick tonight, my beach-waved blonde hair. I've no need for fake tan as the sea breeze has given me a most wonderful glow.

'Dance with me, Annie,' Senan says, and his face brightens up as the band in the cosy little bar we find after dinner strikes up an Eighties classic love song. 'Just once. Please dance with me.'

He raises an eyebrow and leans across the table, taking my hand. My stomach swirls. This is not the type of evening I'd imagined earlier when I was speaking with my mother-in-law on the phone.

My initial reaction is to freeze and say no, but then I picture myself in just over a week's time, hunkered down in the chicken pen in my grubby dungarees, pale again, wrought with loneliness and another world away. Am I doing the right thing? Am I being selfish if I say yes?

My head spins a little and I nod my response, then Senan leads me onto the tiny dance floor in front of a makeshift stage in this glorious hotel bar. The place is dark and quiet, thank goodness, and so far no one seems to have recognized him. In fact he appears to have forgotten his own fame for a moment.

And for the next few minutes, I've forgotten who I am too.

We are both consenting adults. We both know there's been attraction fizzling beneath the surface, growing stronger and stronger as the days and nights together passed by this week.

We both know we each have a huge wound where our hearts once were, and we both know how hungry and starved we've been of human touch and the joy of feeling loved again.

We both also know that we're extremely vulnerable, and how we are living right now in this blissful bubble isn't what real life is like for either of us.

The intensity between us heightens, my pulse races as

he holds me close, and I know I need to leave before we do something we'll regret.

'I'll take you home,' he says. 'My God, I want to kiss you so badly.'

My heart doesn't know whether to sing or cry when he looks into my eyes on the tiny dance floor.

I lick my lips, ever so slowly.

'I think that might be a good idea.'

'What, kissing you? Please say yes.'

'I mean you should probably take me home.'

We gather our coats as I shake inside, and make our way towards the exit. Just as we reach the door of the bar, Senan's phone rings, taking us both by surprise. It's almost midnight.

He stares at it, as if he's afraid to answer in front of me.

'Take the call,' I say, folding my arms against the late-night breeze that comes off the sea in the distance. 'It might be your agent in America?'

'It's not my agent.'

Of course it isn't. I don't have to see the name on the screen to know it's probably a woman making a late-night booty call, or another group of hangers-on wanting a party. And so what if it is? It's none of my business.

He puts the phone back into his jacket pocket until it eventually rings off.

'No. This time last week I would have taken the call, but not now when I'm with you,' he tells me. Our eyes lock. My heart beats so rapidly.

'Why?'

'Because I have no desire to take it,' he whispers, touching my face with the cup of his hand. 'I don't want to say goodbye tonight, and I don't think you do either . . . but I know it's the right thing to do.'

'It is,' I agree, but my hand is in his now, and I feel the midnight sky whirl above me. I feel the strength of his arm as he gently pulls me closer to him by the waist. I feel like a woman again when he parts my lips and kisses me right there and then, and I gasp for air as endorphins wake up and fill me from head to toe at the rush of his kiss.

Oh God, I'm so nervous, but I'm so thirsty for more. He inhales slowly and his smile when he looks into my eyes says it all.

'This wasn't meant to happen,' I murmur, letting my eyes fall closed again, my face tilted up to meet his.

'But what if it was?' he says in return, and then he kisses me again. 'What if it always was meant to be?'

We make it back to the beach house, into the vast living room where we've spent almost every hour of every day of the past week together, and soon our clothes are strewn all over the polished floor.

My navy dress, my silver sandals, his white shirt, his grey trousers, and then his black boxer shorts along with my white underwear. Every time he touches my bare skin, he gives me goose bumps all over, but still I can't help but shed a tear for the range of emotions that flood my barren body.

I'd almost forgotten the sheer joy of human touch between two people who have such a strong physical desire for their bodies to meet as one.

I'm only forty years old, but I haven't been kissed or touched like this in seven long, lonely years. I haven't been kissed or touched like this by anyone in my whole life and God help me if I'm wrong, but this feels so damn good. Senan is as intense a lover as he can be in person, and his eyes are a heightened version of how he looks at me when we're working or eating or when he's showing me something like how to surf or the joys of sea swimming. It's like he's been dreaming of this, and I can't lie. So have I.

He leads me to his bedroom. We are both naked, yet so at ease as he takes me by the hand, and I feel so free in a way I've never felt before.

We don't close our eyes, not even for a second, so eager are we to take in every second of this blissful pleasure. His hands gently explore me, sliding down my breasts and along my waist, sending shivers right through me with every gentle then firm caress. I hold onto his back, finding his neck and hair, then he lifts my leg up and kisses my neck with a hunger I can easily match.

'I'm so sorry if this is wrong,' I whisper to him as he pulls me closer for more on top of the bed. 'But I want it so badly.'

'So do I, baby,' he says, his lips against my collarbone as my back arches and I welcome him deeply. 'We both want this, but we need it even more.'

And yes, I do need this.

I need to be loved physically. I need to be admired and seduced by someone who makes me go weak at the knees with skin on skin, or a look in his eye. I need to be told I'm beautiful, and that I'm worth going that extra mile for. As tears roll down my face, I tell myself that I still deserve to be with someone who lights up when he sees me, or whose stories I find intriguing while he does mine too. I deserve to laugh and dance and dine under the moonlight, and under the sun, like we have done so many times now. I still deserve to feel the urgency of a lover who wants only me.

'You're so beautiful,' he tells me as his eyes drink in my body. 'I don't ever want to say goodbye. Not next week. Not ever.'

I gasp under his watchful gaze, knowing that – right now – I don't want to think of that moment just yet either. I choose to live in this moment in time. I choose to savour every taste and smell of this delicious moment, even if tomorrow might show everything up in a very different light.

I will wait until then and deal with whatever comes my way but, for now, this is heavenly. For now, this feels so right.

@mumoftwo_missing you

*I didn't see it coming, but then, neither did you or
so you told me.*

You had an emotional affair, and even though I
begged you to tell me who she was, you played
it down and begged my forgiveness until I
finally let it go.

At least I pretended I did, but it ate me up
inside. Who was she? Did you sleep with her?
Even once? Did you?

I blamed how easy it is nowadays. I
blamed mobile phones, I blamed the internet,
I blamed our busy work schedules, and I
blamed our money struggles. I blamed my
attention on our two young children, but
never once did I want to blame you.

Nothing happened between you two, you
said. Nothing physical happened, anyhow. It

was only conversation that had gone too far, you told me. She was just a friend. She was someone who listened when I was obsessed with what needed doing around the house, or about how we were going to meet the mortgage payments after topping up once more to renovate the barn. While I was nagging, after an exhausting day in school with pressures mounting in my newly promoted role, you found solace and escape in her ear, when you'd have her full attention with absolutely no sense of reality or responsibility.

She didn't care that you hadn't painted the shed like you said you would, or that we needed to somehow find an extra fifty quid a week to afford the childminder I wanted to move our children to. She didn't care that we'd a burst pipe again, or a stroppy two-year-old who kept us up half the night when she couldn't decide where she wanted to sleep.

You said you'd been foolish and silly, that you'd fallen for an ego boost and used it as an escape from the sometimes mundane daily drag of everyday married life. It was only words that meant nothing; it was only the need for attention – it was nothing important in the wider scheme of things.

Despite all that, I knew I had one thing she would never have, because she wasn't me. Whoever she was, she wasn't me! I knew that whatever did or didn't happen with her, you'd never find someone else who could give you what I could give you in the long term, and that gave me strength to give you the benefit of the doubt.

I honestly believed you when you said you were sorry. Deep down I didn't think you'd risk what we had. I believed you when you said it was nothing. I believed you when you said it would never happen again.

But it did happen again. And it wasn't nothing! I found out all too late but I can never get the answers from you now, can I? It *was* something. It *was* something after all and it almost ruined me for good when I found out that on top of everything else! I hated you for it! I said I'd never do that to you, never!

And I never thought I would, or could.

So why am I doing this now? Why?

Oh God, please help me.

Grid Pic: Moonlight over the Atlantic Ocean
Like: 6,365
Comments: 575

15.

I wake up in Senan's king-size bed and wait for my eyes to adjust to the new surroundings and my brain to kick into gear for what happened the night before.

I can hear him in the shower. He is singing. He sounds happy.

I am not sure how I feel yet, apart from that I might feel a little bit sick if I think about it too much.

'Good morning, gorgeous,' he says with a warm smile as he walks from the en suite, wearing only a white towel around his slender waist. He dries off his dark hair with his head tilted to the side and searches my face for clues as to what this morning might bring. 'It's going to be OK, Annie. Please don't look so scared. Last night was beautiful.'

He crawls on top of the bedsheets and leans his weight on my body, kissing my neck and sending me right to heaven once more.

I tug the bedsheets around my nakedness and feel a shiver run through me. This *is* so beautiful, that's for sure. It's mind-boggling, it's head-spinning, it's orgasmic on so many levels.

But in my mind right now it's also so very wrong.

'I'm a married woman,' I whisper as my face crumples and he stops kissing me immediately. 'Oh Senan, what have I done? What have we done? I'm meant to be working with you not sleeping with you! This is not me! I've never done anything like this in my life!'

He lies down beside me, touching my face and looking at me so attentively. The longing in his face and how he holds my gaze could very swiftly mask my fears, but I can't let this happen again. I need space right now. I need time on my own to digest what happened last night and where on earth we go from here.

A burst of anxiety overcomes me, and I feel sweat form like tiny blisters on my skin and blind panic close in.

'Nothing will change between us if you don't want it to,' he tells me. 'Breathe, Annie. I won't say a word about this to a soul. No one has to know. It can go whatever way you like from this moment on, I promise, but please know that for me it was something really special. And I think it was for you, too.'

I glance at him and swallow, trying to catch my breath.

'I've totally overstepped the line,' I say, my eyes wide as reality bites me hard. 'How did we let this happen? I'm meant to be earning your trust and hearing your voice in my head so I can write down your words, but never in my wildest dreams did I think we'd end up like this.'

'We both knew exactly what we were doing,' he whispers.

'We are both lonely people who found something in each other. It's not like you picked me up on the street?'

He is trying to lighten the tone but I'm not ready for that yet, as a million thoughts race through my mind.

'But look at you!' I exclaim. 'You're gorgeous and fit and rich and famous! I'm forty and married, even if sometimes it doesn't feel like I'm married! I live a million miles away from your lifestyle here. I've two children and a disabled husband who doesn't even know me any more! It's all a big fat mess! We've messed this up, Senan!'

He shakes his head and holds my eye gaze like he always does, looking up at me from where he is hunkered down at the side of the bed.

'OK, OK, let's not panic. We're going to continue as we were and forget this ever happened if that's what you want,' he says slowly. 'My God, I love being with you, Annie! I can't deny I didn't dream as the days passed by this week that this might happen but, like you, it wasn't what I'd planned. I care about you deeply and I'll help you work through whatever your feelings are right now. Just don't panic. Stay calm. We'll work it out, I promise. It's me. It's only ever been me.'

I nod slowly, his soothing words and his gentle touch bringing me slowly down to earth again. I close my eyes but all I can see is Peter, so frail and stiff, staring into space, but there's a new look of sorrow in his eyes like he knows. What have I *done*?

'I need to go back to the B&B and get freshened up,' I say, knowing that at this present moment, I'm not in any fit state to be seen by anyone, never mind Bob and Liam, as I do the walk of shame in my clothes from the night before. 'I need to clear my head. I need to think this through and try and work a way around this, but I don't know how. We have still so much work to do. This was not meant to happen!'

Senan stays beside me, waiting for me to finish speaking.

'Rest up and I'll get you a coffee before you go,' he whispers. 'You're safe with me, Annie, you know that. I can't begin to fathom how you might feel right now, but just know I'm on your side, whatever you want to do.'

'Thank you,' I whisper. 'That would be nice.'

He is such a good person. He is saying all the right things, so I can't be angry at him. I'm only angry at myself.

'Actually, your bathing costume is here from yesterday if you want to go for a swim in the sea before you leave?' he suggests. 'Or, why don't you relax in the hot tub outside and I'll stay out of your way while you have a think to yourself?'

I grab his hand and bite my lip as I stare at him in desperation. 'I'm so sorry.'

'What for?'

'I shouldn't have dragged you into my complicated life,' I say to him, holding his hand as my eyes plead with his. 'Nothing about my life is straightforward, Senan. I should never have taken advantage of your kindness. Last night was something very special with you, but I should have known better.'

'Don't say that, please,' he says, his eyes creasing as he speaks to me. 'We have a special bond, Annie, so please don't diminish it! This isn't some stupid teenage fling, you know! Yes, maybe we took it too far too soon, but I can't tell you how much this week has meant to me. And I think it's been so good for you too. If you truly believe what we did was a mistake, I respect that and it won't ever happen again. Tell me what I can do to ease your pain. Or should I just leave you alone for a while?'

My head spins with so many random things. I close my eyes and I see Peter in his better days, so handsome and in love, then his gaunt face haunts me as he stares into space like he does now. I hear the loud growl he sometimes made in the early years of his illness, the one that always made my blood run cold, and it makes me want to run to Senan. I open my eyes and see Senan's face, so full of life and passion for me. He is saying all the right things, he does make me feel safe and, even though I know I'm wrong, something about what we have together does seem real. At least for now it does.

'What if I leave here next weekend and I never hear from you again?' I say to him, not knowing myself where I'm going with this. He goes around to the side of the bed where he slept and lies beside me again. 'What if this is all some highly charged holiday romance, fuelled by intensity because we're so shut off from the outside world? I'm afraid of growing close to you, Senan. I'm afraid for both of us. I've so much going through my head right now that I don't know where to start. I can't say how I feel, probably because I feel too much. Does that even make sense?'

He puts his hand across my body over the bedclothes and closes his eyes, and then he runs his finger down the side of my face. His touch never fails to make me shiver, and goose bumps rise on my skin.

'Everything about you makes sense to me, Annie,' he whispers. 'You are the most intriguing, talented, darkest, deepest, brightest, most beautiful soul I've ever met and I only want to make you happy.'

I close my eyes and wish I could let this happen. I feel so alive when I'm with him, and so alone when I'm not. I love watching him when he doesn't realize I'm doing it, singing to himself or cursing at the TV, or talking to his agent on the phone or greeting his fans with such tenderness. I love how he looks after Ivy and Sid, and how he gets so upset when he sees Sid's heart breaking as his wife slowly slips away. I love the strength and meaning of every word he says to me, how he pushes me out of my comfort zone and tells me I'm wonderful just exactly when I need to hear it.

I think I might be falling in love him, but how can I be when I love my husband too?

'It's too difficult, I'm so sorry,' I say to him. 'I'd better go to the B&B and get organized, then I'll come back and we'll do some work. I'm so sorry.'

Senan drives me back to the B&B and we barely speak a word on the very short journey down the coastline.

I don't even know if it's a good idea, as I'm trying to slip in without strange looks – at the very least from Bob or Liam – but to my relief the path is clear and I scarper up the stairs and into my room. I close the door and lean against it. I'm so confused. I've sampled a very different way of life here, one that is so energetic and wholesome, a life that is awakening and refreshing. I can't deny it. I adore my time with Senan. We laugh so much, we talk so intensely, we never have a dull moment or a cross word . . . but then who does in the first flush of a romance?

I shudder at the thought of having a sordid, secret romance here. This was meant to be a dream come true. It was to be a chance to work on a lifelong ambition, and most of all it was meant to be a sensible financial move, through which I'd make our lives better. But now I seem to have made my own life worse.

I strip off my clothes, stand under the shower and get under the bedclothes, hoping for some solace and peace of mind, but the demons won't leave my head. I hear Dr McCloskey remind me that Peter is never coming back to me. I see Meg and Danny's faces as they ate pancakes when

I declared I didn't have a husband any more. I see the look of concern on my mother-in-law's face when she sees me stressing and faffing around as the buzzer rings and rings and rings for my attention. I hear Kelly insist that my life can't go on as it is. She is a nurse and even she is struggling with the weight of it all while I'm away, and she doesn't have to look after the children as well, like I do.

Shit, Kelly! I look at the time. She'll be wondering why I haven't called to check in with Peter as I always do in the morning. It's just past nine, which means I'll have missed the children before school, but when I pick up my phone I see I've a message from each of them.

'Double Science today, double boring!' says Meg. 'Have a fun day, Mum! You'll never believe it but I'm all caught up on Maths at last! Jake is a genius – he helped me!'

My heart sings when I read her words, so full of innocence and sincerity. She is truly like a different child. Danny's message is equally wholesome.

'I'm a changed man, Mother,' he says, and I laugh as I can hear his voice as I read it. 'I'm up before Henry the Rooster, chickens all fed, coop cleaned out. You're out of at least one job when you get back. Miss you. Hope you are loving life over there. You deserve it.'

I deserve it.

I've heard that so many times, but what is it I deserve? A break, yes. What I don't deserve is to fall into the arms of another man when I'm still wearing my wedding ring.

What I don't deserve to do is to hurt Senan like I know I'm going to. I need to ring Kelly.

'Hey, love!' she says when she answers the phone after only one ring. 'I was going to give you a wee buzz this morning but wasn't sure what your schedule was – your mum was saying you'd a bit of a night off last night. How did it go?'

My head swims with a flurry of possible answers.

'Fine!' I say, in a voice that even to me sounds unconvincing. 'How's Peter? How are you?'

'Fine?' Kelly echoes. 'No harm, but I'd imagine if you took a poll of red-blooded women who'd had the chance to spend an evening over dinner, drinks and dancing with Senan Donnelly, they'd be saying more than "fine"!'

'It's not like that, Kelly,' I say, my tone taut and firm. 'It was fine.'

She knows me better than that, of course, and I'm sure she can read between the lines, but I'm too tired to go any further, and certainly not on the phone. Maybe I'll tell her when I get home. Maybe I won't ever tell a soul. I feel rotten for my actions, inside and out.

'OK then,' she says, and I can just see her face screw up in disbelief. 'Well, like I said, I was going to ring you this morning at some stage. Now, there's nothing to worry about, but—'

Oh God, no!

'Kelly!'

'Annie, calm down,' she scolds. 'Let me finish. I've been dreading telling you this as I feel I'm letting you down, but I've had to take a day off.'

'Oh . . .'

'But Sorcha, who usually covers for me, is taking over today and maybe tomorrow too,' she explains. 'I'm so sorry. I'm just feeling the pressure of it all, but I'll be back in action on Wednesday. I hope you don't mind. I honestly don't know how you do it.'

I pinch my eyes as I feel hot tears spring up and I don't even know why. There are so many reasons why. I feel bad for Kelly, having to come to that decision, and how hard I know she is finding it to tell me. I feel the blanket of darkness overcome me at the thought of going back to face it all again, day in, day out, night in, night out. The loneliness, the exhaustion, the despair . . .

'Please don't say you're sorry,' I whisper to her, trying to keep my voice steady and calm. 'You've gone way over the extra mile to let me come here. Maybe I should go home early and—'

'See, I knew you would say that!' Kelly says. I've never heard her sound so stressed. 'Don't even go there, Annie. Everything is under control. I just need a short breather, but I think the bigger message is that you do too. If I were you, I'd enjoy every single second of your time in West Cork with the lovely Senan. You'll be back here soon enough, but there will have to be changes made. I see that now more than ever.'

I close my eyes and breathe in long and slowly. Then, when we say goodbye, I fall fast asleep. I sleep right through what was meant to be our afternoon writing session, and when Senan turns up at the B&B to see if I'm all right, I pretend I don't hear the door.

I can't face up to anything right now. I don't know how I'm going to face him in person again.

~Meg~

Dear Daddy,

Oh, I've made a mess of everything, haven't I? This is such a horrible mess!

It was supposed to be just me and you in the room this morning so I could finally say what I had to say to you. No one will ever know how much I had to force myself to go into your room and tell you what I've been meaning to tell you for so long.

I hadn't slept all night thinking about how I'd find the right words to say or how I would even start. Should I just blurt it out, or should I take my time and search my memory for exactly the right words just in case, somewhere in there, you might actually be able to hear me?

I spoke to my music teacher in school yesterday about it all. She's not like a real teacher yet. She's a student who's on placement from university and she really likes me, mainly because I want to sing just like she does too. I told her what I was planning to do today after all this time, and she was so cool about it all. She said to make sure and get it all out of *my system, all seven years of frustration and fear. She said it would make me feel better and that, after I'd done it, I'd feel like a big weight was off my shoulders.*

But it doesn't feel like that at all, Dad. It feels like now I've gone and made everything worse.

It started off just as I'd planned it for ages. I tiptoed downstairs long before Nana called us for breakfast. I listened each morning for her getting up, so I knew it was never before seven in the morning. I even listened at her door to make sure she was still asleep and she was snoring (I'm used to it by now, but sometimes I swear it would make the house rattle). I don't even know why I'm joking. It's not funny.

I was still in my pyjamas and I went downstairs into your room. Your night light was on and your eyes were closed. There was no Bruce Springsteen music this time. The curtains were drawn and the whole place was so quiet but I kept going. I was so afraid, but I just kept breathing as I walked towards you. I put my hand on yours and I closed my eyes tight.

'I'm so sorry, Daddy,' I told you quickly before I changed my mind. 'I'm so sorry I distracted you that day, and I'll never forget the fear on your face just before you fell. But you were wrong too, weren't you? Some of it has to be your fault too! I told you how I heard you on the phone to her. I told you how I'd heard you were going to meet up in secret later that day. You said you just couldn't stop thinking about her. Was she really that special? Why were you thinking about her?'

I caught my breath really sharply.

'You begged me not to tell but I said I would! I was going to tell Mummy everything! You begged again and then I watched in slow motion as your foot slipped and then you screamed and I screamed too. I screamed and screamed even when you stopped and all I remember after that is the pool of dark red that came flowing towards my wellington boots that you'd bought me just that morning.'

'I was only eight years old and you were my hero, Daddy,' I said to you. Tears, real tears at last, flowed down my face and onto the back of my hand as I tried to keep up with them. 'But you loved someone else as well as me and Danny and Mum. I heard you say it to her. I'm so sorry, but you should be sorry too!

It was just then I heard someone shuffle behind me and my heart almost leapt into my throat.

'Oh Meg! What are you saying, darling?'

'What? No! How long have you been standing there?'

My eyes widened and my tears stopped. She was blocking the doorway so I couldn't escape. She was in her nightwear too and she looked ghostly with the light behind her.

'Meg, honey, I didn't hear you come in here,' she said coming towards me. 'You scared me. What's this all about? You can tell me, you know. You can tell me anything.'

I shook my head as I stood there, frozen to the spot. It was Kelly.

'What did you hear?' I screamed. I didn't care if I woke up the entire household in that moment, but then I covered my mouth so I couldn't scream any more.

She took me in her arms and squeezed me so hard and I just know that she heard everything. She heard me! And now she will tell Mum and everything – all of our progress here while she has been away – has been ruined.

I've said too much, Daddy! I'm sorry! Kelly has gone home and I don't think she will ever come back.

x

16.

'You had me worried sick!'

Senan paces the kitchen floor at the beach house on Tuesday morning.

He looks like he hasn't slept a wink all night. After eleven missed calls the evening before, I eventually answered the phone and we talked for over an hour but now, when I see him face to face, I can sense he isn't quite ready to let it go.

'I totally understand,' I say to him from where I sit in my usual place on the Chesterfield sofa across from him. By this stage of our morning, I'd usually have my shoes off. I'd be curled on the sofa post-swim, with a full breakfast in my belly and a coffee by my side. Senan would be either on the sofa opposite or he'd sit beside me, and we'd freely chat the afternoon away, but today everything has changed, of course. Today I sit on the edge of the seat, my hand on my leather satchel strap. The coffee he has made me has gone cold. There was no morning swim together. There was no hearty breakfast. There is no laughter and no easy chat. Everything has changed.

'You haven't eaten a thing since Sunday night, Annie!' he reminds me. 'Look, put the schoolbag away, will you? I'm worried about you and we need to throttle this out.'

'Why?'

'Why? Because you can't just disappear for a day, go on some sort of hunger strike and then try to pretend we can just start working again – because we can't.'

I shake my head. 'We can. We have to work. We just have to.'

My voice is monotone and calm, but I slowly begin to relax when I see how much he cares.

'Not before you at least eat something, for goodness' sake. And relax. You're starting to look like a stiff-upper-lipped teacher again.'

I can't help it. My lip curls into a smile when he says that. Everything about him puts me at ease, no matter how much I try to fight it. I was so terrified of any 'elephant in the room' feeling between us, but it simply isn't there. I may feel like hell in ways but, deep inside, something tells me that Senan and I have an invisible force between us that is simply undeniable.

'Look at you, all caring about me,' I say, teasing him. 'Where did this come from?'

He catches my eye, still so serious.

'Probably because I *do* care so much about you,' he says, as if it's the most obvious thing in the world. 'I know we talked on the phone but, Annie, yesterday was a very

and I'm hoping to widen my scope by going for some grittier, more challenging roles. I need something really big. I need a quality director to put some faith in me so that the industry will take me seriously again.'

I lean back on the sand and watch the sunset in the distance as it comes down in shades of pink, red and yellow onto the sparkling blue water.

'And personally?'

'Is this a trick question?' he asks me. He leans on his elbow, stretched out on the sand to face me. 'Wanting something on a personal level and getting it is very different, Annie. I've realized more and more that I can't always get what I want, no matter how much I once thought I could.'

I glance at him, he locks me in, and we hold each other's stare. Our bodies are close. I know at that moment he wants to kiss me.

'So, what about you?' he asks, breaking the moment. 'Same question. What's next for the beautiful, intriguing lady that is Annie Madden?'

I contemplate my answer, doing my best to be realistic. I think of the conversation with Kelly yesterday and a wave of sadness overcomes me.

'My future, I've come to realize, is not in my hands on any level,' I say to him. 'In fact, I don't think any of us can control as much as we think we can. I once thought my future was all paved out and it was just a matter of joining the dots.'

'Of course,' he replies as he draws shapes in the sand. 'The woman who won't plan ahead. That could be the title of your novel.'

He laughs at his own joke.

'Very good! I *would* love to write more of course,' I say, trying to brighten up a little. 'I'd like to write my own novel one day.'

'I know a good love story you could write.'

My stomach flips when he uses the word 'love'.

'Oh Senan,' is all I can muster. 'You'll soon forget about me.'

He sits up and leans forward, staring out onto the water in the distance.

'You don't really know me at all,' he says. 'Not if you think that.'

'But of course you will,' I say, looking right at him now. 'This isn't the real me. I sometimes let myself drift off and pretend this is real life, but the real me is a lot more ordinary, believe me.'

He looks at me and smiles, and then rolls his eyes.

'Don't start again about how in real life you spend your days feeding chickens in mucky dungarees,' he jokes with me. 'And how your kids need to do real-life stuff like homework and sports and after-school clubs, or that you have to do mundane things like grocery shopping, or fixing up your farmhouse. Imagine!'

'Very funny,' I say to him. 'Nice to hear you've been

listening to me all this time, but what I was trying to say to you is that I'm just a very ordinary woman.'

He throws his head back and watches the sky.

'You are not ordinary to me.'

I feel a rush through my veins when he turns to me and smiles.

'That's nice of you to say.'

'I'm serious. Life is short, Annie,' he tells me as he looks up at the stars again. 'I've learned a lot in a very short space of time with you, and I've realized that meeting someone like you is one of the best things that has ever happened to me, and I don't say that lightly. I've been round the block a few times, but I know something special when I find it. Just because this isn't your real life right now, it doesn't mean you haven't found the real you again.'

I lie down on the sand and stare at the same evening sky, smiling at his humour as well as his meaningful words. Is this the real me? Am I longing to feel like this again?

'You're a very special person to me too, Senan,' I say. 'And you always will be.'

'But you'll forget about me when you're back cleaning out the chicken coop,' he replies.

'Never,' I tell him, and I really mean it. 'All joking aside, I will never forget this and I'll never forget you, no matter what happens next.'

He joins me on the sand and we lie there, side by side, staring at the sky. He reaches for my hand and I allow myself just one more glorious moment to feel his touch. We breathe in synchronicity, just the two of us lost in this precious time, where nothing is real, perhaps, but everything is just as it should be.

Until we hear someone calling Senan's name in the distance. It's a frail, faraway sound, but it's enough to make us both spring up on the sand and listen.

'Oh my God!' says Senan, barely taking time to find his feet on the sand beneath him. 'It's Ivy! Oh no. Come with me, Annie!'

I follow him as he runs, both of us in bare feet towards the home of the elderly couple who Senan loves so dearly, where – sure enough – we meet Ivy wandering around outside, unable to work out which direction to go in to find Senan.

'What is it, darling? Where's Sid?' Senan asks, crouching down a little and holding both of Ivy's arms as though they are delicate bone china. Her wrinkled lips purse tight as if she can't think of the words to say, and instead she points towards the house. Senan scrambles towards the steps and I take Ivy by the hand, leading her back inside to see what's going on.

But I don't get too far before I hear Senan shout back to me. 'Call an ambulance, Annie! Quickly! It's number 3 Beach Lane! I think Sid is having a heart attack.'

With my hands trembling, I let go of Ivy to make the call and then bring her inside and put a blanket over her legs on the sofa as Senan kneels on the floor, desperately giving mouth-to-mouth to Sid between chest compressions. Beads of sweat form on his forehead as he does so, and he talks to his friend as much as he can between his attempts to keep him alive.

'Come on, buddy!' he says, wiping the sweat from his brow. 'You're going to be fine. The ambulance is on its way. Sid, I'm here with you and so are Ivy and Annie. Don't be scared. We're going to get you to hospital real soon, pal!'

Senan glances at me and I bite my lip when I see the tears in his eyes. I grasp Ivy's hand and she returns my grip, as she repeats a soft prayer with her eyes closed. The progress of her Alzheimer's may be rapid, yet I can tell she knows exactly what is going on right now with her precious husband.

'Where are they, Annie? Should you call again? They need to get here quickly! I'm losing him!'

I get the phone again to dial for help but, just before I do, we hear sirens in the distance and wait for the next few agonizing minutes until they reach Sid and Ivy's home. Well, I wait with Ivy as she prays beside me, but Senan doesn't spare a second. I blank out the flashbacks the sounds give me, or the sight of the blue light reflecting in the windows, or the medical jargon spoken as they burst through the doors.

The paramedics swarm in, two lads who ask only a few questions as they take over, and before we know it, Sid is stretchered and off into the ambulance.

'Is he going to—?'

Senan's voice is shaking as he speaks to the crew member at the door as they load Sid into the back.

'Call the hospital in a few hours for an update, but good work, sir,' says the paramedic quickly. 'You've done all you can to make sure this old guy will be coming home to his good lady again.'

I try to make myself useful by getting some hot sweet tea, as Senan does his best to explain what just happened. The way he looks at her so tenderly, the way he holds her hand with delicate finesse and the way his voice breaks a little when he says we'll stay with her tonight stops me in my tracks.

'He will be back soon, yes?' says Ivy with huge, innocent eyes. 'We've never really been apart, you know. Did you tell them not to give him oats for breakfast? He only ever takes eggs.'

'I'm sure Sid will keep them right when he wakes up after a good rest,' Senan tries to reassure her, as he passes her a cup of tea. 'He's going to be fine, just you wait and see.'

Senan looks up at me as if he isn't quite sure what he is saying is all true.

'You heard the paramedic just now,' I whisper to him softly. 'It looks like you may have saved his life, Senan. You saved Sid's life.'

'I really hope I did,' he says to me. 'Forget the tea, darling. I'll see if Sid has any brandy.'

17.

It's Wednesday, and time starts to speed up as Senan and I work our way through the last elements of his life story. We manage to fall into a somewhat different routine, which is midway between the cosy, almost cuddled-up cocoon we'd been inhabiting, and the distant way we worked last Monday when we started.

We visit Sid at the hospital in the morning and then go to see Ivy at the care home where she'll stay for the near future. We lock up their home and check on it daily. As we do, I can't decide if this huge distraction is making us grow closer, or if it's brushing how we really feel under the carpet. Either way, I know I have never before experienced anyone saving a life right before my eyes, and seeing Senan's strength at the time and how he has organized everything for Ivy since has given me more insight into the man than I ever thought I'd witness in such a short time together.

There is still space to keep on top of our best behaviour, yet still a sense of depth and closeness in the air that simply cannot disappear, yet something has changed. It's like his mind is elsewhere, and I can only assume that it's still shock from what he witnessed having almost lost Sid.

'I keep having these insane nightmares,' he finally confesses to me one day. 'Like I can hear Ivy calling me but I can't find her. I'm running up and down the beach but I can't find the house and I can't find her. I'm exhausted, Annie.'

He puts his head back on the sofa and I so want to go and sit with him so I can soothe his distress, but I'm trying so hard not to let our emotions spill over into something physical again.

'Will you stay with me?' he asks, and his words are like an electric shock.

'What? Tonight?' I reply. 'What do you mean, stay?'

He stares at the ceiling.

'Forget about it,' he replies. 'Sorry, I shouldn't be saying those things. Right, back to work. Where were we?'

'I'm married, Senan,' I remind him as much as I'm reminding myself. 'You know I want you. My God, I want you so badly but—'

'You can't, yes I know, I know! I'm sorry,' he says with a smile. 'OK, so back to the rehab chapter. Where was I?'

We do our best to stay focused. Sid's hospitalization and the subsequent insertion of stents – not to mention all the to-ing and fro-ing with clothes and belongings for both Sid and Ivy – has left us both on a strange wavelength. It would be so easy to just fall into bed and forget the world, but time is ticking against us and we've come this far now.

I feel Senan's pain when he speaks about his time in the rehabilitation clinic and how he found solace there, so much so that he feared reality afterwards.

'Institutionalized . . . I think that's what you call it?' he explains to me when he digs a little deeper. 'I was determined to reinvent myself in there, and even more when I left, but there was a strange sense of safety for those six weeks. It was like I was cocooned from the outside world and everything was stripped back to simple things, with a rigid routine that I clung to. I got to know myself more than ever, and I knew it was time for change, so when my time was up, I sold my apartment in Shoreditch and moved here to start again.'

I think of the way he was when I found him, just ten days ago, when he was so lonely, in despair over Ivy's diagnosis, hungover, and the house was an unrecognizable mess.

'Even though I'd learned so much about myself back then,' he says, 'it's very easy for the old demons to slip back when loneliness finds a way in, Annie. I was on a bit of a pity mission just before you got here, and I probably would have continued to go on self-destruct if you hadn't . . .'

I wait for him to continue.

'If you hadn't . . . I didn't expect for you to show up the next day, Annie,' he says to me, as his eyes search my soul. 'In a way I didn't want you to, because I knew by spending so much time together, I could easily get close to you and that it was going to be hard to let go when the time would come. I thought it would be easier to push you away early.'

I am taken aback by his revelation.

'Why would you want to push me away? I was here to write your book. You said in London you were happy to work with me?'

'I was,' he tells me. 'But I was afraid, because I think I knew from that very first day I'd grow close to you.'

I scrunch up my face in disbelief.

'It's true,' he continues. 'You were such a force that day. I felt it was like we were the only two people in that poky room, which is why I made a swift exit. It scared me a bit. You had such a beauty that I'd never seen before. You were fragile and vulnerable, yet strong and determined, and I now know how much it took for you to make that journey away from reality to push your own limits and boundaries. I also knew when I saw you that I might want you. That scared me then, and it does even more now.'

We sit there in silence as I absorb what he is telling me. There I was, plodding into that meeting, almost fainting with the heat and totally overcome with nerves, yet he saw something in me that I'd never believed existed.

'That's . . . that's a lot to take in,' I say, trying to pull the conversation into line. 'But we are where we are now, and we've only a few days left to tie up the detail of your more recent years, so we should probably keep going. We should stay focused on the book.'

We breathe, not taking our eyes off each other. He takes my hand and I hold it to my face. I close my eyes. I take a deep breath and I let go of him slowly. I need to keep my mind on the job at hand, but my voice is quivering.

'You left the clinic, you bought this place, but your career slowed down as a result.' I continue with my pen poised, even though my hands are shaking. I want him so badly. 'Why do you think that was? Do you blame the media?'

He takes a moment to think his answer through.

'I don't blame anyone,' he explains, with deep sadness and disappointment in his eyes. 'I tried to at first, but now I'm just too exhausted with it all. Agnes and I were both to blame. We simply weren't right together, not like you and I are.'

I gulp. Obviously I won't be using that line in the book, that's for sure.

'Anyhow, with Catherine, all those years ago, I tried my best and so did she to make it work. But we were young and naïve. She wanted the suburban lifestyle in North London, where our parents lived, and she found it eventually,' he says with a smile. 'I'm so happy for her. But Agnes was fast-moving and clever. She was always one step ahead, in a way that would make people around her dizzy. I could never keep up with her. Look, I'm totally not claiming to have been easy back then. I was probably a prize asshole, as fame had gone to my head as much as it had to hers, but if she was out to get me, she succeeded in many ways. My phone stopped ringing after that. I feared trust and I deliberately pushed people away before they got close. It was my fault for getting carried away with a situation that wasn't healthy for either of us, and I paid the price, quite literally. But we were both to blame to some extent; after realizing how I feel about you, I can really see that now.'

'Wow,' I say, my pen moving across my notebook as fast I can, trying to get the words down quickly, but I have tears in my eyes when I see the despair on his gorgeous face. I want to touch him again. I want to hold him and tell him he doesn't have to push everyone away. I want to tell him I'll always be there for him.

But I need to keep it professional. If he kisses me again, there'll be no turning back, and I can't risk that.

'Tell me one thing, Annie.'

'Of course.'

'If you weren't married . . . what do you think might happen with us?'

I wait before I answer, as our eyes lock together and the world stops around us, just like it always seems to.

'If I wasn't married, I've no doubt I'd go running to you the minute this job is over and that we'd be so good together. That's what I think would happen.'

'Oh God.'

'You've brought out so much of me to the surface,' I say, doing my best not to physically touch him as we sit so close now. 'You've made me believe in myself again, Senan, not only as a writer but as a person. You've shown me passion, you've pushed my boundaries into doing things I never thought I could or would. You've made me laugh and sing and dance again. You made my heart skip a beat when I thought it had stopped for ever. You've shown me that not everyone is as they seem – and only in a good way; and most of all, you've shown me how to save a life, and I'm not just talking about Sid.'

I take a breath.

'You've brought *me* back to life too, Senan,' I tell him. 'Nothing will ever change that.'

I lean my head on his shoulder and he leans into me, and we absorb all the honesty between us. Once again his hand finds mine, but this time I don't take it. He tries to kiss me but I quickly stand up and walk away.

'Please don't. Right now I can't do this, Senan,' I tell him. He goes to protest but I interrupt. 'You deserve better than this and I'm sorry, I really am. You deserve someone who can give you everything in life, not someone like me who is still married and who has so much responsibility. I feel like I'm leading you on and I don't ever want to hurt you.'

He stands up and shakes his head. 'No!'

'It's true!' I tell him. 'I'm not what you need right now. I can't give you what you need!'

'But how can you possibly know what I want or need?' he asks as he walks to the window. 'That's for me to decide, not you or anyone else. What if I'm happy to wait for you?'

'You can't do that!' I plead with him. 'Wait for what? For me? What are you waiting to happen? I'm trying to keep this real, Senan.'

'You're trying to tell me how I feel,' he says back. 'You think you can analyse me, Annie, but you can't. Don't tell me what I need and what I don't need. You don't even know what you need for yourself, so don't patronize me.'

'It wasn't meant to be patronizing!'

'Save it for your kids at home,' he tells me. 'You think you know what's best for me, but you don't even know what's best for yourself, Annie Madden. You're living a lie, trapped in a situation you can't get out of. You're clinging on to a marriage that doesn't even exist any more.'

'Stop!'

'No! You're a vibrant young woman, but you live like a martyr, tending to everyone but yourself in life. Even your mother-in-law can see it,' he continues, and his words hit me hard. 'Your marriage wasn't perfect! No one is perfect, yet you're so desperate to live a life you think you should and not the life you really want to. You're still wishing Peter back to life, but it's never going to happen!'

His words hit me like a bolt of lightning.

'My husband isn't dead!' I shout at the top of my voice. I lift my notebook and pen, and then stuff it into my bag. 'How dare you! My husband isn't dead!'

I look right at him and, even though he doesn't say it, I imagine what he must be thinking. *If he isn't dead, why were you acting like he was when you were in bed with me?*

'I'm sorry, I didn't mean any of that,' he pleads. 'Don't go, Annie! I didn't mean it!'

'I've heard enough,' I say as I put on my coat, biting my lip as the reality of what I've done hits me like a huge slap on my face. I lift my phone and the keys of the B&B as tears run down my cheeks. 'You seem to have me well summed up, and I have you, Senan. I'll ask the publishers to be in touch. I'll have to run away like the rest did, after all. I'm out.'

18.

'What happened? Annie, you sound like you're in a terrible state! I'm so sorry!'

Martha rings me as soon as I send her the text to say I'm off the job, just as I should have expected she would, but I'm in no mood to talk, nor am I in the mood to explain in any detail how Senan and I got into such a tangle, quite literally.

I'm sitting on a summer seat looking out onto the water, just halfway between the beach house and the B&B, and I'd happily sit here all evening rather than go in either direction.

Bob is already suspicious after my no-show at breakfast on Monday morning, which was followed by my hibernation in my room until the next day, and – even though I thought I'd slipped through the hallway after my sleepover with Senan – it turns out I was spotted by Liam, who dropped a hint when he saw me this morning. I managed to bluff it off that we'd worked late into the night and that I'd simply crashed there. Not that it was any of his business, which I tartly reminded him.

'Things just aren't working out with us here, Martha,' I told her, trying to give as vague an excuse as possible. 'Ironically we were so close to reaching the end. In fact, I imagine if I passed it your way, you could probably make a good stab at fixing it up yourself based on what I've done so far. You could talk him through the rest on the phone and—'

'What?'

'Or maybe Caroline could?' I suggest. 'I just can't take any more, Martha. I'm ready for home at this stage. I'm sorry.'

'But – but I know nothing about Senan Donnelly and, even if I did, I'm not a writer, Annie. You're the writer,' Martha tells me, her voice remaining very calm as our conversation builds. 'Are things really that bad? Did you have a row?'

'It's complicated!'

Still Martha barely breaks a sweat as she speaks. 'I thought you and Senan were having a whale of a time,' she continues. 'Was he rude to you? He didn't hurt you in any way, did he, Annie? I mean, I don't know much about him personally but—'

'No, no, Senan would never hurt me,' I say to her. 'Not in the way you're implying. We just hit a dead end and said some stuff to each other. We can't work together. It's just far too complicated.'

I pinch the top of my nose as stress builds, just as I used

to at home. Claustrophobia wraps around me like a smothering weighted blanket and I feel my hands shake. I want to go home. I want to be anywhere but here.

'Maybe I was out of my depth by taking this on, just as I'd initially feared from day one?' I say to her. 'Maybe the job is simply too big for someone like me, with no experience in writing something so personal, never mind spending two weeks away from home when I've never been known to do such a thing.'

I hear Senan's 'martyr' accusation ring in my ears and it stings.

My mind blurs as Martha calmly goes into practical mode, explaining how it's Wednesday now and if I can just stick it out until Saturday, she could arrange for a flight home then, rather than edge it out until Sunday like we were meant to. If I manage to get the last few bits wrapped up by then, I could fill in the gaps at home over the next few weeks. There is still plenty of time.

'Is Senan drinking?'

'No.' I take a deep breath as my lip wobbles.

There's no way I can tell Martha the truth. I hardly know her, for goodness' sake, and how unprofessional would it sound if I tried to explain that Senan and I had become far too close and had ended up sharing a bed, only for him to want more when I can't give it.

I can't tell her that deep down I *do* want to be with him in so many ways, yet I'm so incredibly torn and eaten up

with guilt because I'm still married to a man who tragically
. . . I can't even bring myself to think of what I'd say next
to that.

At the same time, I can't lie. I can't tell her that Senan is
drinking heavily or out of control when he isn't.

'No, no, it's not Senan's drinking,' I whisper. I feel my
voice shaking. I feel so stupid, like one of my former pupils
when they've been caught in the act making out behind
the bike sheds or smoking at the bus stop. 'It's hard to
explain, Martha.'

'Try me.'

I take a deep breath. An old lady comes towards the
bench, so I gesture for her to sit while I get up and lean
across a pillar to explain out of earshot.

'Like I said, we had a row this afternoon and we both
said pretty hurtful things to each other,' I explain to Martha.
'It got personal. I stormed out when he mentioned Peter
because he really hit a nerve and upset me even more. Look,
I know I'm being vague, but believe me when I say I don't
think I can face him any more. I think it's better we stay
apart before we hurt each other any further.'

But Martha isn't buying any of my 'it's personal' story,
even if it's as close to the truth as I can muster up for now.

She sighs and then she responds, sounding like she has
just run a marathon and is pushing out the last mile.

'Annie, I believe so much in your ability as a writer and
your strength as a person,' she tells me, and I try not to roll

my eyes when I hear the word 'strength' being bandied about again. 'I have bright hopes for your future as a writer, and I'm not only talking about this particular job. I'm thinking long term. Try and grit your teeth and get what you need to finish the story. Sleep on it. Stay out of each other's way for the rest of the day, but please do your best to set this to the side when you've come this far.'

I swallow hard as her words resonate with me. She is right, of course. We are so close to the finishing point, and I'd be a total fool to ruin my future as a writer because of this, but it's so damn messy right now.

Never in my wildest dreams did I ever think I'd be in this position, where I'd be presented with a book deal, where I'd be represented by a literary agent who had my back like Martha does, or where I'd be told I had a bright future as a writer. I'm forty years old. Opportunities like this don't come my way very often, and if life begins at forty, then this is how it will truly 'begin' for me.

It was me who walked away from Senan. He did say sorry, if I recall. He did ask me not to leave. He's been to hell and back over the past few days, so maybe I should have cut him some slack and tried to stay professional, even when he tried to kiss me again. Therefore, it's probably up to me to go back and try to mend our relationship before it's ruined for ever. But not now . . . I need to sleep on it first, just as Martha says. I will approach him, but I'll wait until tomorrow.

'OK, OK, I'll speak to him when we both calm down and see if we can tolerate each other for another few days,' I tell her. 'I shouldn't have reacted in such a knee-jerk way by messaging you when I was in such a tizzy, but things got very heated with Senan and me, and we are both equally to blame. I won't let it linger, nor will I bail out on you. I'm sorry for sending you that off-the-cuff message before I'd really thought this through.'

I can hear the relief in Martha's voice when she replies. 'I know you can do this,' she sighs. 'I know you can make a great job of it like no one else ever could. You're only human, so I suppose when working in such intense circumstances and so closely with someone, things can easily heat up and boil over.'

I rub my forehead. That's one way of putting it.

'Well, I've plenty of stuff from this afternoon to go and write up now, so I'll go back to the B&B and do that,' I tell her. 'Hopefully, after we've both slept on it, we can make a fresh start in the morning.'

~ Meg ~

Dear Daddy,

Nana knew something was up with me, of course she did.

I refused to come out of my room for days, pretending it was 'girl stuff' and while she bought it at first, it wasn't long before she was sitting at the edge of the bed as I sobbed like a baby and told her everything I'd kept to myself for seven whole years.

'He looked at me and shook his head and then his foot slipped, Nana,' I cried. I don't think I've ever cried so hard in my whole life, and I mean that. Not even when I split my head open or broke my elbow when I fell off my bike during a stupid sponsored cycle to raise money for our school. And believe me, I cried a lot back then.

And no one can stop me crying now. Not Mum (who isn't here of course), not Kelly (who I have told a lot of stuff to down the years), not Danny (who wouldn't listen anyhow as all he cares about these days is what tractor he is going to buy with his savings), and not even Nana (who normally knows the cure for everything).

'You've got to give your head peace, my precious girl,' Nana told me as I sobbed into her chest. She smelled like she always did, of fruity perfume and a faint hint of cigarette smoke. I know she still sneaks a puff when there's no one around to catch her. 'You were just a little girl, only eight years old. You can't go on believing you could have caused such a tragedy. I'm so glad you're getting this all off your chest, once and for all.'

'But what if Kelly tells Mum?' I said between heaving sobs. 'What if she comes back here so happy and refreshed, thinking we've all learned how we should pull up our socks around the house, only to find out she wouldn't be living like this if it weren't for me?'

Nana shushed me and rocked me like a baby in her arms. I'd cried so hard that when I closed my eyes, I think I might have been so exhausted that I drifted off to sleep a little, but a gentle knock on the door brought me back again.

It was Kelly.

'Sorry, I didn't realize you were in here, Bernice,' she whispered. 'I was looking to see Meg, but I'll catch up with her later.'

'Let's all have a good catch-up now,' said Nana in her best 'Nana will fix things' voice. It was a tone that not even Kelly could argue with, and she took a seat on my beanbag across from the bed. I didn't think to tell her that it was covered in dog hair, but she would soon find that out for herself.

'I'm back,' said Kelly, as if we might fear it was a hologram we were seeing. 'And I didn't mean to run away from all this,

239

Meg, I hope you know that. I just needed some time out to get my head around everything. This household can be very intense.'

'No shit,' I said, and Nana shot me a warning glance for my choice of language.

'But it's your family and you are most important in all this, not me,' Kelly continued. 'So, I'd just like to say that although your mum is my very best friend in the whole world, and your dad is my patient, I'm not part of this family. You are.'

Nana nodded and I had a feeling they might have discussed this all already.

'We have made such great progress since your mum left for Cork,' Nana chirped in quickly before I started bawling again. 'You were laughing so much lately, Meg, like I haven't seen you laughing in a long time. And you know why I think that is?'

I shrugged like any teenager would when asked such a question.

'I think it's because, for the first time in a very long time, you think your mum may have found some happiness again. You were happy because your mum was happy.'

I wiped my tears away.

'I don't want her to be miserable,' I admitted to them. 'But I think she deserves to know the truth about me and about Dad – about why he fell. Or about the other . . . the other person he'd been seeing. Don't you?'

Nana tapped her nose the way she used to when Danny and I were smaller and we asked too many questions.

'Why don't you let us grown-ups deal with that?' she

suggested, reaching out to me for another cuddle. 'From now on, this house will be full of fun and laughter, just like you all need it to be so badly. Just you wait and see.'

Kelly slipped off to see to you just then, while Nana let me rest on her chest for just a little while longer.

There's only one thing better than a hug from your nan, and that's a hug from your mother. I can't wait to give mine the biggest cuddle, as well as the biggest smile, when she gets home. I've a feeling she needs one now even more than I do.

x

19.

I don't hear from Senan on Wednesday evening after my chat with Martha, and when Thursday comes I sleep in after a restless night full of mixed-up dreams in which I go home and Peter is standing there at our front door with a bunch of flowers to welcome me back.

He isn't sick any more in my dream. He is bright-eyed, fit and handsome, and he has no idea what I got up to when I was here in West Cork. I run to him, but just as I get his length, he steps to the side and I fall on my face and he laughs and laughs until he disappears. The children are laughing too, and so are Mum and Kelly. I call out his name. I scream for him to come back, but he is gone.

In another dream I see Senan, who is shaking his head at me, taunting me that I was never good enough for him anyway. It was just a holiday fling, he tells me. I was just something to release the boredom and loneliness, he teases. I was just another of his regular callers, someone he didn't have to try hard for. Then he is in a glossy magazine and he's telling everyone how easy I was. I see his face everywhere.

He hates me, he says, as he is photographed with his arms around Agnes Patrice, the supermodel ex-wife.

I'm glad to wake up and, after a long, hot shower, I put on a long red summer dress, fix my hair as best I can and make my way down for breakfast. I check my phone for messages from Senan, but there is nothing. I stare at the phone, willing and hoping for a message to come through but it doesn't.

Maybe I should call ahead to tell him about my conversation with Martha and how important it is that – despite our differences – we knuckle down and finish the book, no matter what? We have only three days left really, as Sunday will be spent packing up and travelling home, so we should be making the most of this time together, even as friends, as who knows when our paths will cross again? Next year, perhaps, when the book hits the shelves? Probably not. I'm not even sure how much, if any, role a ghost-writer plays when it comes to publication.

I chicken out and send a quick text instead.

'Senan, we need to talk,' I say to him. 'I'll pop over if that's OK? I shouldn't have stormed off as we need to stay professional and finish the book, no matter what. Hopefully see you soon.'

Bob plonks down at my breakfast table just as I'm finishing my coffee.

'I'm not prying!' he says, with both hands up in surrender. 'I know you were cross with Liam for asking too many questions yesterday, so I'm not going to even go down that road. I just want to check to see if you are OK? Nice dress, by the way, considering it looks like rain – but darling, you seem exhausted.'

I do my best to keep a straight face. 'That's another way of saying I look like shit.'

'Never!'

'Oh Bob, I know you are wetting yourself for information,' I say to him, my mouth twitching into a smile. 'The two of you have been like hens on a hot griddle ever since I was spotted doing my walk of shame when I arrived here the other morning, then Senan turned up here looking for me . . . but you can quit while you're ahead. There's no gossip, no news to report and nothing for you to worry about. I've been working hard, that's all. My time here is almost up, so I need to make the most of every hour. That's why I'm exhausted.'

He shakes his head to tell me I'm on the wrong path.

'Well, I know you think we're prying, but actually we love having you here and don't want to see you hurting,' he says, raising an eyebrow. 'We're looking out for you, that's all. Now, are you still sea-swimming in the mornings? I can't say I'm the most active person in West Cork, but I do know it's supposed to be wonderful for clearing the mind, if that's what you need to do.'

'No, I haven't done so for the past two or three days actually, but I'm heading that way now,' I say, checking the time. 'I'd imagine Senan will already have had his swim, but I'm itching to get back in the water and clear my head before our working day begins. If it begins . . .'

He pauses, sits back and folds his arms.

'Maria says she hasn't seen either of you in a while at the restaurant.'

'We have been cooking at the beach house and trying out new places,' I say, jumping in. 'No need to worry.'

'But then Senan was in there last night on his own,' he says, pursing his lips, as if he has just disclosed prize under-cover information. 'I was beginning to think you two were physically joined at the hip.'

I shake my head and stand up from my regular breakfast seat at the bay window of the B&B.

'I'm contracted to write his life story, not to be with him twenty-four/seven,' I say to Bob, who looks at me like he is reading between the lines. I must admit my stomach did leap when I pictured him there last night alone. 'You know, you two should run a detective agency on the side here. Bob and Liam, Seaside Private Eyes at your service!'

Bob waves his hand and throws his head back in a hearty cackle.

'It's not like that at all, honey,' he says to me then, with sincerity in his big round brown eyes. 'But if it was the case, then thankfully the first mystery is solved. You haven't fallen out, and Senan Donnelly isn't the cocky ass I thought he was. Case closed. Is that a fair enough conclusion?'

I put on my fleecy jacket as I notice a light fall of rain outside. The weather has turned, but it won't stop me jumping into the Atlantic Ocean before I put pen to paper today, that's if Senan is agreeable to me using his shower afterwards.

'He is the very opposite of a cocky ass, believe me,' I tell Bob before I leave the dining area, ready for my working day ahead. I feel suddenly protective of Senan, despite our row on Wednesday. 'He is an absolute gem of a man, a very handsome on the outside man but an even more beautiful, caring and incredibly strong person on the inside.'

I drift off briefly as little flashbacks of our time together run through my head.

'I see,' says Bob, changing his stance to one of true wonder.

'I'd better get going,' I tell him.

Now it's my turn to wave at him. I leave him standing on the doorstep in his Mickey Mouse apron with all sorts of conclusions, no doubt, running through his concerned mind.

I check my phone as I take the left turn off the main road and down the little pathway that leads to the beach house.

Still no word of Senan, which is very strange . . . maybe this is a way of him seeking revenge after I disappeared on Monday evening for hours, leaving him worried and wondering where I was, or for storming off yesterday after he pleaded with me not to leave.

I climb the wooden steps and go to his door, but before I get the chance to knock, it's opened by one of the girls I recognize from last week.

'Oh. Hello,' I mumble, while at the same time wanting to turn on my heels and run.

'Hi?' she says it as if it's a question, folding her slender arms and leaning on the doorframe. She looks like a young Seventies rock star with her heavy dark fringe, and she wears only a long grey T-shirt that skims her tanned legs.

'Is . . . is Senan here?' I ask him. 'I'm his – I'm his—'

'I know. You're the English teacher.'

I take a step back. The other girl comes walking towards her friend from behind. She's very much a carbon copy, only a red-haired version, and her choice of morning attire is the same, only shorter.

'He's asleep. I think,' says the red-haired girl. 'Is he expecting you?'

I feel like a frumpy fish out of water as I stand in front of these two youngsters with my brown leather satchel on one shoulder and my straw bag full of swimming gear on the other. Is he expecting me? Well, probably not is the answer, as the last conversation we had I'd told him I quit, but I'd sent him a text since then and I'd tried to call. And seeing that the two of them are here, it looks like I'm the last person on his mind.

'No, no, he probably isn't expecting me if he hasn't checked his phone,' I mutter, looking in my bag for I don't know what. I snap back and get the urge to run again. 'I'll leave you all to it. Have a nice day.'

I walk away from the beach house with my heart in my mouth, a million thoughts racing through my mind and the sound of two young Memphis Minnies, who are standing on the doorstep giggling, just as they did before. I want to cry but I've no right to cry or feel sorry for myself after all, have I? I made it very clear yesterday that I was off the job. I even told Martha, and if she hadn't talked me round I'd probably be home by now. Senan owes me nothing. He can party with his so-called 'acquaintances' all he wants. That's what he does here. It's what he did before I came into his life and it's what he'll continue to do when I leave.

As far as he's concerned, I'm gone. I have no right to expect anything else from him.

Bob and Liam are in the breakfast room by the window having their post-'breakfast rush' coffee together when I come past and go to the front door.

'Shit,' I say aloud as I fumble with my front-door key. Liam comes to the rescue.

'You're back, darling?' he says, puzzled. 'What did you forget? Don't worry, my head is like a sieve these days too.'

'I've had a change of plans,' I mutter, unable to look him in the eye for fear he might see the truth. 'I'm just going to my room. Excuse me.'

He steps aside and I make my way up the narrow stair-case, then take a right down the corridor and go into the bedroom, where I plonk down on the edge of the bed, still wearing my coat and still holding both bags on my shoulders. I get ready for the dam to burst, and it does.

In my head I'm back in the downstairs bathroom at home, where I'm allowing myself three carefully timed minutes behind closed doors to let my true feelings out before I put my mask back on to face the world. I let the tears flow, silently of course, but I won't sit here for any longer than a few minutes, just as I do at home. I have this whole crying game down to a fine art. I'll get up and wash my face, I'll dab under my eyes gently so they don't get too red and puffy, and I'll gain control of my breathing.

Usually at home, after my little stint in the bathroom, I go out to face my children and it's business as usual, but today I realize that I don't have to face anyone, only myself.

I can cry if I want to. I can feel sorry for myself if I want to. I don't have to answer to anyone, so why am I still forcing myself to keep everything in? And, more importantly, what the hell am I crying for?

Senan? Peter? Me?

I drop my bags onto the floor and take my coat off. I look around the room, pushing tears off my cheeks as I try to make sense of what exactly is going through my head. Do I feel betrayed by Senan? Am I jealous or angry at him entertaining young ladies when I've made it very clear to him where I stand? Am I mad at myself for landing there unannounced after my big grand departure yesterday? Am I afraid of being unable to fulfil my contract and finish the book? Will I let myself down, and – more importantly – will I let my family down if I don't see this through? They're so excited for me with this opportunity, yet they've no idea of my new reality here. I've really made a fine mess of everything, haven't I?

A knock on my door makes me catch my breath.

'Don't move if you don't want to, lovely. I'm just leaving a tray by the door.' It's Bob of course. 'No need to come out. It's some freshly brewed tea and a scone with jam. I don't know about you, but sometimes I find a nice cup of tea puts the world at right.'

I open my room door and his eyes widen when he looks at me. My face crumples.

'Oh Bob!'

'Ah, darling!' he replies.

'I'm so fed up of always holding everything in!' I say as the words spill uncontrollably out of my mouth. 'I'm fed up of hiding in the bathroom at home for three minutes, or suffocating as I try to stop my emotions from getting through. I'm so done with closed doors and pretending I'm OK when I'm anything but bloody well OK!'

'Ah, you poor baby!' says Bob. He steps over the tray he has so delicately prepared, and wraps his chubby arms around me. 'You don't need to hold anything back here. You're among friends, I promise.'

He lets me sob into his shoulder, and then, when I finally let him go, he takes the tray and puts it on the little table by the window and pours me a cup of tea. He quietly opens the window and pushes back the curtains fully, so a cool breeze floats around the room.

'Tea and fresh air,' he says with a warm smile. 'The best cures for anything, according to my late grandmother – even heartache. You've fallen for each other, haven't you, Annie? I won't tell anyone, not even Liam.'

He crosses his heart and closes his eyes as he says so.

'I don't even know what has happened, but it's all a terrible mess.'

I'm on the edge of the bed, holding my cup of tea for dear life as Bob sits at my writing desk opposite, staring at me now with his head tilted to the side. The breeze is really helping with the throbbing sensation in my head but, no matter how I try to control the tears that drip off my cheeks, I can't get a grip on the crying like I usually do. Three minutes have long gone so why can't I stop?

'Cry if you want to, Annie!' he tells me. 'You don't have to hold back in front of me!'

The truth is I couldn't stop, not for love nor money. Not this time.

'I don't know what's going on but, whatever it is, I feel totally out of control and I don't like it,' I tell my new friend. 'Coming here was meant to be life-changing for me. It was meant to give me a break from all the emotional turmoil I have going on at home. It was supposed to be an eye-opener, a chance to glance out of my bubble, where I'd realize how there's still so much else to live for, so much that I've chosen to shut myself off from. But instead all I've done is make everything in my own head a whole lot worse. And for what? For nothing!'

Bob shifts in his seat. He clasps his hands around his knee and leans back in thought.

'I know it's the furthest thing from your mind right now, Annie, but try and go easy on yourself,' he whispers. 'You've had a really, really difficult and long seven years since your whole life was tipped on its axis. Your entire future was taken from you. You gave up your career, your friends, your ambitions, and all your hopes and dreams were shattered. Not only that, you lost the man you love.'

'But that doesn't mean I should—'

'Who knows what anything in life means?' he exclaims. 'Who are any of us to judge? You lost your life partner and you've watched him live in a locked-in, lonely world ever since, where all you can do is watch on helplessly while trying to look after your children too. Your plate of life has overflowed, my darling. You don't need to hold anything in any more.'

Bob gets up and sits on the bed beside me. He puts his arm around me, squeezing me closer like a concerned uncle.

'And so you let all of that responsibility, all of that worry and all of that pressure go for a few days when you were here,' he says softly, before letting his voice rise a little. 'So what? You were swept away by the drop-dead gorgeous Senan Donnelly, who would make a nun go weak at the knees, never mind a married woman! Don't even dare be hard on yourself for that! He's good to you. He's kind. He makes you smile and feel safe. You said he's caring and strong. Isn't that a good thing, after all you've been through?'

I laugh at his nun reference, knowing he isn't far off the mark.

'You enjoyed the companionship you've been starved off for far too long,' he continues, turning serious again. 'Your heart flipped when he looked at you seductively, or when he brushed past, or even better when he took your hand. Your mind danced with joy when you talked into the night and shared secrets and stories, never mind fun and games or food and drink together. You felt like a woman again. Am I right?'

To my relief my tears are drying up now. Everything Bob is saying is true.

'And you allowed yourself – for just those glorious few days – to be that woman again,' he whispers. 'You found yourself. The woman you once were before everything was taken from you – a writer, a friend, a confidante, a person who enjoyed laughter and fun. A woman who liked to dance and eat good food in nice places . . . a woman adored by her man . . . a woman whose conversation stimulated others . . . a woman who took pride in herself, who believed in herself, who challenged herself and who knew her own worth.'

I nod in agreement as I play with a damp tissue in my hand, still staring at the floor. Bob pushes my hair behind my ear.

'You may only see mistakes when you look at yourself right now, Annie, but I see change for the better. Not long ago I saw the timid, quiet, nervous person you were when you first walked through my doors last Sunday evening, and now you are unrecognizable in every way.'

I turn to face him now.

'Really?'

His eyes widen for effect.

'Totally!' he says. 'You walk taller now. You smile more, for sure. You're brighter in your face and you radiate happiness and warmth to everyone you meet since you got here. Maria in the restaurant thinks you're a beauty inside and out. Young Johnny the waiter does too. We all love you here and I'm guessing, even though he must have let you down in some way today, that Senan Donnelly does too. In fact, he knows you better than any of us do by now, so maybe he's hurting just as much as you are? Maybe he just has a different way of dealing with it? We all react to hurt in our own, sometimes selfish, ways.'

I look Bob in the eye and manage a smile.

'You could be a therapist and a detective all in one go,' I say to him. 'But don't ever give up the B&B, Bob. I want to come back here again and again and again. You've been a great friend to me and, even when you're wearing that Mickey Mouse apron, I can still take you seriously.'

Bob straightens up and pouts a little.

'I have been told I'm wasting my time slaving over Full Irish breakfasts, but I wouldn't change it for the world,' he says. 'Oh, my phone is vibrating, give me a second. It's Liam.'

He rolls his eyes and says hello.

'Oh, yes OK, I'll tell her. Yes, I'm with her upstairs. She hasn't been looking at her phone. We've been talking – you know, face to face, person to person. Oh is he? Good! Right well, that's nice. OK, bye, bye, bye.'

He turns to face me as my stomach churns and I scramble for my phone.

'Senan is downstairs, darling,' he says. He stands up and takes off his apron, then goes to the mirror and fixes his hair, or at least what's left of it. 'He's looking for you, not me obviously, but it does no harm to look one's best. Right, go put on some mascara and then go and talk to him. Then, after that, for goodness' sake finish what you came here to do! Get that book written, no matter what! Do you hear me?'

I nod, feeling perspiration rise in every crevice. He is here. I look in the mirror. Oh God, I resemble some sort of horror-movie character with my puffy eyes and red streaks. I dab on some concealer under my eyes, whisk on some mascara and spray on a bit of perfume then fix my hair with my fingers.

255

'Take him into the good room if you want,' Bob whispers when he opens the bedroom door for me. 'Remember, you're both only human, and whatever is done is done. Sort it out like adults and on Sunday you'll have to say goodbye and it will all be over. Nobody died. Nothing has been done that isn't repairable. So, hold that head up high, Annie Madden. And if you ever need another appointment with Dr Bob, just ask!'

'Thank you.'

I walk down the stairs, only wishing I felt as confident as Bob tells me I am, but then I think of how far I have come since I arrived here, all the good times I've had along the way and I know he is right. I will not give up on this job I came here to do and I will not give up on myself.

My heart does a somersault when I see Senan standing in the hallway, holding a bunch of sweet peas in his left hand. He rubs his chin with the other and watches my every move as I walk down the stairs.

Everything about him physically makes my head spin and I can't deny it.

'I picked these from someone's garden, but my mum always told me they grow back very quickly,' he tells me. 'I've missed you.'

He smells of stale alcohol again, just as he did that first day I met him in London.

'I called you this morning a few times, but I noticed

you've been busy,' I reply. My pulse is racing. 'Why are you here, Senan?'

He bites his lip and looks at me so deeply, so pleadingly. I want him to reach out and pull me close but at the same time I want to run away so I'm never tempted to fall into his arms again.

'I thought you'd gone,' he tells me in a whisper. 'I honestly thought you'd gone and I needed to numb the pain.'

I lead him into the little drawing room, remembering how Bob gave me permission to, plus I don't want anyone eavesdropping on our conversation.

'What? So you just went back to your party-boy life with your "acquaintances"?' I ask him. I sit down on a bottle-green leather sofa. He sits beside me. 'It didn't take you long to revert back to your old ways. In fact, you're very quick.'

He looks confused.

'Rachel and whatever her name is?' I say, prodding his memory.

'Oh, with those two? Gosh, no!' he tells me. 'No way, it's not like that! I checked in on Sid and Ivy then had a few drinks by myself after dinner at Maria's, but I left my phone in the pub.'

I fold my arms. 'That old chestnut.'

'I did!' he pleads. 'I went to grab it just now and when I saw your message and missed calls, I came straight here to see you in person. Yes, I had a few drinks last night but only because I was feeling sorry for myself. If I'd been sober,

I'd never have let those girls stay again. They're just hangers-on. They're not . . . I just want to be with you, Annie. I think I've told you at least once before. I'm so glad you're still here.'

He is so close to me now. He takes my arm and pulls me towards him, putting his lips to my forehead. I want to stop him but I can't. He keeps his lips there and I close my eyes.

'What on earth are we going to do?' I whisper. 'I am so confused, Senan. I've missed you too, but I don't want to feel this way.'

'Ssh,' he whispers, then he raises my chin with his finger and I think he is going to kiss me properly but he doesn't. 'We have a few days left and still some work to do. That's the most important thing for now, isn't it? I don't want to mess anything up for you. And I'm so sorry for what I said.'

'I know you are,' I say to him. 'And I'm sorry for adding on to that in my own mixed-up head.'

'Let's just take it one day at a time from here on in,' he tells me. 'No pressure, no expectations. You mean the world to me, and if that means putting my feelings to the side for now, that's what I'm going to have to do.'

I nod in agreement.

'Thank you. I think that's what both of us are going to have to do,' I tell him. My heart is racing but as always his presence puts me at ease so quickly. 'Actually, why don't we work here this afternoon for a change? If it's OK with Bob, it might shake us up a little and keep our mind on the task at hand?'

'I think that's a really good idea,' Senan says, smiling at me as if a weight has been lifted off his shoulders. I get up to ask Bob's permission but he stops me in my tracks.

'You know something, Annie?' he says, with pain etched on his face. 'I know it's only been two weeks, but I need to tell you that . . . I think I might already have fallen . . . I think that I really love—'

I shake my head quickly for him to stop talking as butterflies dance in my tummy.

'A coffee? Is that what you were going to say?'

He takes a deep breath and smiles back at me.

'That's exactly what I was going to say,' he tells me, his eyes crinkling at the sides. 'I'd really love a coffee. I just wanted you to know that.'

'Good thinking, because I'd love a coffee too.'

20.

It's a bittersweet feeling as my time to go home creeps up on us. I've only been here for two weeks but I feel like so much has changed within me; it will take me quite a while to digest it all.

The precious final days go by in a flash, but we manage to pack in hours and hours of writing, hours and hours of talking, and hours and hours of just holding each other as time ticks away.

'I'm going to shelve these last two weeks in my memory bank as the most precious time I've ever spent with anyone,' Senan tells me as we sit around a campfire on the beach on our last night together. 'You've made me see the world in a very different way, Annie. My heart is aching at the thought of saying goodbye.'

We set aims for our future – not plans, just aims – both long term and short term, and even write them down for each other so we can check up and encourage, if only from a distance, along the way.

'I'm going to use the money I earn from this book to

do something nice with the children,' I tell him, writing it down as my number one short-term goal. 'We are so long overdue some fun.'

'That's a great idea,' he says. 'I'm sure you can't wait to see them.'

'I really can't,' I smile, picturing Meg and Danny's precious faces when I get home again.

Senan's list includes cutting out the bullshit in his life, stopping using alcohol as an easy crutch, and allowing only true friends into his home. He is going to really focus on his career, as well as spending as much time as he can with his mum up in London, especially after the scare with Sid and Ivy's heart-breaking diagnosis.

'I'd love to be cast as a hero for once, instead of always playing the rugged bad boy,' he says, writing it down. I look on at him as he does so with such tenderness. Never did I think I'd get to know him so well. Never did I think I'd get to feel so close to him.

He also pledges to cook at home at least four times a week, now that he has mastered the basics, not to mention my version of spaghetti bolognese, chicken curry, and of course my old favourite, shepherd's pie.

I'm going to fix up the farmhouse and find myself some new hobbies, which just might include swimming in a safe part of the lough, and I'm going to do my best to form some new quality friendships, though I know I'll never have a bond with anyone like I do now with Senan.

This is something on a very different level to anything I'll ever find at home.

'And if you ever need a handyman, I'm your guy,' he says with confidence. 'If the acting career doesn't take off, I know I'll be able to make myself useful in other ways.'

'Or you could casually go round and help paramedics out when people have heart attacks,' I jest. 'You really are amazing, Senan Donnelly. And I don't say that lightly.'

He rubs his jaw in a fleeting act of modesty and rolls his eyes, then looks at me more seriously.

'Annie, I know it was only two weeks and I know it was so far from real life,' he says, clasping both my hands in his when midnight comes, just before I leave him to go back to the B&B. 'But two weeks and almost twenty-four hours a day together is enough for me to know that what we shared wasn't just some holiday-type romance. I've no doubt that I have truly loved you, and that was a privilege, even if I was only allowed to for a little while.'

I take his hands and bring them up to my cheek. I close my eyes then I kiss his fingers as my stomach fills with butterflies.

'I can't bear the thought of saying goodbye tomorrow,' I whisper to him. 'It just doesn't feel right.'

We stand in the moonlight after one last walk along the sand in front of the beach house.

'We can still talk every day?' he suggests, his eyes lighting up in a plea with the very possibility. 'We can still be really good friends from a distance?'

I shake my head and look down at the sand.

'I don't know if my heart would settle for that,' I say to him, blinking back tears. 'Trying not to hold you or touch you properly again since the night we spent together has been so, so hard. I need to be honest with you, Senan.'

'What do you mean?' he asks.

I try my best to explain as I watch his face crumple.

'I think . . . I think to have you in my life from a distance and just as a friend after all we have shared is going to be an absolute killer. I don't know if my heart could take it.'

He steps back. He takes a deep breath.

'Well, what if we are more than friends, then?' he suggests, taking my hand now and pulling me close to him. The warmth of his body takes my breath away. 'What if we make a proper go of things? Annie, no one could deny you this chance of happiness. I could come and see you a few times a month, and maybe when you get Peter settled into a routine back home, you could come here and stay sometimes? Bring the kids too. I can't say goodbye to you. I don't want to, and I know you feel the same way too.'

When he says this, for a fleeting moment it all seems doable, something I'd like to at least try. I think of what Kelly said when she invited me out to dinner on the night I first met Martha. She said, 'You can but you don't.' Could

I make this happen? Could I make the best of both worlds, where I look after Peter like I've been doing but still make time for being with Senan in such a way that I can love him as I want to? He is right about one big thing. Everyone *does* keep telling me I have to make changes, and now here I am, presented with this second chance of love? Is this it? Is this the change I need to make?

'I . . . you've no idea how much I'd love to make that happen,' I say to him, breathing in his deep, musky smell as I rest my head on his chest.

'I'm waiting on the "but",' he replies, kissing my forehead.

'But I can't make a decision right away,' I say, holding him tighter. 'And I don't want to lead you on, so I'll really think about this and let you know before I go tomorrow. I've an early start and I haven't even properly packed yet.'

He takes a deep breath and I cry in his arms. Then, when he kisses me properly, so softly and tenderly on the lips, I almost lose my breath at the thought he could be doing it for the very last time.

I need to make a decision. It's going to be a long night.

'So, do you have everything?' Bob asks me, fussing around me like a clucky mother before I leave the next morning. 'Did you take your phone charger? If I had a pound for every phone charger left behind, I'd never have to fry an egg again!'

'I have,' I say, patting my wheelie suitcase. 'It's all in here.'

I've decided to leave a little bit earlier. Three hours earlier, to be precise, so I can avoid any long goodbyes with Senan, who I imagine is still fast asleep at the beach house.

'What about the souvenir tea towels from Maria's? asks Liam. 'And the chocolate for the kids I gave you? Is it all packed away?'

'Everything has been checked and double-checked, don't worry. Oh, thank you so much, you guys!' I say as we form a group hug in the hallway. 'You really did make my stay here just like being at home. Well, with a lot less washing-up, but you know what I mean!'

Liam carries my case to the car while Bob and I have a last few moments together.

'We are going to miss you so, so much, Annie,' he says as he bear-hugs me at the pink door of the B&B. 'People come and go from here all the time, but I think we bonded a lot. Do you think we bonded?'

I pretend to think about it.

'I'm kidding, of course we did! And I'll never look at a game of Scrabble in the same way again. Ah Bob, I've made such amazing friends during my stay here, but don't worry, you're not getting rid of me that easily,' I say to him. 'I really hope you'll let me return your wonderful hospitality by coming to see us all one day very soon.'

He clasps his hands to his chest.

'I'm getting emotional,' he says as his eyes fill up. 'And it's not even about saying goodbye to you, because that hasn't properly hit me yet. I'm just picturing you arriving home at your farmhouse, greeting your two children and your mum-in-law and Peter – oh Annie, what about Senan? Did you sort everything out?'

I put my finger to my lips and close my eyes.

'Don't make me cry,' I whisper, almost holding my breath. 'I'm just hoping I've made the right decision.'

'Which is?'

I shrug and blink back tears, giving him one last hug before I go. Then I turn around and stand on the doorstep, watching as Liam waits for me at the car, and I take one last look at the view from the place I've called home for what has been only two weeks but feels like a lot longer.

The sea in the distance where Senan and I swam and surfed . . . the shoreline I walked along every morning to go to the beach house . . . the sand where we sat around a campfire and put the world to rights as the waves lapped in the distance.

It's been wonderful.

I take a deep breath and think about going home.

I can't wait to snuggle Meg and to laugh with Danny. I can't wait to talk everything through with Bernice and Kelly. I can't wait to sit with Peter, even if it's only to watch TV with him.

But at the same time, I dread the changes I have to face. And I dread how much I'll miss seeing Senan every day.

'How do you like your goodbyes?' asks Liam when I

reach the car. 'Long and dragged out? Or fast, like removing a sticky plaster?'

It's a glorious Sunday morning and Bernice told me the weather has been kind at home too, which is nice to hear. Meg and Danny have been so excited, all set for our big reunion. It's the only thing that's keeping me from a total meltdown as the reality of leaving Senan begins to hit home.

'I think I'm usually the long and dragged-out type, to be honest, which makes everything harder, so let's make it quick,' I say to Liam. 'Before I go, can you make sure Senan gets this? Do you mind?'

Liam looks back at me, puzzled, as he takes the sealed envelope from my shaking hands. I know right then for sure that Bob has kept his promise to keep our brief romance a secret because Liam, even if he suspects something, doesn't show it in his face.

'I'll deliver it personally,' he says. 'That, I promise. Now, you take good care of your wonderful family, and of yourself, Annie. Safe journey home. Make sure and text us all when you get there.'

'I will,' I say as I lift the handle of my suitcase.

Then as I drive away, leaving the Atlantic Ocean a faint whisper in the distance, I hear my own voice in the words I wrote to Senan and I do my best to hold it all together for my journey home, trying my best not to imagine his face when he reads it.

Dear Senan,

I have tossed and turned all night. I've gone over so many scenarios in my mind and every single one of them is breaking my heart. Please believe me when I say that.

I need you so badly, but I don't want to need you, because I know that right now I can't have you.

I'm falling in love with you, but I don't want to love you when I know I can't have you.

Thank you for all the love we shared. Thank you for everything. Thank you for being the most wonderful companion, Senan, and thank you for helping me find the real me after such a long time searching.

Please remember that although time will pass, days will go by, weeks will disappear, please know that every single moment spent with you was so full of love and beauty. But now, I have to say goodbye for good.

The truth is that my family needs me more than I need you, and as much as I want you, I know I have no choice but to let you go.

You truly have brought me back to life, I will cherish our memories, and I will never stop loving you, if only ever from afar.

Annie x

@mumoftwo_missingyou
Everything changed.

My daughter woke me up that morning even earlier than she usually did.

Her chubby hands patted my face all over until I opened my eyes, while my son bounced on the bottom of the bed, making sure we didn't sleep on any longer.

'It's not even a school day,' I mumbled with one eye still shut as I reached for my phone to check the time. 'Please darling, it's your turn. I need more sleep. Please.'

My husband sprang up in the bed like only he could at that time of the morning, and wrestled with our two little monsters, tickling them until they squealed while I put my pillow over my head to drown out our six- and eight-year-old alarm clocks. We'd bought a rooster and his family a few days before, but these two had us awake well before even the cock crowed.

'Who's for a big greasy fry-up?' he asked, knowing he'd hear me moan in disgust in response. We'd stayed up a little too late the night before, watching the last episodes of a box set, and I'd slightly overindulged with wine, which was not ideal as we'd planned to do so much today. The new chickens needed tending to, my husband had checked the forecast to see there was no rain, so he'd pledged to finally attack the hole in the roof of the barn, and we'd a table booked at our local restaurant that evening, which was the furthest thing from my mind at that ungodly hour.

'The very thought of food so early is enough to make me gag,' I said as he pulled on his old jeans and his favourite jumper. It was navy with a hood, and I used to tease him that it made him look like an overgrown toddler, which of course made him wear it all the more often.

'Your nausea is everything to do with the early hour and nothing to do with the wine,' he'd teased, carrying the kids out of the bedroom, one under each arm as they kicked and giggled.

I fell back to sleep again as soon as their chattering voices faded down the stairs. When I woke up what felt like only moments later, he'd left a note beside the bed with a glass of water, two painkillers, and a bacon butty.

'Chickens all still alive and fed – off to the lough for a walk for an hour – enjoy the peace x'

I yawned, stretched and pulled myself up on the bed. The house was still and silent at first, which was so unusual; I wasn't sure if I liked it. I took a sip of the water, then washed back the painkillers, and I'd just bitten into the sandwich when I thought I heard our daughter cry from a distance through the unusual quiet. She was quite the drama queen, even then at only eight years old, and I imagined her stomping her feet, demanding that her dad should carry her up the lane on the way back from the park. I checked the time. It was almost eleven! I hadn't slept that long in years! And they'd be back from the park by now, surely?

I swung my legs out of the bed and strained my ears.

The scream came again, only closer this time. The back door opened – I'll never forget the sound of what I'd later learn was my son bursting into the kitchen downstairs.

'Mum! Quickly!' he called, and my blood ran cold.

'Is it your sister? What happened? Is she OK?'

The shock kicked in immediately and I don't remember how I managed to find my dressing gown or make it downstairs. I don't remember going through the hall or into the kitchen, nor do I remember my son telling me to follow him to the barn as he ran towards his sister's cry which had turned to deafening screams. I don't remember who called the ambulance or how long it took for them to find us in our remote little piece of heaven, where dreams had been built but a nightmare had just begun.

I do remember kneeling by my husband's side where he lay on the concrete floor, curled up in a foetal position. His navy hoodie was soaked in blood. It was thick, dark and syrupy. My daughter screamed more and I screamed harder. My son ran to the end of the lane to wave the ambulance in. He said later he wanted to make sure they didn't miss the turn.

He'd been on the roof, they later said. The beams were damp and rotted, they later said. They'd never have held a child up, never mind a fully grown man, and you should have known that, they later said.

They took him away after calling someone from my phone to come and take over at home.

I had no idea what to do next. What hospital would they take him to? How would I get to him? I was in no fit state to stand up straight, never mind drive. What would I do with the children? How long would he be gone for? Should I cancel our dinner booking? Who was going to wake me up and tell me this was only a bad dream?

The following days were a hazy blur, like a living wake where villagers and well-meaning family members, some of whom I hadn't seen in years, flocked to our house with food offerings and whispers of babysitting, even though the children only wanted me and their daddy, of course. Looking back, I don't even know who looked after them some of the time. It didn't feel real. Everything was like an out-of-body experience, where this was all happening to someone else's family. This type of thing happened to other people or to characters on the TV. It would never happen to us in real life.

My mother-in-law shouted at the doctor when she called us together, demanding she should draw a diagram of the brain and that she should write everything down in simple language so we could try and understand what was going on behind all the medical jargon.

She begged the doctor for some hope to cling to. Her daughter-in-law couldn't be a young widow – that had happened more than once in our family already. It couldn't happen again! The doctor explained how if he'd hit his head one centimetre either side, it would have been fatal. He had literally escaped death by the skin of his teeth. We sighed with relief and hugged and cried, but then she stopped us to say about the severe paralysis, about the stroke that had followed, taking the last of his movements except for two fingers on his 'good side'. She told us gently about the likelihood that he'd never speak again, that he'd definitely never walk again and that his memory would fade in time. He'd need full-time care for the rest of his life, however long that might be.

She told me it might be a few years. It might be a few more.

But I heard none of that. I zoned out long before.

All I heard was that he was still alive, and that was enough for me to carry on. We still had him, even if only physically, and I'd wait for the day when that would change. I truly believed that one day it would change. He'd prove the doctors wrong. I researched and read,

I googled and I even prayed. He could do it. He could defy all the odds, just like they did in the movies. It was just a matter of time until he got better.

I'd wait for ever if I had to, and no one was going to tell me any different, even if my heart was broken into a million pieces.

And then one day I decided to check your phone, just to read your words, just to connect with you again. I didn't realize that my heart could break even more, but it did when I saw that you hadn't let her go after all.

She was there, right there in your inbox, with all your plans to meet up that day, right before our dinner date. You didn't use her real name on your phone. You were both too clever for that, but I knew it was your old friend from before.

I still couldn't find out who she was, and it has been killing me inside since but I chose forgiveness in the long run, not for you, but for me.

I forgave you because I wanted to. I forgave you because I had to, for my own sanity, as I looked into a very bleak future if I didn't.

But I could never forget it, until now. I can finally let it go as I realize it's time to stop asking myself why. I've forgiven myself, too, for believing I had done something to drive you into her arms.

I can't ever let her go completely until I know who she is, but I can wait for that day to come. It *will* come.

And though I may not be able to let you go from my heart, I can, and I will learn to live again. I now know that for sure.

Grid Pic: A distant fisherman on Lough Neagh
Likes: 6,754
Comments: 356

21.

Kelly greets my car at the gate at the end of our lane, both arms waving in the air, almost levitating as she dances around, much to Meg and Danny's amusement.

She holds a home-made banner which says, *Welcome home! We even washed the dishes!* in blue bubble writing, which makes me chuckle and settles my nervous energy just a little.

The sun is shining and the lough glistens in the distance as I take the left turn up the bumpy lane towards the farmhouse, after stopping to acknowledge my very enthusiastic welcoming party through the car window.

'Welcome home, Mum!' says Meg with the brightest smile as she runs to greet me. I feel my heart is going to burst as she wraps her arms around my waist and snuggles in so tightly.

Danny follows suit.

'I'll swear you have grown, baby boy!' I exclaim. 'Oh, I've missed you both so, so much!'

'They've been hyper all morning,' Bernice tells me as she

takes my case from the car boot. 'Super excited! You'll have a lot of listening to do over the next few hours, but first, let's make time for tea.'

'Oh, I'll just pop down and say a quick hello to Peter first,' I reply, feeling a familiar urgency and panic as soon as I get out of the car.

Kelly, who makes it on foot to catch up behind us, and Bernice both exchange looks when I mention Peter, before Kelly goes into an overly enthusiastic update on lengthy sleeping patterns, eating schedules, and all the glorious walks they've enjoyed in my absence.

'That's great,' I tell them, even if the knot in my stomach tells me different. 'Thank you both from the bottom of my heart. I'll go and let him know I'm home.'

I walk from the sun-drenched kitchen into the cool of the north-facing hallway and into the darkness that reflects the way I feel inside, the grip of reality clawing at my gut again now that I'm home. I'm not unhappy to be back. In fact, everything about being here is a reminder of all I have to be grateful for, but a thick fog lies inside of me: the sadness I feel for Peter and for how life has dealt him this cruel blow, as well as the tug of guilt at the wonderful two weeks I've just experienced away from here.

I have a message from Senan on my phone that I've been building up to opening since I got here, but every time I've try to read it until now, I've felt a pang in my heart for how much I've hurt him and how much I miss him already.

'I understand,' he wrote to me. 'I'm not going to try and change your mind, but instead I'll dust myself down and focus on those aims I made. There are lots of positives and beautiful memories I'll always hold onto from our time together. Your family are so lucky to have you. All my love, Senan.'

I swallow hard after reading it and straighten my shoulders. Here we go . . .

It's like stepping back in time as I walk past our family photos on the wall, past the staircase where I know every stain on the wood. I run my hand along the panelling we put on the walls after we first moved in here. I look at the rugs we chose, scattered under my feet, as I walk along the floor that was once polished but is now just faded and bare. And then I get to the door of Peter's room.

Before I go inside, I remember what Bob said to me in my bedroom at the B&B just a few days ago.

He said that being with Senan was perhaps like I'd awakened the woman I used to be – the woman I could have been. Something clicked inside my mind when I heard that.

Being with Senan had been mind-blowing in so many ways, like the past had caught up with the present at last. It was like a cruel tease too, but it was also a life-changing lesson because I realize now, after stepping back from the life I've been living, being *that* woman again was what I've been waiting for, for all these years.

I've been waiting to be loved again even more than I've

been longing for it. I've been waiting for the day to come when I'd laugh with my husband, when I'd dance with him, when we'd eat and cook and drink wine together again. I've been waiting to try new things with him, to meet new people and to see new places. I've been waiting for him to kiss me, to hold me, to ask me how my day was again. I've been waiting for debates and discussions on what to watch on TV, or what not to make for dinner, or where not to go on holiday. I've been waiting and waiting and waiting.

Despite what the doctor or my family thought, I hadn't just been hoping, or wanting or needing.

I'd been waiting.

I honestly believed that if I waited long enough, one day this nightmare would be over and we'd be able to pick up from where we left off. But now, after seven painful, lonely years, I've finally realized the wait is over.

It's never going to happen. And the biggest awakening of all is that I can still do all of those things again many times over, but never with the one person I'd been wanting to and waiting for. That's the cruel part. I can still do all of that, but not with him, and I never will again.

I open the door gently, and I stand there just for a short moment in the doorway, watching my husband sleep. He lies on his back, arms straight down by his side on the hospital-style adjustable bed, the pale blue sheets doing nothing for the pasty colour of his face. I go to his side and touch his hand, finding my way onto the armchair beside him. I sink into it, and its softness welcomes me like I'd never left it.

'I'm home, Peter,' I whisper into the dim light of this tiny room. The curtains are closed. Everything is dark and still. The clock ticks in the background. The room smells sterile and clean. Nothing in this room has changed. Everything about me has.

'I'm really sorry,' I tell him, fighting as best I can against all the guilt, the fear, but most of all, the realization I now have inside. 'I'm so sorry our life ended up like this, Peter. Most of all, I'm sorry your life ended up like this, even though I know nothing about us was perfect.'

I look up to see Kelly in the doorway. She is holding a mug of tea, which she brings over to me, a look of deep concern and sorrow on her face.

'Sit with him if that's what you want to do right now,' she tells me, 'but – just so you know – he's been sleeping a lot longer these days. It might be a while before he wakes. Just do whatever is best for you now, Annie.'

She hands me the cup of tea and leaves me to it, but before she closes the door behind her, she stops again and looks my way.

'I hope you don't mind me saying so,' she says gently, 'but whatever it is you are sorry for, I don't think you should be. None of this was ever your fault. None of this is what you ever would have wished for – not for you, not for Peter, and not for your beautiful family who deserved so much more.'

She smiles sadly, but I can't look her in the eye.

Instead I just hold the cup of tea and sit there in the darkness, watching Peter breathe slowly as he sleeps. Soon, my tea is cold, and I'm still staring and he is still sleeping. I hear conversation from the kitchen, hushed whispers interrupted by brief laughter from the children, or the sound of a TV theme tune in the distance.

I should probably join them so at least Bernice and Kelly feel they can now go home, but I can't bring myself to leave Peter just yet. I feel like I've been time-travelling, or that I'm jet-lagged, not that I've ever known what it feels like to be jet-lagged, I've never travelled that far. But now I seem to have travelled to the moon and back in my own mind. I need to stay here with him to feel grounded, and to let this very real world I live in sink right in, once and for all.

I sit with him for at least an hour, until eventually his eyes flicker and he opens them slowly. My heart leaps and I take his hand again.

'Peter, it's me,' I whisper. I turn on the bedside lamp, but even the change in lighting doesn't make him flinch. 'I just got home.'

I swallow, feeling my hand shaking as I hold onto his. The clock sounds as if it's ticking louder than usual. The room looks smaller than I remember.

I stand up and lean forward so I can be in his eyeline but he still doesn't flicker.

'Give me a squeeze if you know I'm here, Peter,' I say as my lip trembles. 'Just one light squeeze? Or you can blink and I'll know you can hear me? Peter?'

Nothing.

I sit back down on the armchair and put my head in my hands, trying to smother the choking tears that threaten to drown my words as they always do. Nothing has changed here, and it never will. Usually by now I would have come up with some quick excuse to leave the room so I can take my three-minute break in the bathroom, just to let this weight lift and to hide my true feelings from him or the children, but I don't this time. I am not going to run and hide. I need to explain to him how sorry I am, and I'm not talking about what happened in West Cork.

I'm talking about how I've been feeling for all those years since his accident.

'You see, every single day I wished that all this would change,' I say to him, my voice cracked and low. 'And that was wrong of me, because it's not going to change, is it Peter? You can't make it change and I can't make it change. No one can. It's going to stay like this every single day, or become worse than this. And everything we had, all those wonderful times we spent together, are always only going to be memories now.'

I take a deep breath.

'But they're brilliant memories, Peter. We had some fantastic times and I thank you for that.' I say to him. 'We

283

weren't perfect, no. There is no such thing as perfect, but we had many, many times that were as perfect as they could be. I hope you know that. I hope you know that all those years will never, ever be forgotten. They're in my heart for ever and I know they're in yours too. Aren't they?'

I wait again for an answer, and then it sinks in one last time.

I needed to take a step back from everything I've known for the past few years to finally learn to accept that. And although I know it's a good sign that this truth has become absolutely clear to me now, it's still a very, very bitter pill to swallow.

'You look like a totally different person, yet I can't pinpoint exactly what it is that makes you so.'

'Bernice said that too,' I reply to Kelly, who has been hanging around for much longer than she needs to. 'I'm trying to figure out if it's a good thing or a bad thing, but she didn't indulge me at all.'

I said goodbye to my mother-in-law just moments ago, seeing her off with a bag full of souvenirs from Cork and a million thank-you hugs. I know she hated leaving us. She could see right through me, just as Kelly can now too.

I look like a different person because I am a different person. I am not the stubborn, frantic, worn-out woman I was before I left here. I am still frightened; I am still scared to death of the future, but I am also gracious in defeat. I am not able to do all this any more.

Kelly checks the time on her phone.

'Joel will be waiting on you with open arms,' I say to her as she stalls again before leaving. 'He must be so happy today has finally come.'

Kelly smiles. 'He will be glad to have me back,' she tells me. 'But are you sure you don't—'

'I'm fine, Kelly!' I interrupt her gently. 'It's going to take me a few hours to readjust, but once you go I'll be back on duty and it will be like I've never been away in the first place.'

Kelly lifts her overnight bag and swings it over her shoulder.

'If you're sure,' she says gently. 'I can see so clearly how tough it is on you to come back and face up to all of this. It makes perfect sense, so please don't beat yourself up about it.'

'It is very tough,' I say, refusing to deny the obvious for once. 'But I've had quite an awakening at last when it comes to my coping levels. I'm sad to the core, but it's been a long time coming. You were right. You all were right. It's too much for me now and the children need me back in full swing, not some shadow version who they hear crying into the night.'

Kelly gives me a quick hug. 'You know, I've always thought of you with such wonder, but now . . . now that I've spent two full weeks in your shoes, I see the utterly brave, absolute superwoman you've truly been.'

'No.'

'Annie, if that was Joel, I'd be on the floor howling and screaming, but you've managed with such grace,' she tells me. 'What you've been doing on a daily basis here isn't for the faint-hearted. I'm so glad you have come to accept that it's never going to get any better, but I'm also heartsore for you too. Time for change, eh? For everyone's sake? Especially those two wonderful children, who are so delighted to have their mother home and looking happy. If you are happy, they are, Annie. Go and be happy for them.'

'I will. It's time for change,' I say, feeling my knees go weak at the thought of it. 'Whether I like it or not, I need help, Kelly. I really need help.'

She puts her hands on my shoulders, tilts her head and smiles.

'Annie Madden! That's the bravest, most courageous thing I've ever heard you say.'

22.

The days pass by and I quickly fall into my old routine, almost as if I was never away. Well, at least that's how it would seem to the outside world, but of course inside I'm very different.

Inside I'm yearning for Senan's touch, for his laughter, for the carefree times we spent together. I hear his voice when I'm working on his book, and at times I have to stop and breathe when the pain of wanting him so badly overcomes me.

I still go from hot to cold when it comes to making arrangements for Peter's new care regime, but I also learn that seeking help is not quite as straightforward as it seems. There are waiting lists the length of my arm. There are only certain places that can offer the necessary levels of attention that Peter will need. There are financial implications also, and I spend any free time I have working out the maths as to how much each option might cost.

'Peter could need this type of care, and more, for many years,' I say to Kelly as we share a late lunch together one

Tuesday afternoon. 'I need to make sure the money is there to see it through. At the moment it's looking as though I can afford one weekend a month, which is something, I suppose. In fact, it's more than something. It's a start.'

'Yes, it's a start,' she agrees, 'but I really think you need more time than that. You look exhausted already, Annie, and you've only been home a week. This can't go on.'

She is right, of course. I am utterly shattered, and everything about West Cork and the working break I had feels like a world away.

After a very early wake-up this morning, where I panicked as I hadn't heard Peter during the night, I came downstairs to find him lying awake in silence. He hasn't rung the buzzer since yesterday, and I've found myself straining my ears, checking on him every fifteen minutes when he sleeps to make sure he isn't just lying in bed staring at the ceiling. I don't want to think he might be feeling frightened or alone. I've seen tiny changes ever since I got back, and if those are a sign of what's to come, then looking after him is going to get a whole lot harder. At least I can admit to that now.

'So, have you heard from Senan much since you got back?' Kelly casually asks as I clear the table after our quick bite to eat. 'You don't talk about him much. I thought you'd be gushing over spending so much time with someone like him.'

I freeze, the cloth which I was using to wipe the table dangling from my hand in mid-air.

'Don't I? Give me a sec. I'll just go and check Peter,' I say, my eyes like saucers at her unexpected question. I find him still fast asleep, but when I come back to the kitchen Kelly is still waiting on an answer.

'Sorry if I said something wrong,' she says. 'I'm just being nosey, I suppose. I was hoping you'd end up best buddies with him and that you'd invite him over so we could all have a bit of a gawp at him in the flesh.'

I flick back my hair, doing my best to look cool about it all, but I know it's not working. I feel as if I'm acting like someone else as I try to perform some sort of charade once more to my best friend when the subject of Senan comes up. I feel like I'm lying, then I realize that's because I am, and I don't want to tell lies. Not to her, not to anyone. Mostly, I don't want to tell lies to myself.

Have I heard from him much? Yes, I have had the most heart-wrenching text messages. Have I wanted to hear from him? Yes, damn right I have – so, so badly. Do I miss him? More than I could ever put into words. Do I feel bad for feeling like this? Yes, which is why I haven't told anyone.

The more I pine for Senan, the more I don't recognize who I am, yet in the same breath I never felt more like myself than I did when I was with him.

I sit down at the table as Kelly watches my every move.

'What's going on, Annie? You know you can tell me absolutely anything and it will never cross my lips again.'

I hear Meg upstairs, singing as usual.

'You've no idea how good it is to hear her sing these days,' I say to Kelly. 'She sings morning, noon and night lately, be it into the mirror or as she dances around her bedroom, yet if I asked her to sing for me or anyone else, she'd cower like she didn't know what you were talking about. But still, I can see changes and it's so good.'

I'm digressing again and I know it.

'Annie?' she says, raising an eyebrow. 'I honestly was only just asking to make conversation but now I'm starting to think you're avoiding any mention of Senan. Don't tell me if you don't want to.'

She knows I want to. I do want to. I'm bursting to tell someone that at long last I feel alive again, and while I know I shouldn't need another person to make me feel so, something about Senan has awakened me and it feels so good. I'm yearning for him in my sleep, when I'm awake, and all I can think of is what I'd give to spend just one more day in his arms.

'Senan and I . . . Look, Kelly, it's like this. We agreed before I left that we probably shouldn't talk unless it was something urgent about the book,' I say to my best friend. 'But no matter how much I try to let him go from my head, I think he's found his way in here and I'm so scared, Kell.'

I point to my heart while Kelly's hand clasps her mouth.

'I swear I had an idea this would happen,' she whispers. 'Oh God, Annie! Did you fall in love with him? Is that what you're saying?'

I bite my lip and squeeze the dishcloth which I left on the table moments before.

'We had a very intense two weeks together,' I say to her, feeling already like a huge weight is lifting off my shoulders by finally being honest. 'Kelly, it was so perfect. We had an undeniable connection, a real energy between us that was like magic sometimes. We talked for hours and hours, and not just because of the book. We talked in depth. He listened to me, Kelly. He took in every word I said and he helped me release so much of the emotion that has spent most of the past seven years pent up inside me.'

'Oh, Annie.'

'We spent a lot more time together than we needed to, and I enjoyed every single second of it. I know I can't have him, yet I feel like I want him and need him so much,' I confess. 'Is it wrong? He writes to me and sends me messages almost every day. He wants to talk but I feel I need to keep my distance. What do you think? What do you think I should do?'

She stares at me with tear-filled eyes, then she reaches across the table and takes my hand in hers. She shakes her head.

'It's not wrong, honey,' she tells me softly. 'Look at you! You're lighting up when you talk about him, even though you're trying so hard not to show your hand!'

'Am I?'

'Yes, you are!' she replies. 'Annie, my heart breaks for your loneliness here. It kills me to see you struggle every day

291

with the cards you've been dealt, and of course you want more of that wonderful feeling you experienced with Senan. What human being wouldn't want to feel that force of uncontrollable energy, that powerful connection, or that wondering if something was meant to be? It's the best feeling in the world, and you've suffered so much without it for far too long.'

'But Peter?'

Kelly pauses for a moment.

'I know how painful this must be for you, Annie,' she says. 'But Peter is never going to come back to you. I think you know that now, so please don't throw away any little glimmer of happiness that comes your way while waiting for your life here to get better. I'm not saying to rush into anything with Senan, but just take your time and enjoy getting to know him, even from afar. Things here are never going to change, but you are changing. I can see it in your eyes. You are allowed to grow and change and develop your life down different paths. No one could dare judge you for that. Just take your time and tread carefully. Getting to know Senan Donnelly, and feeling that glow of whatever you want to call it inside does not mean you're abandoning your duties here. You are worth it all, and more, Annie. But God help him if he hurts you.'

I smile and laugh a little.

'I'm glad I told you,' I say to her. 'I'm not the type of person to live a lie, and I'm certainly not the type to ride off into the sunset while leaving a trail of destruction behind. My duties are here, first and foremost, with Peter, and they will be for ever. It's just nice to know someone out there cares enough to like me so much again.'

At that I unexpectedly burst out crying.

'Oh no, what did I say?' Kelly asks me. 'Was it the bit about him hurting you? I was only trying to sound like a big bravado friend! Annie, what is it?'

I try to control my heaving sobs, and when I finally do I spill out another truth to Kelly, one that I wasn't expecting to.

'I really miss him, Kelly!' I tell her. 'I feel so bad saying it, but I miss him so much and I want him even more. And then I feel so guilty. I feel so guilty that I've wronged Peter!'

'You haven't!' she tells me, standing up now to give me a hug. 'Don't deny that feeling, darling! Talk to Senan if you want to. Do what you have to do! Hell, invite him over and go to see him somewhere if you want! Meet up with him and talk it out with him face to face.'

'No, no, I couldn't,' I sniffle, grasping onto her arms. 'I just needed to say it out loud. I miss him and I want him, but I can't have him. That's all I needed to say.'

No matter how much I stick to my guns by not conversing with Senan, I find myself looking forward to his messages and one-way ramblings on what he has been up to. I don't need to wonder how it feels for him to get nothing in return, as he tells me how tough it is, but some days this one-direction communication takes the edge off missing him, whereas on others it makes me want to run to him even more.

'I've been cooking up a storm here but it's not the same without you,' he tells me in his latest email. 'Maria jokes with me saying her profits have dipped since I met you and you've turned me into a wannabe Jamie Oliver. I go grocery shopping now, which means a lot more selfies but it's all good fun. I'm so glad I met you, Annie. I spend so much time remembering the moments we shared, but most of all I treasure every memory and use them all to inspire me going forward. I hope you're working through those aims for the future! I know you aren't a big believer in planning too far ahead, but I live in faith that one day I'll see your face again. I'm working on accepting how you can never be mine, but I'd still love to share some time again with you one day. Until that day, I'm thinking of you always. Senan.'

He signs off sometimes as if it's the last time I'll hear from him, but then I'll get a 'Good morning. Have a lovely day', or a similar message at night to wish me sweet dreams. He'll send me photos of his cookery efforts or of his view over West Cork as he watches the sun go down.

'Every time I look out of the window I see you running and I hear you laughing on your way to the shoreline. I hear you singing in my kitchen. I feel you beside me on the sofa at night. I taste your skin on my lips and I feel closer to you when I cook the food you used to when you were here. I can't help missing you. I can't help loving you still.'

They fill me up and they keep me connected to him, but I know they won't last for ever. I write to him also, but I never press send.

'Dear Senan,' I type into my laptop to send him an email. 'I want to talk to you so much. You're breaking my heart, Senan. I want you to hold me again. I want to hear your sweet voice and your terrible singing. I want to lie with you on the beach by the campfire. I want to swim with you in the sea, and then eat breakfast again on the deck like we did so many times. I want to see your eyes light up when you tell me a story from your past. I'm still working on the final draft of your life story, and I hear your voice in every word. You've taken a piece of my broken heart and you've made it feel brand-new again. Please look after it for me, and please keep talking to me. I can't bring myself to reply but I think of you every single day. Annie.'

I write it and I save it as a draft in a folder on my computer which I've filed under his name. They are mini love letters in a way, and it helps me get rid of some of the angst and loneliness I feel when I think of him.

I always feel better when I've done that. Then I can get up and get on with my day. I dress Peter and take him for a walk. I wash his clothes and cook for him. I liquidize the food. I check his oxygen levels. I talk to him and watch TV for a while. I read to him and make sure his room is clean and tidy. Then I make dinner for the children, check up on their school days and their worries. I clean the kitchen and do some more laundry. I check on the animals, I pay the bills. I do more food shopping and I see something else around here that needs repairing.

Then, when everyone is asleep, I polish up more of Senan's story. Sitting alone in the living room, I pour a glass of wine. I flick through the TV. I long for someone to talk to. I check my phone to read a late-night message from Senan, but I won't reply.

No matter how much I want to, no matter how much my heart bleeds for him, how much my mind yearns for him and how much my body aches for him, I know I have to slowly let him go.

I may have only loved him for a short time, but it's a heavy weight I'll carry with me for a very long time.

I really wish I could let him go.

23.

I deliver Senan's life story to Caroline, via Martha, on the same morning that Peter will spend his very first weekend in respite care.

It's been a bumpy few weeks. I have almost torn my hair out checking on availability in different care homes, measuring quality of care against cost, and what I can afford from the life-assurance policy to pay for it all. In the end, after several phone calls, numerous visits and endless research, I chose Beechwood Manor for one weekend every fortnight. Now the day has come, though, I am absolutely dreading making the first move.

'You've been an absolute pleasure to work with,' Caroline tells me when she phones to say the manuscript has been received and accepted, a bit ahead of schedule. 'I know you've a lot going on at home, so you've really shown us all what you're capable of, Annie. The book is heartfelt, honest and a real page-turner, just as we'd hoped it would be. Congratulations.'

I allow myself a little moment to glow with pride and

achievement as I sit at my kitchen table in the summer sunshine. I picture the scene where I'll nip into town on an errand and slowly drive past Corners, the bookshop, where Eileen the elderly owner will have it in the window, pride of place, just as she told me she would on my last visit. It may not be the novel I'd dreamt of, but it's a published work and it gives me goose bumps to think of the day I'll hold it in my hands.

'I always knew you'd be a writer,' she'd said to me one day before I left for West Cork when I told her the news that I'd be ghost-writing Senan's story. 'You've been one of my best customers since you were a little girl. You devoured every book you could find. Oh, I remember when you couldn't even see above the counter, and look at you now. I'm so proud of you, Annie!'

It's the end of June and the children are at school for the last week of term. A long, eight-week break awaits us all. I'm not sure if today feels like a deeply sad end of an era or a frightening new beginning, but I'm just taking every hour at a time.

'I'm so happy you like it,' I said to Caroline, thinking of all the late nights I've spent since I got home from West Cork, editing and polishing. It was a bittersweet experience, going through Senan's story, and so many times I felt like giving in and calling him just to hear his soothing voice and words of reassurance, but it just didn't feel right with Peter by my side as I worked.

I could hear Senan's voice as I typed, I could see how his face lights up when he laughs, and I could feel his pain as I read over sections describing some of the more challenging times of his life.

And sometimes at night, when I'd go to bed and my head was so full of him, I'd allow myself to remember his smell and his touch. I'd imagine his strong arms around me again. I'd shiver under the warmth of his kiss, but only in my mind.

'And of course the best news of all is that Senan is absolutely thrilled with it,' chirps Caroline. My stomach leaps when I hear his name said aloud. 'We're talking about cover photoshoots next, so we've a few nice ideas – not that it will be difficult with such an easy subject matter to photograph. The media are gagging for extracts. I really think this is going to do wonders for his career, so well done for playing such a pivotal role. I spoke to him just this morning and he's super excited for all that's to come.'

I close my eyes and grip the phone. Senan still sends me the odd text message just to say hello, and I've read them back so many times to ease the pain of missing him. I sometimes now send a short reply back, but I've done everything in my power not to engage in lengthy conversation. My heart just couldn't take it. Neither could my conscience.

'I'm so delighted for him,' I say, feeling my voice shake a little when I think of him. 'Is he keeping well?'

She pauses.

'You made quite an impact on him, Annie,' she tells me. 'It seems like working with you has been very good for him, so yes, he is well.'

'It was very good for us both, that's for sure,' I say to Caroline. 'Thank you for such a wonderful opportunity.'

When I hang up the phone after saying goodbye, I open the window and breathe in the fresh air, hoping something as simple as that will keep driving me on to get through this day.

Kelly will be here soon to help me take Peter to the care home where he'll spend his first weekend, and I really wish she would get here soon. It's not in her job description to do this, but she is doing it as my friend. I only hope I can see this through with dignity. I fear, as the morning goes on, I'm going to change my mind, but I know that's not the avenue I should go down, not now when I've come so far.

I can barely look at Peter all morning.

He has stopped ringing the buzzer these days. He lives in a world of utter silence now that none of us can break through. It's mentally challenging, it's utterly frightening, but most of all it's so unbearably sad. Every time I look at him I feel my heart break a little more when I think of how different his life should have been.

I go to his room and I sit with him, trying not to break down when I see the leather weekend bag I've packed for him sitting at the bottom of the bed. The care home is fully equipped for all his needs, so getting him ready was easy from the physical point of view. It's the emotional turmoil that's the worst. I wept as I ironed his T-shirts and the loose jogging bottoms he wears every day. I felt my heart bleed as I folded them and packed the bag. For some reason, it was the moment when I arranged his washbag with his shaving foam, his razors, his aftershave that really got me. He always loved to be well-groomed and he always spent a fortune on expensive aftershave. It was his one little luxury, and it's something I've kept up even after all these years when he can no longer choose it for himself.

'It's only for a few days,' I say to him now as I sit by the bedside waiting for Kelly. 'The room they've chosen for you has a beautiful woodland view. It's not the lough, but it's as close to nature as I could find for you, so I really hope you like it.'

My lip quivers at the thought of leaving him there, no matter how much I dress it up.

'I've left in some framed photos of you with the kids, and I bought a new frame for a copy of our wedding picture – you know, the one on the jetty with the boat in the distance?' I say, trying my best to sound bright. 'You loved that photograph. And your tartan blanket, of course. I'll bring that home again on Monday when I go to pick you up. Do you think I've remembered everything? I really hope I have.'

I was going to keep the children off school today, but decided in retrospect it would be too ceremonious. This is a big deal for me, but for them it's best if I play it down as something positive for all of us, including Peter. And just as I think of that again, my stomach jolts as fear claws my insides.

Is this really better for him?

'You're doing the right thing,' Kelly says as she knocks on the bedroom door and comes in.

I jump. 'Gosh, I didn't even hear you. I've been hoping you'd get here soon.'

She goes to the other side of the bed and speaks directly to Peter in her upbeat, jolly way.

'All right buddy?' she says, ruffling his hair a little. 'It's hardly Costa del Sol but it will be a nice wee break for everyone, especially you. My friend Natalie works there and I've told her to take none of your bad manners, do you hear? Best behaviour all the way?'

My mood lifts immediately now that Kelly is here to guide us through this and to keep our spirits up.

'And what about you, missy?' she asks me. 'What do you have planned for the weekend?'

I stutter out excuses for not being organized, despite all my grand plans for day trips to the beach, or a full day in the city shopping with the children.

'One step at a time,' smiles Kelly. 'Nice and easy does it. You'll soon find a new routine, don't worry.'

I know of course – even though I've nothing planned for tomorrow or Sunday – that I won't be left alone to fester in my thoughts. Bernice is likely to arrive with Jake, so I'd imagine they'll drag us out to dinner somewhere nice, and there's been a whisper of a surprise visit from my only sister, which would be a lovely distraction. She lives so far away now we don't see her very often, but it's always a real occasion when she manages to come and see us with her three young whirlwind children.

'So will we make a move then?' Kelly asks me. I realize I haven't been able to string a competent sentence together since she arrived. I feel as if I'm in a bit of a daze right now. One step at a time is the only way, so I do as I'm told and follow Kelly's lead.

As we take Peter out of our farmhouse to begin this new adventure, I pray for the strength I need to see it through. I try not to look at the swing he built in the garden for the children, or the greenhouse he had such high hopes for. I see him bouncing on the trampoline with the children at the bottom of the garden, before it almost blew away in a storm one night and we spent the day searching hedges and fields, only to find it in our neighbour's garden. I hear him singing as he fixed up fences and filled in potholes on the lane.

I glance at every spot around the place we call home, but I don't look at where the barn used to be. I can't bring myself to look in that direction today.

I fix him into the car with some small talk about how fine the weather is, and then climb into the driver's seat beside him as Kelly joins us in the back.

* * *

Beechwood Manor is a twelve-mile drive from our home, so not too far away, or so I keep telling myself.

Just like the brochure promised, it really does have a homely environment which emphasizes individual nursing care packages tailored to meet each patient's needs. I could recite every line from their website, every quote from families of the residents and every box I ticked when trying to decide what is best for Peter.

He will have oxygen on standby twenty-four/seven just like he does at home. His food will be liquidized for easy swallowing, as choking is becoming more likely now as each day passes by. I've seen so many changes in him lately and, even though I've embraced each new challenge with as much strength as I possibly can, there's no denying that it's all too much for me to deal with alone, especially at night when I fear something might go wrong.

'I know you're feeling guilty right now,' Kelly says from the back seat as we drive away from the farmhouse and out onto the open road. 'It's very normal to do so, but please try not to, darling. We've been over all of this, but just keep reminding yourself that if you don't get out there and get a life, then the aftermath of that accident has robbed you too and it's got two for the price of one.'

I focus on the road ahead. I focus on the music that sings from the car stereo. I hear the presenter on BBC Radio Ulster talk about the weather and all the promise of a great summer that's on the way, and I pine for better days, but at the moment all I can feel is that I'm driving on a road that is leading Peter away from me, the first step towards a long-term goodbye.

Then a song comes on that reminds me of my time with Senan and I gasp out loud, much to Kelly's bemusement when I glance in the rear-view mirror. I can see me with Senan, walking on the beach, laughing and smiling, but most of all feeling so alive. Who was I back then? Is this why I'm doing this? Am I trading Peter off so I can find Senan and all the happiness I had with him again?

What if he doesn't like it there? What if they don't know how he likes to watch some TV just before bedtime? Or, at least, that he used to. What does he like these days? No one knows. If I don't know, how can strangers know?

'No, no I can't do this!' I say out loud. 'I can't leave him!'

I indicate left and pull the car in onto the grass verge at the side of the road, skimming a hedge as I do so. I slam my hands on the steering wheel when the car stops, and I try to control the overwhelming urge to turn back.

'Annie, what's wrong, love?' Kelly asks. 'Would it be better if I drive? What's going on? Annie, talk to me!'

'This is awful, Kelly!' I tell her. 'I feel like I'm betraying him if I take him away from home! I feel like a total traitor. How can I hand him over to other people? I'm going against everything we promised we'd be to each other. I feel so fucking selfish. It's like I'm abandoning him!'

Kelly shakes her head and hushes me like you would a child.

'All of this is so normal,' she whispers in her always reassuring tones. She puts her hand on my shoulder from the back seat. 'But it's good to get all of those feelings out. You know you can scream and cry to me anytime you want. This is a major moment for you, but you're not alone, Annie. We're all going to try and make this happen as smoothly as we can.'

But there's something else deep within me that tells me to go back.

'Kelly, I think . . .' I say, turning towards my husband who sits beside me in the front seat.

'What is it?'

'Since . . . since I came back from West Cork, I don't know if it's gut instinct or if it's guilt, or if it has taken me to step away to see things more clearly, but I see him declining more and more rapidly as each day goes by.' I try to explain. 'It's like a slippery slope that he's going down so fast.'

'And that's exactly why you can't be expected to care for him at home any more!'

'I know that, but it's like . . .' I want to say what I'm so frightened of, but I can't get the words out. 'I wish I could see Dr McCloskey once more to get a clearer picture of where we are right now, but I've a feeling in my stomach that's telling me to take him home.'

Kelly doesn't argue with me this time. Instead she takes out her phone and makes a call right there in front of me.

'Hi Cher, it's Kelly. Is Patricia free?' she says, looking into my eyes as she does so. I'm craned around from the front seat, wondering what she is up to now. 'Patricia, thanks so much for taking my call. I'm with Annie and Peter. Yes, Annie Madden. Would there be any chance of a quick word to put Annie's mind at ease before she leaves Peter in care for the first time today? As you know, it's a huge step, and she may have a few questions for you that might help ease her feelings.'

She hands the phone across to me. I hear Dr McCloskey's familiar voice and immediately feel my heart rate settle.

'I just think, doctor – I have an awful feeling that Peter's condition is getting worse by the day now, so rapidly, and I'm not sure now is the time for me to make these changes,' I whisper, biting my lip as I speak. I hold Peter's hand as I do so. 'Do you still think this is the best thing for him?'

Dr McCloskey sounds as if she has heard this all before, but I'll take anything from her . . . anything that might steer me in the right direction.

'Annie, the last time I looked at Peter's scan, as I explained to you, there were signs of mini strokes that to the naked eye on a daily basis, even as his primary carer, you might not notice the repercussions of,' she tells me. 'Now that you've been away from the whole situation for a short while, you're seeing things a lot more clearly, and that's a good thing. You're absolutely right. His condition is diminishing at a much more rapid pace than we'd have liked, but with a brain injury of his type, even someone relatively young doesn't necessarily have time on their side.'

I take a deep breath. I have a question I need to ask, but finding the words is proving impossible as seconds tick by. In the end I just blurt it out.

'Just tell me . . . is my husband dying, Dr McCloskey?' I ask her, my hand going straight to my mouth as I utter those words. I swallow. 'Please tell me the truth. Is he dying?'

Kelly puts her head in her hands as the world around us goes on. Cars race by outside as time stands still here in my car. Dr McCloskey doesn't wait long before she answers my question.

'I'm so sorry, Annie,' she tells me. 'Peter is slowly slipping away, and he has been doing so for a while now. Like I said to you before, this is never going to get any better. Every day he is getting closer to the inevitable, and it may not be long. I'm so sorry.'

I nod my head slowly.

'Thank you,' I tell her. 'That's all I need to know.'

I say goodbye to Dr McCloskey, feeling strange at saying thank you to her for delivering what is the worst news I can imagine hearing. I hand the phone back to Kelly. Cars keep driving by, the world goes on, yet mine once again has been stopped.

My husband is going to die.

'The only other option I can think of,' whispers Kelly, with tears in her eyes, 'is to have someone professional come and stay in your home for a few nights a week? A nurse, I mean. It will work out more financially, but I can help you look into it if it sounds like a better plan at this stage?'

I nod, praying and pleading with myself not to crumble. I feel the whole world is closing in on me, a sense of doom that I knew was coming, but I'm still not ready to face up to.

'I want to take him home.'

24.

The next few weeks feel like everyone is walking on eggshells.

Patti, our new night nurse, takes over three nights a week, which allows me to get a full night's sleep but, even with Kelly's couple of hours during the day, I still feel emotionally and physically exhausted. I don't know whether it's knowing the inevitable isn't too far away, or that now I've taken my foot off full throttle, everything I've been coping with for seven years is hitting me like a runaway freight train.

I receive my second chunk of payment from Senan's book, which will come in handier than ever now, and to try to distract my mind I start making a proper to-do list where I plan to finally fix up the farmhouse. I need to work on the laneway first. There are potholes that would take the wheels off a car if approached at any speed, and the hedges that run alongside it need to be trimmed back. But no matter how much I try to make a start on any of these tasks, I find I don't have the energy or inclination to see them through.

One More Day

Martha is keen for me to start brainstorming ideas for a novel, but the best I can do is write down my feelings every day before I go to sleep. I'm in no place to write anything more than that at the moment, which thankfully she understands.

Instead I spend my days wallowing in my loneliness and grief, so far away from all the ambitious resolutions I'd made for my future to Senan. It's as if I'm walking towards an oncoming doom that's going to hit me on a given day. I cling to memories; I lie awake at night wrestling with my own thoughts and fears, and during the day I revert back to pretending that I'm fine when everyone around me knows I'm anything but fine. And then there's Senan . . . I miss his words and his touch so badly, which spins me into circles of guilt and fear that I've betrayed everyone I love the most by still wanting him.

'Fancy a walk?' Meg says to me unexpectedly one afternoon when she finds me staring into space.

I look back at her with wild eyes. I can see how frightened she is. You can feel the fear in the air in our home, worse than it ever was before.

'Don't worry, it was just a stupid idea,' she says, slipping off from the place where she sits on the worktop.

'I'll go! Yes, let's go!' I tell her quickly before she disappears. 'Meg? Thank you, darling. Let's go for a walk, just you and me.

* * *

Meg links into my arm as we saunter up the country lane that runs beside our home and I do my best to savour this moment, amidst all our sadness, and how far we have come in a very short time. My daughter wanted to walk with me. She wants to be close to me physically too, and I am reminded of how much she needs me right now. Even when she was storming off and eating in her bedroom, or avoiding my eye, or sulking into her headphones, she needed me.

'Penny for your thoughts,' I say to her when we stop by a hedgerow to admire a new foal in the lush green field before us. 'I remember how you used to love coming up here to pick gooseberries along this hedge, and you'd peep through the gate to see if you could spot any new horses. You were such a curious child.'

I push her hair back from her face and watch as she inhales my physical touch. I've been missing moments like this much more than I had paused to realize.

'When you were away,' she says, her eyes flickering as she looks up at me, 'I told Dad that I was sorry, and now I need to tell you too.'

'What?'

My heart skips a beat, but my automatic reaction is to wrap my arms around my baby girl and take whatever is worrying her right out of her heart and into mine, where I will feel her pain instead.

'I made him fall that day,' she gasps as her eyes fill up with tears. 'It was my fault, Mum, and even though Nana said I didn't have to tell you, I really do. I distracted him. I told him I knew something about him, and it made him fall.'

I squeeze my daughter so tightly I fear I might injure her, and I close my eyes, cursing myself, wondering how I didn't know about this much sooner. How many nights has she tortured herself over this? How many days has she been distracted, so full of remorse for what could have been?

'No, no, please Meg,' I whisper into her hair as it sticks to my face, damp with both her tears and mine. 'You must never, ever blame yourself for anything that happened that day. Your dad wouldn't want you to and neither do I. It was no one's fault. It was not his, it was not mine, and it definitely wasn't yours. We love you so much, Meg. My precious, precious girl.'

She sobs into me until her arms go limp and she can cry no more. I look up to the heavens, into the pale blue sky, and I thank God that Meg found the strength to tell me what she has been going through.

'Every day, from now on, I want you to know how loved you are and how special you are to all of us,' I say to her, holding her beautiful face in my hands. 'You don't need to worry about a thing. Not about Dad, not about Danny and most definitely not about me. We grown-ups make mistakes. We are all only human. Your dad made mistakes and I did too, but that doesn't mean we love each other any less.'

She smiles through her puffy red eyes, and I can see her shoulders drop as the weight she was carrying leaves her once and for all.

'So you knew then? About the other—'

'I knew,' I nod, linking her arm again as we make our way back home. 'I might never know who, but yes, I knew.'

Senan sends me an occasional cheery, upbeat message, asking how I am and what I'm up to, but I can't face any sort of explanation, so I don't respond to him as much as I'd like to. I keep our correspondence short, sweet and above level, passing on my regards to Sid and Ivy, or to Bob and Liam in case he should ever bump into them in Maria's. He doesn't know Peter is dying. He has no clue what I'm going through here and, no matter how much I long for him, it would be too easy to hurl all my fears in his direction. He lives in a completely parallel world that is so different from mine – a world I still often escape to in my lonely mind.

Now, do you understand? I feel like saying to him. *Now do you know why I pushed you away from me? You don't want to be part of this. No one would.*

I consider blocking his number to take away the pain of still yearning for him in so many ways, and yet resenting him in others, but I can't. None of this is his fault, is it?

'I just hope you're OK,' he tells me in his most recent

message. 'You're never far from my thoughts, Annie. You deserve the best.'

But what I deserve is the furthest thing from my mind these days. I feel like I've made huge progress with my daughter, yet when I think of the future I feel totally lost, more confused than ever and broken inside.

'*Why?*' I scream into nowhere one day when I'm far enough away from the house in the chicken coop again. 'Why did this happen? *Why?*'

I think no one can hear me, but when I look up and see Danny staring at me with tears in his eyes, I know I have to try to pull myself together. I pray but I don't even know what I'm praying for. I go from wanting to wrap my arms around Peter and wish him back to life, to wanting to jump on a plane and find Senan and the beach house again so I can forget this horror we are all facing here.

'It's going to be OK, Mum,' Danny mumbles in his newly broken voice.

'Of course it is, honey. We are strong together. We'll always be strong.'

I stand up and fall into my son's arms, doing my best to believe what I'm saying is true.

And I know I am shutting out everyone who cares for me, which is doing none of us any good. I've shut off from Bernice, I've gone quiet on Kelly, I don't answer Senan and I just want to hold my children. Even when Bob calls me to see how I am, I deliberately ignore him.

The days turn into weeks, the weeks into months and, when the summer drifts in, as pleasant as the weatherman promised it would be, the blue skies still can't stop me seeing everything in grey.

25.

Summer trickles by and the kids spend most days down by the lough with their friends, fishing and swimming, while I read in the garden alone or listen to the radio to pass the day by. They seem happier these days, which should perk me up a little, but I still keep myself to myself, preferring to hide away from reality for as long as I can.

They'll be back to school by September and maybe then I'll find a proper routine, but for now it's like every day is the same and the wonder of West Cork is the only thing I want to keep me company as I spend my time on the farm or behind closed doors.

I sometimes stare at Peter in a lengthy daze, holding his hand like I'm a living widow, frozen in time as the world goes on around me.

Kelly says I've gone backwards, but I don't think I have. I think I'm stuck.

I'm just stuck.

* * *

A knock on my bedroom door one Saturday morning in August arouses me from a dream where I'm in my wedding dress at the local chapel. Peter and I are getting married. I'm waiting on him at the top of the aisle, even though I know it should be the other way around. The groom is meant to be waiting on the bride, or so tradition says. I wait longer. I see our guests shift in their seats, and then I watch on as the faces of our friends and family turn to dread. The clock ticks time by. I hear them all whisper, and I see them shake their heads. He isn't coming, I repeat to myself. I'm waiting and waiting but he isn't going to show up.

Then I see him in our local bar. He is with a woman. She is very beautiful to look at, much younger and more exciting than me. She is trying not to touch him but they can't resist. I see her face. Oh God, I see her face. Is that her? No! Could it really be . . .? No!

'I'm so sorry to wake you, Mrs Madden.'

Patti, the retired nurse who now spends half a week in my house, yet who I've been determined not to get close to on any sort of personal level, insists on calling me Mrs Madden. I haven't been called that since I was teaching at school, but I accept her doing so: it acts as a formal barrier between us that suits me quite well.

'Yes? Can I get you something?' I glance at my watch and see it is four a.m., and I'm still only half-awake when it clicks in that something is obviously very urgent to need my attention at this early hour.

'What's happening? What's going on?' I ask her, as a weight of dread sinks to my stomach.

'I think you might want to come and sit with Peter now,' she tells me. 'I've already called the doctor. He's on his way.'

'No!'

I have known this moment was coming for three months now, yet I slide down to the floor, my hands skimming the doorframe of what was once the entrance to our marital bedroom. I hold onto it, feeling any ounce of energy I had left within me disappear, and I lean my head there for a moment, trying to think of what I'm supposed to do next. I'd pictured this moment many times. I'd wondered where I would be when the day would come, in the way I used to imagine where I'd be when I went into labour with my children.

I've played it all out in my head so many times, so I should be more prepared, but I'm not. This is one part of my immediate future I knew was coming, yet so far I'm not handling it in the way I'd practised in my own mind.

'Call my mother-in-law, please,' I whisper, conscious of waking the children. They don't need any drama in the middle of the night. 'And can you call Nurse Gallagher too, please? Yes, call Kelly. Call them quickly please.'

I put on my dressing gown and slippers, knowing I don't have the physical strength to get properly dressed, and I make my way downstairs, holding on to the banister with every step I take.

I walk across the hallway and slowly open Peter's bedroom door. I hear Patti talking to Bernice on the phone from the kitchen. Maybe I shouldn't have alerted her during the night? Maybe I should have waited until morning.

'Oh Peter,' I gasp when I see him.

I take my usual seat beside him, my face etched with a permanent frown as it seems to always be these days. I stand up again, knowing I want to look at his face for as long as I can while he still breathes beside me. His handsome face is almost entirely covered with an oxygen mask. I can see his lips are blue and his skin is a deathly shade, almost porcelain, but he is still warm to touch. I put my head lightly onto his chest and I listen to his heartbeat.

It's slow and faint, but it's still there.

I take his hand. I need to talk to him. There's so much more I want to say.

'It's going to be OK, Peter,' I whisper, nodding constantly as if I'm trying to convince myself as well as him. 'Please don't worry. I'm here with you. Everything is fine, just fine.'

I remember how he used to soothe me at night if I ever felt anxious or frightened in life. He'd rub my hair and tell me a story of better times and, within moments, I'd feel better already.

'Remember the time we went on our first proper holiday?' I whisper now to him, hoping I can return the feeling he used to give me with his words and memories. 'We were so nervous, weren't we? We were only going to Salthill in

Galway, about two hundred miles away. There were no aeroplanes or big expense involved, but to us it was a true adventure. It was like going to the other side of the world.'

I've no idea why this memory just came to me, but I find myself talking to Peter the way he did for me so many times, or the way I used to tell our children a bedtime story off the top of my head; they'd drift away to sleep before I'd finished. He would tell me they'd do that because they felt so safe at the sound of my voice.

I hope I can make him feel safe now.

'You were so nervous driving that day,' I smile. I sit down on the arm of the chair so I can see him as I speak. 'We had a map, a proper old-fashioned map covered in blue pen marks, and I did my best to call out directions, much to your frustration. I'd never been to Salthill before and neither had you. We had no idea what to expect, but we hoped when we got there it would be as beautiful as everyone had told us it would be.'

I take a deep breath. I hear the doctor arrive in the kitchen on the other side of the wall. I hear the soft whispers of our parish priest, Father Brendan, who arrives seconds behind him.

'Peter, we have had so many wonderful adventures that I will always cherish,' I tell my husband as tears stream down my face. 'You were a fabulous husband to me, even when we didn't always see things the same way. Even when you messed up at the end of our time together, I still loved you. Even now that I still don't know who she was, I still love you. I loved you then and I'll always love you with every breath I take, for ever. You've been the best father to Meg and Danny. I promise you that we'll keep your memory alive in so many ways. I'll make sure of that.'

The doctor opens the bedroom door. He puts his head around and nods his arrival, but I haven't finished yet so I keep talking as he makes his way in. He stands at the other side of the raised bed now and takes Peter's left wrist between his finger and thumb, glancing at me as he does so. The priest mutters a prayer for the dying softly at the same time, and anoints Peter by blessing his forehead and then his hands.

'You're on your way to heaven now, Peter,' I sob. 'I know I don't have a map this time to try and help you along the way, but remember when we saw the ocean at Salthill and how we knew we'd found a little piece of heaven all on our own? You're on your way to heaven. It might be scary going there when you don't know what to expect, but I'm here right beside you. I'll stay right here until you find your way and I'll meet you there some day. I love you, Peter. I will never find anyone else like you, no matter where I go next, or no matter what I do. Look after us all, won't you?'

I look at the doctor's face again and he smiles gently.

'I'm so sorry. He's gone, Annie,' he whispers as Patti, who has slipped in to the room, quietly checks her watch and discreetly writes down what I assume is the time of death.

'He fought a long, brave battle, as did you all, but your husband is at peace now.'

He is gone. That's what he said, isn't it? Peter, my husband, is gone.

26.

We get ready to say our last goodbye to Peter on a warm morning in late August.

The sky is bright blue with cotton-wool clouds scattered above us, the birds are singing outside, and I hear tractors bounce along the nearby road as normal life goes on around us.

It's a very strange state of mind I'm in right now. The past two days have been like a fog in some ways, yet comforting and restful in others. I go from being plunged into a sense of deep sadness in my heart, to relief that Peter's pain is over, then to desperation as I realize my whole identity of the past seven years is now up for review and renewal. Knowing I'll never sit with Peter again and read to him, I'll never touch his face again, I'll never plan his meals or scurry around as he sleeps to get things done, the future feels both alien and frightening.

'Did you sleep OK?' I ask Danny. He is fully dressed already in his sharp black suit. I'll swear he has grown a few inches over the past while.

He used to shrug and sigh when I asked him such 'boring' questions, but he's much more attentive to me now.

'I woke just once,' he tells me. 'I'd a really weird dream, plus did you hear Grandma Joan snore? She would wake the dead!'

We both pause when he realizes what he has said and then we burst out laughing. I give him a hug. He feels so big and manly and he smells like his father, which stops me in my tracks.

'You're wearing Dad's aftershave?' I say to him. 'That's a really nice thing to do, Danny.'

'I took it when they were clearing out his bedroom for the wake,' he tells me. 'I hope you don't mind?'

'I don't mind at all, darling,' I say to my handsome son. 'In fact, I'm delighted you wanted it. He was a fusspot when it came to his cologne collection. Only the best would do, so he'd take great pride in knowing you have similar tastes.'

Ironically, I do believe my children have learned more about their father since he died than they ever did when he was still with us. It's like their interest in him has been piqued and they are thirsty for stories, both old and new.

We've shared memories around the kitchen table, we've looked at photographs of better days gone by, and when my own mum arrived from Spain for the funeral, it's like we started all over again with our grief, going round in circles as emotions bubble and hugs are shared.

Now that the morning has come, there's a sense of

formality in the air. We are all dressed in our best clothes, the house has been cleaned up as best we can, the food we've been nibbling on has been cleared away, and the voices that laughed and cried with us over the last forty-eight hours now drop to a whisper.

'This shouldn't be happening,' my mother says to me quietly as the undertaker closes the coffin and we prepare to leave the house for the church service. 'It's like history is repeating itself and it's far too cruel. You shouldn't have had to suffer like this, and neither should the children. It's unfair.'

She holds me close and I inhale every second with her. I don't see her very often, but there's simply nothing like a hug from your mother to make the world feel better.

I understand what she means. In fact, I've thought the same so many times.

I know I will see reflections of myself and my sister when I look at my children today as they walk behind their father's coffin. We were just a little bit older when our dad was taken from us, and it's too much to imagine that my own children are now going through the same thing as we did.

I know their circumstances are very different to ours, but losing a parent as a young teenager rocks your foundations to the very core. You look at your friends differently from that moment on. You depend on them so much more. You face each milestone of your life differently. People look at you through different eyes for a very long time. You replay last conversations with your parent and wonder were you a good daughter or son. Maybe you were too hard on them at times? Maybe you didn't say you loved them often enough? Then you spend your days longing for their words of wisdom, for the warmth and security of a hug, for just one more chance to tell them everything you need to. You lean on your friends, you feel sorrow for your other parent when you do so, you cover up your real emotions with anger and rage, and you never want to see Mother's Day or Father's Day ever again. You build up a wall of protection, you are vulnerable, needy and sore. And there are wounds that – no matter where you go in life and no matter how you keep searching – you can never, ever heal.

You can learn from them, but they are always there to be picked at, like a scar on your heart that never goes away.

On top of all that, I fear that because Peter was taken from Danny and Meg in so many ways long before this, they'll never know just how much he loved them, or how full of life and joy he was. The truth is, we all lost a lot of Peter a long time ago. Since then, he has been living in a body that no longer worked, and his suffering is over now, yet it's still so hard to say goodbye.

'You're doing so well,' Kelly whispers as I stand at the sink, my hands submersed in soapy water, even though I'm wearing my funeral attire and we need to leave very soon. I just feel the urge to do something mundane and everyday right now, something like wiping down worktops, just to test to see if I can feel some sense of normality again.

'I don't know if I can cry any more, Kelly,' I say to her. 'Should I be crying more than I am or more than I have today? I feel so numb now. It's like I'm all cried out and I'm empty inside.'

She leans her head on my shoulder, and together we stare out through the window onto the back yard of the farmhouse, to the chicken pen in the distance, the greenhouse, the swing, and the vegetable patches that are overgrown and neglected.

'The day is young, but no matter how you handle it, you should have no regrets whatsoever today or any day after this,' she whispers to me. 'You cared for Peter right until the very end of his precious life. You were there for him every single step of the way. You gave him respect, you gave him your time, you gave him your love. Even in the toughest times, you were always patient, gracious and kind, Annie. You have nothing to be afraid of. You did your very best and it was more than enough.'

I look across at Bernice, who keeps going from busying herself with any type of task she can find, to bursts of anger where she curses God for taking good people long before their time. I had to ask her to sit down earlier when I realized she had washed and scrubbed the same coffee cup three times, even though it hadn't been used.

Despite all the commotion and mixed emotions, it is Meg's words to me that really take my breath away when she approaches me just as I'm drying my hands after my spontaneous urge to do something similar.

'I hope you don't mind, Mum, but I have an idea.'

'Tell me what it is, baby,' I say, kissing her hair.

She takes a deep breath.

'Look, it's probably silly and it's probably a bit late to organize it, but you know the way you told me you read a poem at your dad's funeral all those years ago?' she says, holding a sheet of paper in her hands.

She looks up at me with such innocent, pleading eyes.

'Yes?'

'Well . . . do you think it would be all right if I sang a song today for Dad? I'd really like to.'

I hold her face in my hands and look into her brave eyes as tears build in my own again. I may not have been able to cry all morning but now I can. My darling daughter has moved me once more with her sincerity and kindness, a little ray of hope in such a dark day for all of us.

'Meg, that would be the most beautiful thing!' I say to her. 'You're such a kind, wonderful young lady. Don't you ever forget that! And we'll make sure we do your daddy proud. He would be so, so proud of you both today.'

I stand up straighter when I see the smile on her face, knowing she is pushing her own boundaries and fears in order to ensure her father's funeral is as special and as personal as it can possibly be. I feel Peter's energy surround me once more like a warm blanket. I can feel him smiling on us, like he's giving me his approval. We're going to be fine.

The undertaker gives me the nod that it's time to go and I gather my children to my side. They link an arm each and I hear the chapel bell toll in the distance, then we walk out of the house behind Peter's coffin and I hear gasps and sniffles from family members who have travelled to be here with us today.

'Thank you for giving us such precious memories,' I whisper into the sky as the sun shines down on our garden. We may be taking him away from his home in a physical sense, but I can't see this place ever being without Peter. He is still here.

'You OK, Mum?' Danny whispers to me as we make our way down the lane and out to the main road by the lough where cars wait to take mourners to the nearby church.

'I am, you know,' I tell my wonderful son. 'Don't worry about a thing. I am OK and we're all going to be OK.'

He bites his lip and links into my arm a little bit tighter.

'I know I might have complained sometimes,' he says to me, 'but I'm going to miss him being here. This house is going to be so quiet without the nurses and everyone else coming and going.'

'Even Margo the music therapist who can't sing?'

'Even Margo,' he replies. 'It's going to be weird.'

'Weird,' I repeat after him with a smile, remembering that day when he'd said the same word to me at the kitchen table and I'd been so offended. 'It certainly is going to be very weird, Danny, in so many ways, but we still have each other and your dad will watch over us, that's for sure.'

We arrive at the little church moments later and it looks as though the whole village has turned out to pay their respects to Peter. As they watch on with faces strained with sympathy, I've never been prouder of my two children than I am today. Danny suddenly looks like a man instead of a boy. It's like he has grown up all of a sudden, and the way he puts his arm around me and his sister as we follow his father's coffin into the chapel – where one day, eighteen years ago, we took our wedding vows – makes my chest swell with joy.

'Peter's life as he knew it was cruelly sucked from him seven years ago,' Father Brendan tells the packed church congregation when we've taken our seats and the church has filled up with mourners. 'And although things were never the same again for him after that cruel fateful day, nor for those who loved him, it's important to remember him for the exceptional man he was up until that life-changing moment. He was a dedicated father who adored young Danny and Meg. He was a devoted husband to his childhood sweetheart, Annie. He was a loving son, a brother, a son-in-law, an uncle and a friend. Peter Madden had a razor-sharp sense of humour with his witty one-liners and practical-joking ways. He was a force to be reckoned with on the football field, where he wore his club colours with such pride. He was a proud man of the lough like his father and grandfather had been for many years before him. On top of all that, he was a handsome divil too, and didn't he know it!'

We all manage to laugh at that. I close my eyes as the priest reads his homily, seeing Peter smiling all the while I do so.

'I ask you all to remember Peter for the strong, athletic, kind and gentle person that he was,' he continues. 'Remember his contribution to our community. Who could ever forget the village tractor run of 1997 when he soared to victory and took great delight in milking it at the local pub when the prize was a few free pints? Or the one and only beauty pageant we held when his future wife Annie was the winner? Oh, I can still see the look of delight on his face. He really was the cat that got the cream that day!'

I look at Meg and Danny beside me as they drink in every word Father Brendan has to say about their dad, and my heart feels like it could burst for them.

'We will celebrate Peter's life today, not mourn his passing, because Peter's body may have been taken from us but his spirit will live on here in this lough-side village in so many ways,' he finishes. 'It will live on in his children, the most precious legacy he has left during his short time in this world. Let's celebrate Peter today and let us thank God for all the goodness he brought to each and every one of us. Let us pray for his soul and thank God for the grace of having him in our lives and for the memories we will cherish for ever.'

The congregation trickles out a light round of applause, and even Bernice is smiling through her tears at Father

Brendan's words of comfort. The atmosphere is positive and commemorative, but when Meg sings at the end of the service, the church falls totally silent again.

I watch her walk from our front-row pew in the church, her little hands shaking as she unfolds the piece of paper with the lyrics of an Irish ballad and her eyes darting around until she finds me again. I smile and try to reassure her with my eyes that she can do this.

And she does. She is absolutely perfect.

'That was beautiful,' Mum whispers to me. 'Every single thing about today has been beautiful, Annie.'

'It really has. It's exactly how he would have liked it.'

We carry Peter to his resting place in the little cemetery that skims Lough Neagh. A sense of peace overcomes me for how much love is shown for him here today from our whole community. Schoolchildren in uniform form a guard of honour, the local Gaelic football team do the same in their club colours and, just like on the day of my own father's funeral, the fishermen from the lough down their nets and bow their heads to show their respect as we pass by.

He was so loved. He will always be loved. We are broken now without him, but I'll do my best to fix our children's hearts and to make their futures the very best they can be, just as he would have wanted.

A piper plays a tune in the breeze by his graveside as we make our way out, back to the farmhouse where all our memories lie. As we leave his grave, I glance back at the lough, and part of me knows that no matter when I need Peter, he will always be here. He is still in my heart, and he will be for ever.

A small group of close family and friends gather back at the farmhouse where I've arranged for tea and sandwiches to be delivered after the service, and when I get a moment to myself, I slip off into Peter's bedroom and take a moment to reflect as the utter finality of this all begins to sink in.

I open the curtains and the window, seeing the deep blue of the rugged lough in the near distance. The bed he lay in has been taken away to make room for the wake. I'm glad I didn't see it being removed from the house. Instead two small sofas were placed where it used to be. Memorial cards offering words of comfort and sorrow sit on the side table where the books I used to read to him once sat. Bunches of flowers in vases are scattered all around the house, including a beautiful bunch of white roses from Senan and a burst of summer blooms from Bob and Liam. I lost count of the people who called us, but when the dust settles I'll get round to reading every message that has been sent, every note on each bouquet and every card that was delivered either by hand or by post since Peter's passing.

Senan stopped with his daily messages as soon as the word filtered through to him, apart from one quick text to offer his deep sympathies.

'Dear Annie, I'm so sorry to hear of the sad news (Caroline

told me this morning). I know how much you loved Peter. You spoke about him with such warmth and pride. Please take good care and know I'm thinking of you all at this sad time. I will leave you to mourn and grieve for your terrible loss, but I'm always here if you ever need me. Senan.'

This time though, I did reply.

I thanked him for his kind words, and wished him well from the bottom of my heart, and I encouraged him to find the happiness he deserves, far away from the baggage I will carry for a long time after Peter's death. As much as I've withheld the urge to talk to him lately, I like to think I'm not the type of person to blank out someone who is offering words of sympathy, even when I'm trying to protect my own feelings, plus it feels like closure, which is best for us both.

I've been thinking quite a lot lately about the type of person I used to be and the person I've become over the past seven years.

I often wonder what I'd be like now if Peter hadn't fallen so tragically that day. I wonder even more about what type of person would he be? And how would we be together?

Would Peter and I still be in love with each other, or would we have drifted apart like some married couples do over time? Would I ever have found out of his continued meetings with another woman? Would we have stuck together even so? Would we still live here in the farmhouse, or would we have moved on somewhere new? Would we have had any more children like we'd often planned to?

Senan was right when he said I wasn't keen on making big plans for the future. Since the accident, I've heard well-meaning people talk to me with great confidence as they plan for days and years to come, just like Peter and I used to. I hear them say that by the time they are forty they'll have done this, that, or the other; or that this time next year they'll be here, there and everywhere, and I want to tell them, no! Life doesn't work that way, unfortunately. We can hope and dream, we can set goals and targets, but we can never fully control what's coming up next. None of us knows what's round the corner. Nothing is ever guaranteed, not even tomorrow.

We know nothing about tomorrow, until tomorrow comes. We can mourn for the past, we might wonder about our future, but the most important moment will always be now, as frightening as the now might sometimes be.

27.

As the season changes to Autumn after Peter's passing, so does everything around me.

I finally force myself to take up those resolutions I made in West Cork, beginning with fixing up the farm house. I do my best to squeeze in as many repairs as I can before winter comes, which keeps my head busy and my house busy too. We've never been used to quiet, so the sound of a van pulling up outside, a drill or saw being deployed, or someone whistling as they work takes away the silence, going some way to replacing the bustle of the daily visits from Kelly, and the occasional appearance of social workers, physios and occupational therapists. I missed the company, even Margo the music therapist with her eccentric ways.

I arrange for the hallway flooring to be polished up to its former glory and I buy new rugs to protect it. We give the whole house a new lick of paint both inside and out, feeling the benefit of a fresh start and a step away from some of the more painful memories we've been holding on to. I have a walled garden made in Peter's memory on the site of the old barn, where we can now sit on a little bench and think of him amongst nature when we want to. The staircase has been given a revamp, the electrics in my bedroom have been fixed and the leak in the kitchen has been patched up at last.

But no one could have prepared me for how it would feel to pack up Peter's minimal belongings and sort out what we wanted to keep. Danny had his aftershave collection, of course, and I also gave him a ring I'd bought his dad for our first Christmas together. Meg wanted his bookcase, which now sits proudly in her bedroom, and I hope that someday she'll dip into her father's eclectic collection. I packed up his clothes and Kelly kindly took them away for me, but I kept one of his shirts which I couldn't bear to part with. It was an old checked shirt, one he used to joke about as he'd had it for so long but didn't want to let it go.

Then one cool September afternoon, as I snuggle into the shirt, in his pocket, I find something I didn't even know was there. On a piece of paper, I see her name and number. The shock of it almost makes me physically sick.

'Kelly?' I say in an urgent voice that makes me sound as if I am about to either collapse or explode. 'I think there's something you need to tell me.'

Kelly arrives within minutes, her face so pale and ghostly, and immediately I know that it's true.

'I could never find the right moment to tell you. I'm sorry,' she says, but I take a step back when she tries to embrace me. 'It just never seemed appropriate. It wasn't even—'

'You were supposed to be my best friend! I told you everything! I told you all of my fears and you held me while I cried, yet all this time you knew my husband? You knew him before his accident. You knew him before you knew me?'

Kelly puts her hands up in defence and shakes her head. I gasp, trying to find my breath again. I stifle my sobs, hoping my children won't hear any of this. They don't need to know. I didn't need to know either!

'Please sit down. Please let me explain,' says Kelly, her voice quivering almost as much as mine is. 'I only ever met Peter once, in the bar. He turned heads, of course he did. He was exceptionally attractive, and he really stood out amongst all the farmers and fishermen, but I was with Joel. I noticed Peter, yes, but I simply admired from afar and—'

My eyes widen. I think I might be sick.

'We didn't know he was married,' she continues. 'He didn't say. Well, it never came up really, and then I saw them together once more after that. I confronted her. I told her to step away before there was trouble. She fell for him pretty quickly, and on the day of the accident, she was going to tell him she was leaving once and for all. She didn't get to, of course, but she left nonetheless.'

'Your friend from America who left here so suddenly? Lexi?' I whisper, feeling my heart crumble at my own ignorance of what was going on behind my back at a time when

I thought my life was perfect. 'She went back to America because she was in love with my husband?'

Kelly nods as fat tears escape onto her cheeks.

'And then I got the job to look after him,' she whispers. 'I didn't want it at first. I felt as if I'd done something wrong when I really hadn't, Annie. I was so angry at them both, especially when I saw the wonderful wife and family he had, and I suppose I wanted to do my best to make life easier for you in any way I could. I wanted to try and make up for Peter's reckless ways with my friend. I wanted to help you be happy again.'

She comes towards me and this time I don't stiffen up or move away. I always wondered where an angel like Kelly was sent from, and now it all makes sense. Her loyalty and friendship sometimes felt too good to be true, but I understand it all now. I understand why she always went that extra mile.

'Thank you for not telling me,' I say to her, feeling as if a final stage of closure has been reached at last. 'Not knowing her identity was so painful, but I don't think I could have coped with knowing when he was alive, no matter how much I thought I needed to.'

'Are you OK, Annie? I'm so sorry.'

'Yes, I'm OK,' I tell Kelly, and I really am OK. 'Thank you for not telling me who she was, so I could sometimes pretend it wasn't real and so that I could love my husband right until the very end.'

* * *

'Do something positive with the downstairs bedroom,' Bernice tells me one day, her sleeves rolled up and her Marigolds on as she helps me give the house a really good deep clean. It's funny how we've become used to calling it the 'downstairs bedroom' or 'Peter's room' when it had always been a family room before, but one that was only ever used on occasion by his parents and grandparents who lived here before us.

I toy with making it a second living area, like it was before, but it's Danny who comes up with the idea that we end up going along with.

'It could be your writing room, Mum,' he says to me. 'It has one of the best views of the lough and I imagine Dad would love to see you following your dreams by writing your first novel in there.'

And so that's what it will become, and the end result fills me with such inspiration. I paint the walls white, I frame artwork I'd saved from the children's early schooldays and I put it on the walls. I buy a new desk and I plonk it right at the window so I can see the lough in the distance. I decorate the room with some plants and I buy a new little sofa where I can read from the bookshelves I've installed around the far wall. A small stove in what was the old fireplace makes the room very cosy, as does the Keshan-style rug I pick up for a bargain at a second-hand furniture store in town.

As the evenings draw in and the lonely nights creep up on me, I pledge to write my first few chapters by Christmas.

It is healing, it is therapeutic, and most of all it distracts my mind for just a few hours each evening if I struggle with my new routine, or lack of it, without Peter to care for.

'The days feel so much longer,' I tell Kelly, who now calls on social visits only. 'I actually don't know how to fill my day, which is a far cry from what I'm used to.'

'Maybe it's time to think about going back to teaching?' she suggests, but I'm not so sure about that. 'Or features writing? You could work freelance?'

'Not just yet,' I tell her. 'I feel like starting something new. Maybe I can make a go of writing that novel and see where that takes me. Martha still believes I can do it, so who knows?'

And when September ends, I pluck up the courage to show Martha the first few chapters I spent the first month without Peter working on. It's a heartfelt story, or at least I'm hoping it is, where I've taken all the pain of losing Peter, the agony of missing Senan and put it into a fictional love story.

'You've lived out some of this, I can tell,' Martha says when she gives me some initial feedback. 'It's raw, it's emotive and I feel it's got great potential. I love it, Annie. Keep going.'

Meg and Danny are adjusting to our new way of life too, slowly but surely, but not without a few bumps along the way. Schoolwork becomes a challenge, more friends seem to call at the house, which is nice, as they rally round and fill the house with noise, but there are times when they dip and I do my best not to show them how frightened I am as they grieve.

'I feel like I could punch something,' Danny tells me one night, having broken down in what I interpreted as a mixture of teenage hormones and grief all in one go. 'Why am I so angry, Mum? I only remember Dad as someone who sat in that awful chair or lay in bed staring at the walls and it really annoys me. I want to remember more than that. I'm so mad.'

I fill the house with photos of happy times with Peter to try and jog his memory, and I sign us all up for some counselling, which is taking the edge off all our angst. Danny even joins a boxing club, which he now jokes saves him from undoing all the good work we've had done around the house when he feels like punching the walls. Meg has immersed herself in singing, believing she is going to be the next Adele, and I don't put her off her stride.

'It's a perfect distraction for her and a great release,' Mum tells me on one of our daily phone calls. 'None of you need to jump into this new way of life or feel forced to find new routines, my love, but it will happen organically and that's the best way. You're doing well, Annie. You're all doing so well.'

I hope I am. I'm really trying to fill in the gaps of my day when the children are at school, and the weekends when I used never to have a minute to myself.

I find a whole new world right on my doorstep when I discover a unique bunch of ladies who run a swimming club at the lough called the Wild Water Dunkers. Mary, their founder, welcomes me with open arms when I message her online to find out more, and soon I'm wet and wild every Sunday morning with a circle of ladies who make me laugh so heartily. We spend far too long warming up afterwards in a coffee dock by the water where we put the world to rights, and I really feel I've found a tribe to call my own.

Saturdays in autumn are spent window-shopping with Meg, and we treat ourselves to coffee and something sweet, then pop in next door to browse the books in Corners where Eileen always gives us a hearty welcome.

The family-run old-fashioned little cubbyhole-sized treasure chest is where I always used to grab a few minutes when I could, but nowadays Meg and I take it at our leisure, which was something I really had to work hard at doing after being on a timer for so long.

'Not long until we have our own local author's book on the shelves in time for Christmas!' Eileen tells me one Saturday just before Hallowe'en. 'My heart almost over-flowed with pride when I saw the cover in a trade magazine, Annie. They've put your name on the cover. That doesn't always happen when ghost-writing, so well done you!'

Caroline had sent me the cover by email, and it had taken me three days to open it, as I knew seeing Senan's face again would rock my whole world. When I did pluck up the courage, my heart actually leapt when I looked at his rugged, handsome face staring out from the screen. I know it was his idea to put my name up front alongside his. He always said he would insist on it, and it pulls on my heartstrings to see that he was true to his word.

'I think it's a bit of an omen that your book is out on the day of my official retirement,' Eileen tells me. She has a little shake in her voice, reflecting her almost eighty years on the planet and her candyfloss lilac hair looks so good I always want to reach out and touch it. But her announcement takes me by surprise. Despite her age, Eileen has always been evergreen, and I can't imagine Corners without her.

'November the eighteenth?' I say to her in surprise. 'Oh Eileen, please don't tell me you're closing down! It wouldn't be the same here—'

'No, no, my grandson Jack is taking the reins in time for Christmas,' she says with a sparkle in her eye. 'He's been working behind the scenes for years now, but he will need someone on a part-time basis to take up my pew here and greet customers. Maybe you would keep an eye out for someone who might be interested?'

I look at Meg who looks back at me and we both try to find the same words to reply.

'Mum would!'

'I would!' I say to her, and she lights up in response. 'Eileen, if it's a part-time role I'd be absolutely delighted to hear more. I'll leave you my number for Jack. No pressure, at all! But this would be right up my street.'

'There's no better place to be than surrounded by books,' she tells me, with a pink lipstick smile. 'I'll put in a good word for you with the boss!'

Kelly and Bernice are the first to rally round when I get the job, and we raise a glass together in celebration.

'So, when do you start? Oh, you will be in your glory, Annie!' says Kelly, almost levitating with excitement.

'Next week,' I announce with nerves and delight. 'I'll be shadowing Eileen for two weeks, which I'm really looking forward to, then it's over to me from November.'

'The day Senan's book hits the shelves,' says Bernice with wide eyes. 'Imagine, you'll be selling the book you wrote to unsuspecting punters! You've so much to look forward to, darling. I'm thrilled for you!'

'I really hope so, Bernice,' I reply. 'I don't know if it's the seasons changing or just time working its magic, but things are starting to fall into place nice and gently, which is just how I'd hoped they would.'

'Baby steps and new starts,' says Kelly, raising her glass. 'Peter would be very proud of you.'

And no matter how much betrayal I've felt since I heard about Lexi, I really do think that Peter would be proud of me. I forgive him. I always had, but now it feels like I'm really moving on. There are so many new starts coming my way, like tiny new challenges and chapters, and although I sometimes find it overwhelming, it keeps me ticking by and saves me from wallowing in my grief or self-pity.

One More Day

This year has been the end of an era for me and my family, but also the dawn of a whole new beginning. I need to keep charging forward. I need to keep living.

At long last, things are looking brighter.

28.

I'm in my dungarees and wellies in the chicken pen in the November rain as Hilary, Henry and the gang peck around my feet when a delivery van pulls up into the yard.

The first week on my new job, shadowing Mary before she leaves, has been a great success. It gives me a new structure to my routine, making my time to write and my time to look after the kids and the farmhouse so much more pleasurable.

I push my hair off my face, knowing I've probably streaked my cheek with mud, rain, and who knows what else after some digging around in the soil all morning, and go to see what the courier has brought our way.

'Annie Madden?' says the driver as he jumps out of his white van and goes to the back doors. 'Just a second.'

He takes out a medium-sized cardboard box and my heart starts to beat a little bit faster. I know what is inside that box before I open it, and I'm sure the delivery guy is getting a bit of a kick from the look of childlike excitement on my face. It's the copies of Senan's book. There's still a week until publication, but these are my very own copies.

'I wrote a book for someone and this is my first time seeing it, so excuse me if I look a bit stunned,' I tell him. 'Oh, this is so bloody exciting! Meg! Danny!'

The man looks suitably impressed and holds up his car keys as I fumble with the box, putting it down on the doorstep as I try to tear it open.

'Here, let me,' he says, running his key down the middle seal on the box. He does the same thing horizontally and I push back the cardboard flaps to see my very own complimentary copies of Senan's life story right in front of me.

'Meg! Danny!' I feel tears sting my eyes as I wait for my children to share this joyous moment, forgetting for a second that the man who delivered the box is still standing beside me.

'Look at it!' I exclaim, hugging a copy of the book to my chest. It's shiny, it's smooth to touch and I can't help but sniff it. There's nothing like the smell of a new book, especially when it's your own! Well, kind of mine. 'Ah, it's so gorgeous!'

'Senan Donnelly – *Unbroken*,' reads the delivery man over my shoulder. 'You wrote this? Wow. I've seen him on TV. Damn good actor. Congratulations! That's quite the achievement!'

I almost do a dance of delight and resist the urge to hug the stranger who is now whistling on his way back to his van. Meg and Danny arrive at last to the back door where they react in their very own unique and very typical ways.

'Mum! It says your name on the cover!' says Megan, running her fingers down the spine. 'I didn't realize he was such a hottie. I can't wait to tell everyone in school!'

'He isn't *that* good-looking, but he's a cool dude for sure,' says Danny, with a face of total approval. 'Nice work, Mum. You rock!'

They skip off back to their caves, leaving me sitting at the kitchen table beside the box of books, smiling at this little moment of glory on my own. I wish I could talk to Senan right now. I wish I could share this moment with him. We worked so hard on this book and now here it is, in the flesh, yet we are miles apart in more ways than one.

I haven't heard his voice since I left him in West Cork. I've read all his messages and I've replied to some, but I couldn't cope with hearing his voice. I've always felt weak at the thought, but I'm a different person now. I've spent the past three months here reflecting on who I am and who I want to be. I've put all the tools in my box and I've grown and developed so much, using all my life experience, good and bad, to get me to where I am now.

I would love to talk to him.

I take out my phone from my chest pocket on my old faithful, grubby dungarees and I scroll through to find his number, then I stare at it for a while, wondering what he might be doing now. His messages are much more spaced out these days, which is totally understandable when I was so vague with my replies, but I was trying so hard not to hurt him, and not to hurt myself when the timing was so wrong. I wonder has he found a new girlfriend. I wonder is he still living at the beach house. I wonder if he ever managed to find an acting role that cast him as the hero instead of the bad guy. I wonder does he still think of me at all.

I still think of him, every single day.

I press the icon on the phone and close my eyes as I hear the ringtone.

'Annie?'

Oh God. His voice. My eyes fill up already and I grip the phone.

'Senan, yes, it's me,' I reply, unable to hide the nerves in my voice. 'I-I got the book just now. It looks so good. Congratulations.'

I hear him slow down the car as he indicates to stop to take the call.

'Wow, I have to say I wasn't expecting to hear from you,' he says, sounding a little breathless as he speaks. I can picture him right now, rubbing his forehead with his hand. 'Sorry, I'm a bit taken aback. Yes, the book looks fantastic. My family have read it and they gave it the thumbs up, so that's a good start.'

'It's so good to hear your voice.'

We both say this at exactly the same time. I want to see him so badly, but I know I've no right to just turn up out of the blue like this after pushing him away for all this time.

'Anyhow, I just wanted to say—'

'I still miss you, Annie. How are you?'

I gasp and wipe tears away from my eyes, staring at his face on the cover of the book that sits in front of me. I run my finger down his face, wishing with all my heart I could touch him in real life right now.

'I'm doing well, thanks, and I hope you are too, Senan,' I whisper to him. 'I . . . I still miss you too.'

We both sit in silence after that, not really knowing what more to say. There is so much to catch up on, but it's hard to know where to start and I'm not even sure we're in a fit state right now for proper conversation. It feels like the time we spent together deserves more than a phone call.

'I've been hoping you'd change your mind and come to London for the launch event?' he says, with a crack in his voice. 'It's next week. There's a bit of a celebration. I know you already told Caroline you couldn't make it, because it was the first thing I asked her, but maybe . . .'

I close my eyes again, knowing that once more I'm going to let him down.

'I can't come for that, I'm sorry,' I tell him. 'It's just I started a new job and that's the day the lady I'm taking over from leaves. They're having a lunch for her.'

'A new job?' he says, as gracious as ever, even though I can tell he is gutted. 'Congratulations, Annie. I'm happy for you.'

I realize my reason sounds pathetic in the wider scheme of things. I've known about the book launch for a while, of course. I've never been to a book launch before and, even though I want to go more than anything, and I want to see Senan even more, I've been playing it safe and using my part-time job in a little bookshop as an excuse to keep my mind focused on my home life for now.

'It's in the local bookshop,' I tell him, feeling a bit silly now. I wrote a book and I can't attend the launch because I have to go out to lunch with my new boss from our local bookshop and his elderly grandmother. 'God, Senan, I'm so used to not going anywhere. I should have made a decision and made plans to be with you next week. I don't know what I was thinking. I'm trying to stay grounded but I should have planned to—'

'But you don't make big plans, isn't that right, Annie?'

He sounds really pissed off now, and I can't say I blame him.

'I'm still a bit afraid to,' I whisper. 'It's lovely to hear your voice.'

He takes a moment to reply.

'So you said earlier,' he replies. 'Look Annie, I have to be somewhere now, so I'll let you go. Thanks for calling. You take care, OK?'

'I'll go!' I tell him before he hangs up. I stand up and feel a rush of energy fill me up, like I've finally realized it's now or never.

'Senan, I'll be there. I'll plan it right now. I can't miss this, no way.'

'You sure?' he asks, switching off the engine of his car. 'Annie, I swear I'm dying to see you. Are you sure?'

'Yes, I'm sure, Senan!' I tell him. 'I just don't know how I'm going to wait until then, but I'll be there by your side just as I should be. I'll see you in seven days. Oh God, I can't wait.'

We say goodbye and I feel like I could run laps of the garden with delight. I haven't thought of how I'll get there or what the cost will be. I haven't thought of where I'll stay in London, and I haven't even thought of what I'll do with the kids as it's a school night.

But I'll be there. For once in a very long time, I'm making a plan for next week, and nothing is going to get in my way.

29.

'Operation book launch!' Meg announces we need to go shopping for something new for me to wear. 'I'm thinking sophisticated but sultry, and you should definitely get a haircut and colour, Mum.'

'What would I do without your heartfelt honesty about my appearance, darling daughter?'

Meg's new interest in fashion is never far off the mark, though. Sophisticated and sultry does sound good. I've gone over the scene in my mind so many times, picturing the moment when I see Senan at the book launch, and what I'm wearing always plays such an important role, of course.

We have talked for hours on end since we reconnected last weekend, and my heart skips a beat every time I think of seeing him again, even though we've both agreed to get to know each other again very slowly.

'I keep picturing it in my mind too,' he tells me one night as I lie in bed with his face on my phone screen. The snow is pelting down outside and I feel a sense of warmth and cosiness that I haven't done in such a long time. 'But I can't bear the thought of being in the same city for a whole day and waiting until the book launch in the evening. Sod it, I'll pick you up at the airport.'

'That would be lovely,' I say, trying to contain my joy as I imagine it all.

'I just can't wait to hang out with you again,' he says. 'I know you've been to hell and back since we last met, so I want to look after you and show you a really nice time.'

I touch his face on the small phone screen.

'You really are a sweetheart,' I say to him, wishing the days would pass quicker. 'A break away is just what I need, and to get to spend it with one of my favourite people is a huge bonus.'

We lie there staring and giggling like starstruck teenagers, saying nothing a lot of the time, but I always try to steer the conversation back to reality when I feel we are getting caught up in romantic notions too soon again.

'I'm still grieving and will be for a long time,' I whisper to him. 'I'm so afraid of letting this life and love I've always known go, and I've had a lot to absorb lately.'

He nods, his eyes full of empathy.

'Of course you have,' he says to me. 'There's no rush. We can just get to know each other again and see how it goes from there. We'll go for dinner in London. Maybe do some shopping. We'll catch up on all the things we've been up to, and I promise it can be at a snail's pace if that's how you want it.'

When I hang up the phone every night after speaking to Senan, I feel so full up inside again, like a whole new lease of life has come my way. I have so much to tell him, as he will have to tell me too, but we've agreed that we'll save it until we are at least in the same room, when we can laugh and cry together, rather than spill it all out over a phone call.

I want to see his face when I show him pictures of me swimming in Lough Neagh with the Wild Water Dunkers, I want to hear his opinion when I show him extracts from the novel I've been working on. I want to describe everything about the cosy bookshop where I now get to hang out a few days a week, where I'm surrounded by thousands and thousands of words to inspire my biggest dreams.

And I want to hear his biggest dreams too, some of which are too good to wait until we meet up again, and he just can't resist telling me already.

'I've got this amazing opportunity with my new agent,' he tells me two days before the book launch. I've just finished breakfast at my kitchen table. 'She's got me a final audition for a big budget series on Netflix. It's really last minute, so I'm literally on standby to hear more.'

'That's magic! Wow, I'm so thrilled for you!'

I feel my heart rise with delight for him and I grin from ear to ear.

'I just had to call you and tell you first,' he says, his voice booming with excitement. 'It's potentially massive, Annie.

357

With the book coming out and now this, I feel my life is starting all over again. And then there's you . . . my God, I can't wait to see you.'

I grip the phone and feel a rush of adrenaline fill my veins.

'I wish Saturday would hurry up too,' I say to him with a real spring in my step. 'Not long now, Senan. Oh, I can't wait.'

Meg and I manage to squeeze in some shopping each afternoon – once school and work is done – in preparation for my weekend away, and when Friday comes, Bernice and Jake surprise us with an early evening visit to make sure I'm all set.

'I'm sure Eileen and Jack totally understand you needed a couple of days off, even if it's her big leaving day,' Bernice says, in between admiring my new hairstyle and dress with great awe. 'It's not every day you get to see a book you've written go out into the big bad world, and Eileen of all people would be only too delighted to make sure you were there.'

Of course Eileen understood perfectly. She wouldn't hear of any apologies at all, and rushed me home to make arrangements, even offering to look after Danny and Meg, bless her.

'Go and try everything on so I can see what you'll look like! Think of it as a dress rehearsal!' Bernice says. 'Oh, I'm so proud of you, Annie!'

'Great idea!' I reply to her, butterflies whooshing around my tummy every time I think of being face to face with Senan again. I put on my new green velvet dress, feeling it snug around the curves of my body, and allow myself – just momentarily – to bend the rules I've set in my mind where we take it very slowly. I imagine him caressing my skin. I slip my toes into stiletto heels that make me feel tall and elegant, a far cry from the wellies and dungarees I'm so used to. I clasp a delicate necklace at the back of my neck and tilt my head to the side, longing for his lips on my collarbone.

I dab on perfume, slowly anointing my wrists, and I imagine hot, passionate kisses, where our mouths will meet again at last. Shivers cascade up and down my spine when I think of finding his fingers intertwined in mine again.

Then I look in the mirror and I'm so pleased with what I see in front of me. I am brand-new inside and out. I take a deep breath and smile at my reflection, and then I go downstairs to show off to my family.

'Ta-daaa!' I say, holding a copy of Senan's book in my hand for effect. 'Do I look like a writer? I feel like a writer!'

'That's because you are a writer!' Bernice coos, her hands clasped up to her face. Jake folds his arms and nods in agreement. 'You look absolutely radiant, Annie! I haven't seen that beaming smile in so, so long, and by God it looks good!'

'I picked it, of course,' says Meg about the dress. 'I'm thinking of starting a blog to promote my music and fashion sense. I could be on to something.'

Danny joins in with one of his usual quips.

'Any excuse for taking more selfies! Mum, have you seen how much make-up she goes through – she's only sixteen!'

I stand back to admire my two teenage children, fourteen and sixteen years old on their most recent birthdays, and I feel a sense of immense pride in my lot. I'm just about to burst into a speech of how grateful I am for everything when my phone rings.

'It's Senan,' I announce. 'Please excuse me.'

I can't help but beam into a smile when I see his name. I also notice how Bernice watches me with a look of pure joy on her face. I still haven't told her anything about how close Senan and I really are again, and I don't know when I will. There are some things I need to keep to myself for another while.

'Hi Annie!' he says as I make my way to my writing room to take the call. 'I have good news and bad news. Well, amazing news and bad news actually.'

I walk down the hallway, still wearing my book launch attire, and listen to what he has to say.

'Go on,' I say, not knowing what to expect. 'This is a nice, unexpected call to get, and I'm all dressed up here in case you need me to fly off to somewhere exotic at the drop of a hat.'

I'm joking, of course, but Senan is not.

'Funny you should say that but . . . well, the big audition,

Annie,' he tells me as I sit down on the sofa. 'The one I've been waiting to hear about? I'm down to the final two for the part! Annie, this is it. This is the huge role I need to launch my career again, just as the book is out, so it couldn't have worked out any better. I'm tantalizingly close, but . . .'

I stand up again and walk to the window, pacing back and forth as I take in his news.

'But?' I say, throwing my head back in delight. 'How can there be a "but"? This is fantastic.'

'It really is, thanks. It's a bloody massive role,' he tells me. 'It's a title role, Annie, but that's all I can say at the moment. I'm still sworn to secrecy. But then the bad news . . . well, I'm just off the phone to Caroline to say that due to the timing and urgency of this, we're going to have to postpone the celebrations this weekend as I have to travel to the audition.'

'Oh.'

'I'm absolutely gutted. I'm dying to see you, Annie,' he says, but my ears can't really take this in.' You do understand though, don't you? I'll make up for it, I promise.'

'Oh,' is all I can say again, as disappointment ripples through me.

The room spins a little and I make my way to sit down again.

A million thoughts race through my head as I go from elation to sheer sadness, back to delight again for this dreamlike opportunity that has come his way. I touch the green dress and grasp its light material, feeling like Cinderella who didn't quite make the ball, and I try to hide the quiver in my voice.

'Senan, I'm thrilled for you, you know I am,' I say, focusing on my breathing so I don't break down in tears. 'That's really brilliant news, but of course I'm devastated we won't get to see each other.'

There's a pause in the conversation which I'm glad of. It allows me to let my disappointment sink in, and it does to my very toes, and then settles like a sickly feeling in my stomach.

'I'm so gutted about the weekend too,' he whispers. 'I really am.'

'Don't worry, I will be fine,' I say, trying to mask how I really feel inside. 'And besides, it's only one weekend, isn't it? I'm sure we can make up for it soon. Maybe I could go over the following weekend instead? I mean, what about the book launch? Can they reschedule?'

I am already looking at flight times in my mind, but I can tell by his slight hesitation that there's more to come.

'Well, Caroline wanted to look at other dates for the event,' he goes on to explain. 'You can imagine she isn't exactly my biggest fan right now, as she's had so many things to cancel, but the thing is . . . the thing is, if I get this job I could be off the radar for at least six months before I can commit to anything else.'

I gulp and fresh tears sting in my eyes.

'Six months?'

'On set,' he continues. 'The book launch is important, but this is a hundred times bigger, and when I tell you all about it, you'll definitely see why. Its life-changing in more ways than one, I really mean that. I simply can't turn it down.'

'Of course you can't,' I mutter, rubbing my forehead.

I think of all the times I ignored his calls when I got back from West Cork earlier in the year. I think of all the messages he sent me, so full of longing and love. I think of every time I wanted to talk to him but didn't, and now, here I am, finally at a stage of my life where I can run to him if I want to, and there's a chance we'll have to wait another six months. It's like some cruel twist of fate.

Six months off the radar. Six months before I might see him again. I sit down on my writing chair and lift a pen, doodling with it just to give myself something to do as I try to find the right words.

'Senan, you know that even if Caroline or anyone else in your world thinks differently of you right now, I am still your biggest fan and always will be,' I say to him softly. I remember how he pledged one day he would wait for me, but I'm tired of always waiting. 'I'm disappointed, of course I am. I'm absolutely devastated, if the truth be told, but—'

'I am too, Annie, but if you can just wait—'

I close my eyes tight at the thought of waiting again. I've been waiting for Peter to come back to me all these years, but he didn't, and now I'm reminded that Senan Donnelly lives in a very different world from the one I inhabit. My life, no matter what he says, is very ordinary.

'Let's not make any more plans,' I say, reverting to my usual mantra of how life always gets in the way when you do. 'I'm insanely proud of you by getting this far with your audition, and I know that the audition will go brilliantly and the director, whoever he or she is, will choose you for this part. Keep me posted, won't you?'

My voice crackles with pain, as does his when he replies.

'You'll be first to know everything, that goes without saying,' he tells me before we go. 'Just stick with me, Annie. This is really big, I swear to you it is, but if you don't want to wait, as always I will understand.'

I clutch the phone to my chest, I shake my head and I say goodbye, then I take a moment to myself as I let my mind readjust to the direction my week is now going in. I take a deep breath, I remind myself how much disappointment I've already experienced in life, then I flick back my hair and dial Eileen's phone number.

Eileen answers with her friendly tone and I put on my best smile.

'Change of plans, Eileen!' I say, trying to sound as chipper as I can, even though I'm smiling through my tears. 'I won't be going to London after all tomorrow, so I'll be able to work in the bookshop as before and join you for your retirement lunch, if you'll still have me?'

'Annie, what on earth are you talking about?' she says timidly. 'I hope you aren't cancelling this because of me?'

I blink back tears as if she can see me. If only it was as simple as that.

'No, no, it's just a change of plans,' I say to her, doing my best to disguise the pain in my voice. 'Something I'm very much used to by now. The event has been postponed so I don't need to go to London after all. See you Saturday for your big retirement day!'

I look down at my fancy dress, my new shoes, and I touch my freshly styled hair. Plans, I ponder.

No wonder I hate making them.

30.

I'm washing the dishes in a bit of a daze, thinking of what Bernice had to say to me before she left this evening. I don't know how she could tell, but she knew that it was much more than the disappointment of attending a posh event in London that had plunged me into such sadness after Senan's surprise phone call.

'I can read you from a mile off,' she whispered as Jake was warming up the car for her. 'You've fallen for him. I can see that as plain as the nose on your face. But you're afraid to love again. You're afraid to step across the line. You're afraid to put your faith in him so soon after losing Peter.'

I couldn't even find the words to deny it to her.

'Darling, you know after my Bob died, I thought my ability to love had died with him,' she continued. 'You've been coping so well since Peter left us, and I've watched you pick up the pieces from afar with a glow inside of me, but I need to tell you one thing. The human heart is much bigger than we think it is. Just because it's been broken once, doesn't mean there isn't room to love again. If Senan means as much to you as I think he does, please let him in, Annie. You don't have to let go of Peter to let more love in. Do you hear me?'

I nodded from where I stood at the back door, exhausted after today's revelation.

'I really thought I was ready, Bernice,' I told her, my lips twitching as I speak. 'But, just as I was about to give it a chance, I'm told he has to leave for six months. I've realized that Senan and I really do live in parallel worlds, so although my heart may be as big as you say, I need to try to protect it a little more from now on, because it looks as if we aren't meant to be, no matter how much we want it. He's an actor, for crying out loud. I can't compete with that, can I? I'm just an ordinary woman.'

She raised an eyebrow.

'There's nothing ordinary about you, Annie Madden. Nothing ordinary whatsoever.'

'Funny, Senan once said the same,' I said with a bittersweet smile as I saw her off. 'But, compared to the world he lives in, I'm feeling very ordinary and very far away.'

I'm up to my arms in suds now and frozen in time at the sink, thinking of her words, when Meg comes into the kitchen, her eyes wide with excitement.

'Mum, Mum, come quick!' she exclaims. 'Senan's on the telly and he's talking about the book. What if he mentions your name? Come quick!'

I swallow back tears and shake my head.

'Turn it down a little, will you love?' I ask her, full of fear that I might hear what he is saying from where I stand. I just can't bear it right now. 'I have a bit of a headache. I'll catch up later.'

She comes right over to me and looks at my face.

'What's going on, Mum?' she asks me.

'What do you mean?'

'Well, first, the book launch is cancelled, and now you don't even want to watch him talk about the book on TV?'

'I just have a headache, that's all. It's no big deal.'

'Do you miss him or something?' she asks me. 'It's like you keep slipping into some sort of trance now and then, like your mind is miles away. I'm just wondering if you're thinking of him when you drift away.'

My daughter is highly intuitive, there's no denying that. Just as I thought I'd been hiding my pain over Peter for years, she can see right through me, even now.

'I do think of him a lot,' I say, trying my best to be honest, as I always do with both my children. 'You're right. I was really looking forward to seeing him again at the book launch but it wasn't meant to be. There's a new job he really wants, and if he gets it he has to go away to work for six months. He will find out tomorrow.'

She screws up her face.

'I think I'm going to stay single for ever,' she says as she plods away. 'I hate the thought of liking someone so much that you miss them so badly. That's happened to you twice now. It sucks.'

I dry my hands on a tea towel and stand there for a moment by the sink as Senan's voice still hums from the next room. I close my eyes tight to try to blank it out as I wait for Meg to turn it down. She switches the channel, much to my relief.

After our reconnection, the thought of waiting six long months until I can see Senan again is just too much. Meg is right. It really does suck. Maybe he won't get the job? I curse myself for being so selfish as to even think that.

I do want him to get the job more than I want to see him, which means I love him more than I even thought I did.

'If I were you, I'd wear your new dress to work today, Mum,' Meg tells me on Saturday morning as I fix my hair in the mirror in the hallway.

'I suppose it wouldn't look out of place at the Red Fox for lunch, even if I do turn a few heads from punters who have only come in for the latest thriller or autobiography for the weekend.'

'You suit green,' she tells me, before she leaves me to it. She has coursework to catch up on and Danny, to my great delight, has also set today aside to, in his words, 'last-minute cram' for his forthcoming exams.

Despite fearing that I'm still finding my way now I don't have Peter to look after any more, I marvel at how my two children have turned out to be such fine company. They have matured a lot, even in the short time since their dad died, and we've grown into quite a tight little unit, but sometimes they still look at me with such sadness and longing. I do my best to shake it off, to reassure them that I'm absolutely fine and that, in time, they will be too.

Meg and her friend Jodie are studying hard for their GCSEs, and I know that Meg has her eye on a boy in school called Tommy, who sounds like a real character. She has signed up to singing lessons and is even writing out her own lyrics in her free time. Danny is struggling a little bit more behind closed doors, but I need to give him space to grieve for the father he lost such a long time ago. They've had so much to deal with in their very short lives so far.

Meanwhile, I have my new friends from the swimming club; I've Kelly, of course, who hovers around me like a helicopter; I've Mum, who is always there when I need her on the end of the phone; I've still got Bernice, who checks in more than ever, and now I've the prospect of finishing my novel in the not too distant future.

I arrive at work in my book-launch attire, stopping in my tracks to admire young Jack's fine window display, which I know he has done in a bid to soften the blow of the big launch being cancelled today. He has arranged at least twenty copies of Senan's autobiography around various TV-themed decorations, including a video camera, a flat-screen TV and a director's clapper board. I'm very touched by his efforts.

'You look like a Hollywood star,' Eileen tells me when she pops by at lunchtime on her way to the Red Fox for her celebratory do. 'I'm delighted to see some glamour in this shop after years of bookworms having to look at little old me.'

'Everyone loves little old you,' I remind her. 'I've got very big boots to fill in here, and I know it.'

'Ah, thank you, but you and young Jack will breathe new life into this place,' she replies. 'In fact, looking at the window, you already have! Imagine a real author working in Corners! Who needs London? Let's go celebrate over lunch, Annie.'

I tuck my hair behind her ears as I try to let it all sink in. The shop has been busy this morning, and Senan's book has sold well, with some people even asking me to sign a copy, which I do with some hesitation. It's not my story at all, but one day I hope I'll have a shelf-full of novels and I'll hold book signings galore.

'Well, this is your big day more than mine, Eileen, so I must return the compliment by saying it is younger-looking you're getting,' I tell her. She does look so pretty in her lilac dress, matching her hair, and her face as always is powdered to perfection. 'It's a real honour for me to join you today, and I've already put any notions of fancy book launches in London to the back of my mind. I'll make it there one day!'

'That you will, my dear,' she says with her usual sparkling smile.

I lock up the shop, putting our 'Out to lunch' sign in the window, and we shuffle down the street to the Red

Fox, where Jack is waiting for us along with a very carefully selected guest list. Much to Eileen's surprise, there are journalists from the weekly newspaper, some of the more regular customers, and a few neighbouring business owners who have worked alongside her on our little main street for many years.

It makes me blush when Jack announces me as not only their new staff member, but also their 'special guest', and I spend most of the lunch hour answering questions on what Senan is like in real life and how I approached writing his intriguing life story.

'Is he as good-looking in the flesh?' one of the younger female journalists asks me, to which I nod politely. 'I always thought he should have won a second BAFTA for his role as that distraught father, but my favourite will always be *Broken*. It's so good to hear he's back on the scene again.'

'And hopefully he'll be back again on our screens very soon,' pipes another. 'I can't believe you got to work with him so closely!'

I hear my phone bleep in my handbag and excuse myself to use the bathroom, in case it might be Senna with an update on his audition. He had to catch a flight this morning to a top-secret location, so I haven't heard from him since last night, though I know he should be in touch soon.

'Right, here goes, Annie,' he tells me in his message. 'It's just me and the director, so please say a prayer or send lucky vibes my way!'

I message him back quickly.

'You can do this!' I tell him as my heart races for him. 'As clichéd as it may sound, just be yourself and you'll blow him away!'

'Her,' he messages back. 'She's a real powerhouse – this is very exciting! I wish you were here with me. I really do.'

'So do I,' I mutter, before I send another quick good-luck message and go back to my table. I'm thrilled for him, I really am, but I can't help but think how different today could have been for us. I'd have been in London now, probably checking in to my hotel. I'd be nervous as hell, but only to see him again. I've pictured the scene in my head a thousand times, where he would have met me in the hotel lobby after our airport reunion, and we'd travel together to the launch. He'd look handsome in his designer suit and tie. His hair would be as touchable as always, and he'd have a spark in his eyes when he saw me. We'd hold hands in the car on the way to the venue, even though we'd pledged not to; we'd stare at each other like giddy teenagers, and all through the formalities of the evening, we'd steal glances across the room, knowing we were both thinking of what we might get up to later.

'Isn't that right, Annie?'

'Oh, sorry! What was that, Jack?'

I take my seat back at the restaurant table and snap back to reality, where I'm miles away from Senan, as always, and our big reunion is only where it can ever be for a very long time – in my dreams.

'I was just saying that I've read the book already, and he isn't what you'd expect at all,' Jack continues. 'He seems like a really cool guy, and not the mess the media portrayed him to be. I'd say he has huge success on the way after this.'

'Hopefully,' I say, as my stomach twists at the thought of not seeing him for another six months. It's frustrating not to know who this hotshot director is, or where she has taken Senan and the other contender for her leading man, but I'm sure I'll find out soon. I just hope he isn't disappointed today after getting so far down the line.

We finish up lunch and I send a quick text to my two little students at home, who respond in their very own, very different ways.

'Danny is being a pain as usual. He says I left a mess in the kitchen and I didn't.'

I send back a tart reply. 'I don't care who left the mess. Just make sure it isn't there when I get home.'

'Meg is officially bone idle!' Danny writes to me. 'She missed a delivery when I was in the shower because she didn't get to the door on time, but I know she heard it. Lazy!'

'I'll speak to you both when I get home,' I tell him, checking the time as I say so. 'It's two p.m. so I'll see you in two hours. Behave!'

'PS, I'm going for pizza, so don't worry about me for dinner,' he replies. 'And Meg said something about going to Jodie's. Or was it Layla's, which is probably a cover-up meaning she is going to meet Tommy. I can't keep up.'

374

This is my real life, I remind myself with a wry chuckle. Not fancy book launches in London.

Jack drives me back to the bookshop after lunch as the winter snow begins to fall. I can't help but gush once more at how good our little window display looks in this beautiful backdrop. *Unbroken* is tipped to be a big Christmas best-seller, and if my morning is anything to go by, we could be sold out of our existing stock by close of business today.

'It's so good to have you on board,' says Jack as I get out of his car, and I notice how he looks at me with such wonder. 'I'm thrilled to be working with you, Annie. I really am.'

He has a slight twinkle in his eye which does wonders for my confidence, even though I'm almost old enough to be his mother.

'Thanks, Jack,' I tell him as I gather my belongings. 'I think we'll make a great team. I'm excited for the next chapter here at Corners, pardon the pun.'

He drives off and my phone rings just as I'm turning the key in the door at the bookshop. My heart begins to thump in my chest when I see Senan's name on my screen.

'Annie, you'll never believe it,' he tells me, sounding like he has just run a marathon. 'They've just told me and I wanted to tell you first. God, Annie, I'm shaking! I got the job!'

I drop my handbag onto the snowy ground and the key of the shop goes with it. I put my hand on the door to steady myself. I swallow hard, losing my breath momentarily, and then I stand up straight with a beaming smile.

He got the job.

'Senan, I had never any doubt, honey!' I tell him, biting my lip. 'Congratulations! This is only everything you deserve.'

I feel tears of joy in my eyes and try to ignore the pang of longing I have deep inside, knowing it will be next May or so before I get to see him again. A full year from the glorious time we spent in West Cork.

'I need to ring Dad to tell him the good news, and of course Sid and Ivy, so I'll race on, but I'll talk to you again very soon, OK?'

'Of course, go do your thing!' I reply, stooping down to pick up the key for Corners, the little store where my own future lies for now. 'Go tell them the good news. You're amazing, you know that.'

He chuckles at the compliment.

'No, you are,' he says emphatically. 'And I plan to show you just how amazing you are to me as soon as I can.'

He hangs up and I open up the shop, staring at the window display with a pang in my heart as his face stares back at me from the book cover.

Six months.

'OK, Annie Madden, it's time to get real and stop dreaming,' I mumble to myself as I dump my handbag down behind the counter, feeling a bit ridiculous now in my green velvet dress, which is way too fancy for a little family-run bookstore.

At least I don't have to worry about cooking dinner for the kids, I think to myself as I force myself to tidy around some shelves and fix the ladder that slides along the floor. The library ladder is one of my favourite features in this little nook of a shop, and I love when a customer wants a book from the archives or a special edition, so I can climb up and find it, feeling very old-fashioned as I do so.

It's Saturday, my children have a better social life than I do, and the prospect of an evening by the fire – just me, a glass of wine, the telly and a takeaway for company – awaits. Everyone else I know seems to have plans. Of course they do.

I don't want to even think about what I'd be doing in London instead. I don't even want to think about how I'd had my hopes up that life might for once go the way I'd dreamed. Even though I'd been adamant about taking it slowly in terms of getting to know Senan again, I'd never have envisaged him being whisked away to some mysterious corner of the globe for six months, just when I'd finally plucked up the courage to shelve my widow's guilt and meet with him in person. I don't even want to think of how his life will inevitably change when he's on a film set, surrounded by people as gorgeous and talented as he is.

Christmas is coming. It will be our first festive season without Peter, and I want to focus on making it the best it can possibly be under such trying circumstances. Even though it's been years since we all had a proper family Christmas together, the thought of being without his physical presence is enough to make me lose my breath.

I let out a deep sigh, make a cup of tea and sit down behind the small counter with a limited edition copy of *Jane Eyre* that I took from the top shelf, thankful of the company of Charlotte Brontë, whose work always brings me back to my schooldays when I was an A-level English student with Peter by my side.

As I savour each word of my favourite classic, I'm soothed by the slow ticking of the clock, by the sound of the old-fashioned bell when someone comes into the shop. Before I know it, the two hours have passed and, aside from a trickle of people who popped by wanting books on the school curriculum or something 'light for the weekend', it has been relatively quiet, but satisfactory at the same time. Senan's book was popular too, and now, as I turn the sign round on the door to 'Sorry, we're closed', I remember I need to return the copy of Jane Eyre to the top shelf before I lock up and leave for the evening.

I climb up the ladder, run my finger across the row of extra-special leather-bound books until I find its proper place. I slide it in, blow some dust off the shelf, and feel my heart sink as the thought of another lonely Saturday night in front of the TV is all I have to look forward to.

Six months isn't for ever, I know that, but I also know that so much can change in that time, especially if two

people are on different sides of the world. I imagine how
Senan is celebrating right now, somewhere in a strange city
with his new director and maybe his agent. He'll meet the
rest of the cast soon, and while I'm doing school runs and
selling books in my part-time job, he'll be living it up in
some exotic location where everyone wants a piece of the
action.

'I'm sorry, we're closed,' I call when the doorbell rings,
afraid to look down from my dizzy heights. As much as I
love to climb up here, coming back down is always a bit
shaky, and I hold on for grim death as I do so, one slow,
careful step at a time.

'That's a shame,' says a very familiar, very low voice. I
freeze. 'I was looking to speak to the famous local author.
Annie Madden, is that you by any chance?'

My hands grip the wooden ladder. My mouth drops open
at the familiarity in his voice, and I close my eyes, begging
that I'm not dreaming.

'Senan?'

'Please don't fall,' he whispers. 'You're pretty high up
there!'

I try my best to take my time to dismount the thin ridges
that take me back to the floor one careful step at a time
and, when I reach it, I dust off my hands and stare at my
unexpected customer.

'You're here?' is all I can muster up. 'What the . . . what
on earth? Senan!'

I walk slowly towards him, and then I fall into his arms and lean my head against his chest, squeezing him so tightly as tears burst from my eyes. I have so many questions, I don't know where to start.

'I'm here, Annie,' he says, his own eyes glistening too as he takes a step back to look at me while never letting me go.

'My God! How?'

'You've no idea how hard it was to keep this a secret from you,' he says, taking me back closer to him, kissing my hair just like he used to all those months ago. I inhale his familiarity. My head spins with adrenaline and a fear that this might not be real. 'I wanted to tell you so badly, Annie. I wanted to drive here first thing this morning when I landed, but I had to go straight to the audition in Belfast.'

I have no idea what he is talking about but, right now, I don't care. I just want to hold him and I don't ever want to let go, I want to touch him and taste him and listen to his stories all over again. I want to keep him here in my arms and feel his hand through my hair as he kisses my face.

'Six months, Annie,' he says, holding my face so tenderly now as he looks into my eyes. 'I'm going to be filming in Belfast for the next six months, not on the other side of the world like you seemed to think I'd be. But I was sworn to secrecy. I can tell you now that I've got the role, and I'm so glad I can do so in person. I'm going to be working right here, and we can spend all this time getting to know each other all over again.'

I step back and my hand covers my mouth in surprise, then I catch a glimpse of the book that brought us together, where it sits in pride of place in the shop window.

'Annie, we don't need to make big plans,' he whispers, 'but you are worthy of love again and I would like to be the one who proves it to you, if you'll let me?'

I nod and wipe the tears from my eyes, knowing that I probably look as if I've been through the wars as my once carefully applied make-up is smeared, but I don't care.

'I will let you,' I say to him. 'I would love to let you.'

He lights up and his beautiful eyes drink me in.

'Now, I don't know about you,' he says. 'But I think a pretty dress like that deserves an evening of celebration, wouldn't you agree?'

'I would totally agree,' I tell him. 'And believe it or not, I don't have any other plans.'

He kisses me so tenderly.

If this is what it feels like to live in the moment, then this moment is OK.

@**mumoftwo_missingyou**
'Is there ever a time to let love go?'

I often ponder over the question our teacher asked us one day back in high school as the winter wind howled outside and the feeling of Christmas was in the air.

I was seventeen, he was just a little older than me, and I could barely concentrate on the plight of Jane Eyre or anything else to do with A-level English Literature as I was so utterly smitten by his smile. He was sitting over by the window, where it was already falling dark outside.

It may have taken me almost twenty-five years to find my answer to her question, but I think I've got it now at last.

You see, I always feared that I'd have to let my late husband's love go to make room for new love in my life, but I now truly believe that along this sacred journey we meet many people who teach us how to love and be loved in so many different ways.

Life can be an exploration, a voyage, or a cross-country road trip. It can be a wind-in-your-hair quest, but it can also sometimes take you down a very bumpy road. Whatever path we follow, love is the fuel that keeps us going on our way.

And there are so many different kinds of love to discover. Self-love, which can take so long to discover; the love I have for my friends, for my children whom I adore; the love I have for my mother and sister, even though they are so far away; the love I have for Peter even though he is no longer with me, and the overwhelming love I feel for this wonderful man who lies by my side right now.

Being with him, and appreciating all the love I've been so lucky to have known in my first forty years on this planet, means that I'll never be lonely again.

I may have lost my husband, but I've never, ever lost our love. I was angry, I was hurt, I was afraid and I was lost, but only because I loved so deeply to begin with. And now that he is gone, I can accept that I'm still so worthy of being cherished and adored on the rest of my journey here without him by my side.

I'm still worthy of seeing the joy of a new season or the dawn of the new day again. I'm still worthy of holding a hand for support, of feeling the embrace of a loving hug, of the warmth of a kiss again. I'm still worthy of watching the sun rise and set, marvelling at the beginning and end and the privilege of seeing another new day.

I'll always hold in my heart the joys of youth and the years of marriage we shared, Peter, and I will continue to live in magical wonder at how great our life once was.

I have loved, I have lost, my heart has been battered, bruised and broken into a million pieces, but the magical thing is that it is still beating and that means it can still love so much more. Because love and magic are one and the same.

My heart, and all of yours, was made to be loved, and it's big enough to love again and again and again.

The human heart is as big as the ocean.

What a truly beautiful thing to know.

One More Day

Grid Pic: The sun rising on Lough Neagh on Christmas Day
Likes: 3,567
Comments: 283

Author's Note & Acknowledgements

Way back in 2005 when I was a young mum and PR who was truly bitten by the writing bug, my aunt Kathleen waved a magazine at me and urged me to join her in entering a short story competition. The winner's story would be published in *Woman's Way* and the prize was a two-night stay in West Cork, at the magnificent Inchydoney Resort just outside the town of Clonakilty.

Reader, I won, and the rest is history. As well as having written a grand total of fourteen novels since then, I also had the pleasure of returning to Inchydoney for a wedding in recent years where my love of that area was reignited. So, when it came to deciding on a place for Annie to go and write, it seemed the perfect fit.

Closer to home, I've also recently discovered a whole new appreciation for the shores of Lough Neagh, which has a breathtaking beauty and a sense of peace which captured my heart. I took a spin there just before I began writing *One More Day*, and I was filled with so much inspiration on what it would be like to live right beside the lough and the whole way of life it presents.

So, when I wanted to choose a setting for this book, it was an absolute joy to bring these two very special places together and bring Annie from the wild beauty of the lough where she is so at home, to the southern shores of Ireland and the magnificence of West Cork.

I'd like to thank my agent Sarah Hornsley at Peters, Fraser and Dunlop Literary Agency as well as my editor Kate Bradley and the wonderful team at HarperCollins, all of whom helped me bring Annie, Senan and Peter's story to life. Thank you for your ongoing support, your patience, your brainstorming and creative input and for encouraging me every step of the way.

Thanks as always to my wonderful family – Jim, Jordyn, Jade, Adam, Dualta & Sonny, my dad and siblings and everyone in between!

Thanks to all the booksellers across the UK, Ireland, Germany, Hungary, Italy, The Netherlands, the USA and Canada, especially Sheehy's Cookstown in my home county of Tyrone. Thanks to the amazing bloggers who support me year on year on social media and who share such creative photography and wonderful reviews. Thanks to the media both at home and further afield who cover my stories, especially those I've worked with recently including Cliodhna Fullen (*Conversations with Cliodhna*), *The Irish News* (Jenny Lee), *Belfast Telegraph* (Aine Toner), *UTV Life* (Pamela

Ballantine and Petra Ellis), *Tyrone Constitution* (Lauren Sharkey, Darren Beattie), *Ulster Herald* (Conor Coyle, Thomas Maher), *BBC Radio Ulster* (Chris Lindsay, Mark Davenport), and the *Sunday Times* (Henry McDonald). A huge thank you to both Translink and Libraries NI for selecting my books to promote to readers, and also to Tim McKane and all the wonderful members of the NI Business group on Facebook whose support has been phenomenal.

Thanks to Tanya and Sean Maguire and all my 'sisters' at The Player's Conservatory throughout the USA, Canada UK, Ireland, Germany, Brazil, Puerto Rico and France. I'm so, so honoured to have met you (well, virtually!), to teach you, and to get to know you all so dearly. You are a VERY special bunch of people who I now call my friends.

Thanks to Ruth Miller-Anderson for all your last-minute help and to Shane Coleman for answering my questions on life by the lough, including the name of the mountain range in the distance which I couldn't find on google! Thanks also to Erin and Mickey Coleman for the offer to write at their beautiful cottage by Lough Neagh. I dream of doing so one day very soon.

Thanks to the many care-workers, nurses and doctors who answered my plea on Facebook for advice on brain injuries, respite care and options for those who care for loved ones at home.

Most of all thank you to you, my readers, for all your support, your messages of enthusiasm, your 'shelfie' photos in supermarkets and bookshops, your comments and name suggestions for characters and so much more. Whether you listen on audio, borrow from the library, or read in paperback or e-book, I appreciate each and every one of you. Thank you!

Finally, I'd like to dedicate *One More Day* to one of my dearest readers, Aurelia Kelly, who we sadly lost so tragically in late 2021. Aurelia, I will hold your words and sweet messages close to my heart forever. Please hold your family near, and may your wonderful, kind, gentle soul rest in peace.